Agnes Sorel

The Breast And Crotch That Changed History

First Edition

Published by The Nazca Plains Corporation
Las Vegas, Nevada
2009

ISBN: 978-1-934625-71-2

Published by

The Nazca Plains Corporation ®
4640 Paradise Rd, Suite 141
Las Vegas NV 89109-8000

PUBLISHER'S NOTE
Agnes Sorel is a work of fiction created wholly by *Tim Desmondes'* imagination. All
characters are fictional and any resemblance to any persons living or deceased is
purely by accident. No portion of this book reflects any real person or events.

Cover Photos, Iakov Filimonov and Denis Khveshchenik
Art Director, Blake Stephens

Dedication

This book is dedicated to the women who have changed the world.

To those who have changed the world for good, like Florence Nightingale, Mother Theresa, Susan B. Anthony, and hundreds of thousands of others. And let us not forget Agnes Sorel

But it is dedicated as well to those women who have cast dark shadows on history: Lucrezia Borgia, Eva Braun, and Delilah.

Here's to women – all of you.

Including the two women who have changed my life, very much for the better.

Agnes Sorel

The Breast And Crotch That Changed History

First Edition

Tim Desmondes

Introduction

The Battle of Agincourt was fought on October 25, 1415. The English warrior king, Henry V, defeated the army of the French king, Charles VI.

Following the English victory, Charles VI recognized Henry V as his heir and as regent of France. He married his daughter Katharine to Henry and declared his own son, the dauphin, illegitimate.

Shakespeare's great play, Henry V, dramatizes these events.

In 1422, when both Henry V and Charles VI had died, Henry's infant son, Henry VI, was generally recognized as king of France north of the Loire River. Charles VII, the rejected son of the former French king, ruled France south of the Loire.

Shakespeare's play, Henry VI, gives the English view of the ensuing struggle which tipped the scales back towards Charles VII when Joan of Arc raised the siege of Orleans, defeating the English. She then had Charles VII crowned King of France at Rheims.

That coronation was the turning point in the Hundred Years' War.

Joan of Arc was, and is, a great French heroine.

But another woman, Agnes Sorel, "the most beautiful woman in France," who became Charles VII's mistress, played the final pivotal role in bringing closure to the hundred year war between England and France.

Agnes' mastery of France was instrumental in leading not only France, but all of Europe out of the middle ages and into modern times.

The following pages tell Agnes' story.

Tim Desmondes

1

Chapter One

"You are destined to rule a great nation."

The words permeated Agnes' whole being. The moment the words were out of Zèlde's mouth the eighteen year old maid knew they rang true. She was indeed destined to rule a great nation.

Agnes' cousin, Antoinette, was also eighteen years old. And Zèlde, the old sorcière had read her future in the tarot as well. Strange to say, although the cards in the spread were quite different from those in Agnes' reading, the prophecy was somewhat similar. "When one close to you has fulfilled her destiny, you will comfort a monarch."

But whereas Agnes accepted Zèlde's prognostication as entirely valid, Antoinette scoffed. It seemed to her the crazy old sorcière had a single-track mind.

When they were sitting in the rose garden back at Crevecour Castle, the girls' prattle fairly glistened.

"You heard what she said," Agnes chirped. "We're going to be famous, you and I."

"You don't actually believe what the zany sorcière of Beauvais told us, do you?" Antoinette asked. "She's obviously quite mad."

"I know in my heart that she saw our future, Antoinette," Agnes protested. "I knew it then, and I know it now."

"Including that part she added to your fortune and not to mine?" Antoinette responded with a naughty grin.

The friends giggled. There was something both funny and a quite ribald in the proviso Zèlde had added to Agnes' fortune.

"The part about the...maidenhead?" Agnes laughed.

There. She had said it out loud. And that caused an outburst of giggles the gardener at the other end of the garden could hear. The girls' giggles caused him to laugh aloud, good naturedly.

Neither girl mentioned the proviso aloud, but both remembered it verbatim: "If thy maidenhead become ruptured other than by Destiny's passion the Fortune is forfeit."

The young ladies certainly knew the meaning of the terms "maidenhead" and "virginity," and even had some realization of just what was understood by the words "chastity" and "deflower."

When they were together in their secret hideaway in the basement of Crevecour Castle, they always practiced kissing each other. And each of the girls had privately reached a clandestine finger up her own cunt to inspect the "cherry."

And after the prophesy they repaired to the hideaway and checked each other's "maidenhead" with their dainty fingers.

It somehow felt so wicked and so hilarious to do so.

Keeping your cherry from rupturing had something to do with being marriageable in the future and with being nice in the present.

After reassuring each other that they were "unruptured," they laughed so hard they were afraid someone would hear and discover them in their hideaway.

"Well, I think it was great fun to get our fortunes told," Antoinette proclaimed. "And I think it's silly to put our trust in what that old lady says. I don't think she's even Christian."

"What does 'Christian' have to do with it?" Agnes asked with a pout.

Antoinette contested by saying: "I've heard your own priest, Father Jehan, tell us 'Do not put your faith in magic or sorcery. Entrust your faith only to God, the Holy Virgin, the Church, and the Saints.'"

When quoting the good father, Antoinette, a mischievous mimic even when she was being serious, made her voice deep and masculine, and burlesqued the curé's Flemish accent. Both girls sniggered.

Agnes was not convinced by her cousin's take on the situation. And since her cousin had given a comic rendition of Father Jehan's actual statement, she wasn't sure that Antoinette believed it either.

Well, what did the old curé know? Just because he was a man of the cloth didn't mean he knew everything, did it? And she doubted he even knew what a maidenhead was for that matter. Zèlde's prophesy rang truer in Agnes' head than the priest's dry platitudes. Why should she, Agnes, not be a queen?

Queen of what, though? Picardy, the province in which she lived, didn't have a king. During the Hundred Years War, still in progress then in 1434, the province had changed hands between France and England many times. At the moment it was ruled by the English. Her family and friends hoped it would soon revert to France.

To rule a great nation, a female had to be a queen, didn't she? But the king of England, Henry VI, was only a little boy. Everyone knew he was too young to have a queen. And, as to Charles VII, the king of France south of the Loire. He was middle aged, with a wife, and a son, the dauphin. And the dauphin was already married. His was as hopeless a case as the English king. It was all very confusing.

Well, as Father Jehan always said, Agnes would just have to have faith. She hoped it was all right to have faith in Zèlde.

Over the course of the next few months, the meaning of the prophecy became clearer in Agnes' mind. She understood and she believed. She knew she had to remain a virgin until Destiny decreed the moment to yield her maidenhead to a great ruler, so she could rule as well.

She knew boys penises got hard and they wanted to shove their "thing" into her "*ce-que-j'ai*"(which she'd learned to call her cunt).

She had a picture in her mind what her future would be. Her image was a replica of the altarpiece at Saint Vivienne's church. The picture was of the Annunciation. In the striking picture, painted by Jan van Eyck, the angel was announcing to the Virgin that the great moment was at hand.

Agnes believed her great moment would be something like that. But, of course, without the angel Gabriel. Yet, it would be similar. She, Agnes Sorel, would remain a virgin. Which mean she wouldn't let any boy burst her cherry. And one day she would be a queen, like the Holy Mother. It was all too wonderful! Too wonderful to confide to anyone at all. Even in Confession. Particularly in Confession.

Antoinette returned to her home in Maignelay, and Agnes spent several months at home nursing her great secret. She saw herself as a great queen, wearing first one crown and then another. The castle she lived in, Crevecour, began to appear shabby in her eyes. Her father, Jean Sorel, was lord and master of the castle. Whether the English or the French were in possession of Picardy, he retained nominal overlordship of his tiny fiefdom. But Agnes knew that she was born to achieve a greatness that would eclipse Crevecour, and would overshadow even the cities of Beauvais and Amiens.

Agnes was sure her fame would outstrip Picardy itself. She was destined, after all, to rule a great nation. Zèlde had foretold it. And in Agnes' heart, that fortune had taken root.

In May, Agnes' mother, Catherine, Lady Crevecour, went to visit her sister at Maignelay. She left the four boys, Charles, Jean, Vincent and Cyrille back in Crevecour with their father. But, of course, she took Agnes with her.

Agnes and Antoinette were delighted to see each other again. The cousins had much to discuss. And a great deal to laugh and giggle about. Both were somewhat wiser concerning sexual matters than when they had been when together last. They had a secret place in the donjon of Maignelay Castle that was even more secret than the one back at Crevecour. The hiding place had once been a guest room. It had been abandoned and locked during the long war, and Antoinette had discovered the key to the room. The cousins spent hours on end in their secret hiding place opening their souls to each other.

Since they had grown breasts, they played with each other's nipples. And rubbed olive oil on each other's cunts. It was great fun.

"Do you have a boyfriend yet?" Agnes asked her cousin as she slid her oiled hand around to caress her clitoris.

"Kind of."

"What's a 'kind of' boyfriend?"

"Well," Antoinette answered. "There's this older boy, François. He's nineteen. And he's *had* some peasant girls around here. You know what I mean?"

"I'm pretty sure I do," Agnes said breathlessly "So did you let him...You know?"

"Kind of."

"Stop that, silly," Agnes giggled. "Tell me what you let him do."

"No. First, you tell me. Do you have a boyfriend back there in Crevecour?"

"There's no 'kind of' there, Antoinette. No boyfriend. No nothing. And you know my brothers would just about kill me if I let any boys get close to me with their "things" and all. Now, what about this François? Tell me. Come on!"

"Well, we were in the woods, you know. Off the beaten path. And I was asking him to tell me about...you know what."

"Yes, go on!"

"Well, he told me he'd tell me lots if I sat down on this fallen log that was near-by."

"And...?"

"And he talked about how he had felt Yvette's breasts. And how Marie-Laure had let him even kiss her...her..."

"Her what?"

"Her nipples!"

The maids laughed so loud they were worried someone would hear them and discover them in their secret place.

"And then, did you do it?"

"Then, he put his arm around me, and I let him leave it there. Then, he started to feel my breasts. And I didn't stop him."

"Antoinette, you didn't!"

Antoinette smiled and shook her head in reply.

"And did you still have on your blouse?"

"Well, yes. But I unbuttoned it so he could kind of reach his hand in."

Agnes muffled her giggle with her hand. Her eyes teared up with mirth.

"So, that's all you did?"

"Nearly."

"Come on. Don't tease me. Tell me all."

"Well, I let him kiss me."

"On the mouth?"

"Of course on the mouth."

"And did he, you know...What about his tongue?"

"He tried to stick his tongue in my mouth, but I wouldn't let him."

"And that was all?"

"Not quite."

"What then?"

"Well, he kept rubbing my breasts."

"Including your nipples?"

"Yes. Then he guided my hand to where his you-know-what was."

"And...?"

"And I felt it through his codpiece."

"Then what happened?"

"Everything felt...funny and all.

"I was so curious I reached in and pulled out his...his..."

"Cock." Agnes said.

"Then I said I had to get back home," Antoinette said. "He was disappointed that I wouldn't take off my blouse or play with his cock. He actually asked me to suck it. But I wouldn't.

"But then he just kind of grumbled, and I came back here."

"Have you seen him again?"

"Yes. He keeps asking me to walk in the woods with him again. But I don't want to."

"Don't want to?"

"Well, I want to. And I don't want to. I'm afraid that if we went back, I'd end up sucking his cock. And that would lead to other things. And I'd...get into trouble."

"Then François isn't really your boyfriend," Agnes insisted.

"No, I guess not," Antoinette admitted. "I know the peasant girls let him go further with them. He says they let him "do" it to them."

Agnes wanted to use the word. So she blurted it out.

"You mean they let him fuck them."

The girls started giggling.

Then Antoinette continued.

"If I encouraged him he'd expect me to let him go that far with me. And you and I know what that could lead to."

The cousins pondered that situation. They did, indeed, know what that could lead to.

On another occasion, the two maidens were discussing the session they had back in Beauvais with Zèlde.

"Down by the village, we have a sorcière, too," Antoinette told Agnes.

"A real sorcière like Zèlde?"

"Yes. Her name is Ouida. She's real old like Zèlde."

"Did you ever have her tell your fortune?" Agnes asked.

"No. I was afraid to go to her wagon alone."

"Let's go, Antoinette," Agnes urged. "Don't you want to see if she says the same things as Zèlde?"

"We would have to cross her palm with silver," Antoinette warned. "Do you have any coins in your purse?"

Agnes answered: "Father gave me some coins so I could buy some ribbons if we ran into any itinerant merchant while on this visit. How about you? Do *you* have any silver coins?"

"Yes. I have a couple of coins, too. Let's go, Agnes. But I hope you don't take this seriously like you did with that other silly fortune telling."

There was no point in arguing. The fortune Zèlde told back in Beauvais was not in the least silly. But Agnes believed it was best not to get into a row about it.

The girls had to walk through the village to its far border. There was a brightly painted wagon there, a wagon in which the fortune teller obviously lived. An extremely ugly woman, in voluminous multi-colored skirts was sitting on the ground before a fire, boiling some foul smelling mixture in an iron pot behind the wagon. The young ladies approached her with some trepidation.

The old woman cackled a greeting and bade the girls sit on the ground in front of her.

"Well, my pretties. What brings you to visit a poor old woman like me?" she asked.

"We were hoping you could tell our fortunes," Antoinette stammered.

"Fie!" the hag spit out, looking them up and down. "You are lying to me. It is not nice to lie to a helpless old woman."

The cousins were flabbergasted. This was scarcely the greeting they expected. They both swallowed and found themselves speechless.

The sorcière noted their discomfort with glee, and continued.

"You each already know your fortune, do you not? Are you here to tempt fate by asking again?"

The cousins blushed and shook their heads.

"It isn't your fortunes you want to know," the hag admonished. "That has been foretold already. You see, I know these things.

"What you really want is advice on how to assure your destiny. Isn't that so?"

When the maids nodded their heads in agreement, Ouida laughed a most disagreeable snort, displaying a mouth full of rotting teeth.

"You!" she pointed at Agnes. "Get yourself over here and ask me what you want to know. And cross my palm."

Agnes had never been timid. Yet she scooted around the fire apprehensively and sat next to Ouida.

"Cross my palm with silver," the old woman demanded again.

Agnes had the necessary coin in readiness and gave it to the hag.

"Now. What is really on your mind?" Ouida demanded as the coin disappeared into the folds of her skirts.

"I must prepare myself to rule one day," Agnes blurted out.

"Yes, yes. I know that," the hag spat out.

"And I have been given a warning," Agnes stammered. "That I cannot meet that destiny unless..."

Her voice faltered.

"Unless you preserve your treasure intact," the sorcière finished the sentence for her.

Agnes had already equated her "treasure" with her intact maidenhead.

"Yes."

"And you need to learn how to please the lust of men without sacrificing the flower of your maidenhood," Ouida confirmed.

There was the word out in the open.

Agnes had never exactly thought of it in that way. But yes. She suddenly understood the irony of the fact that seduction would be the path that would lead to her dream's fulfillment.

"You must learn to keep your swains happy and fulfilled, as you learn the arts of love," the fortune-teller informed her. "You can learn those arts only by practice. You can learn such things only from the males of our species. Do you understand?"

Agnes did not fully understand, but nodded her head.

"You must satisfy your lovers, and yet keep your knees together until the moment of destiny. Do you understand?"

Agnes nodded again, feeling that she nearly comprehended what she was being told.

It kind of equated to how her cousin had let François play with her titties while she actually handled his cock.

"Keep the hands and lips of your swain busy exploring that nubile body that has developed so temptingly," the sorcière continued. "While he is thus engaged, learn to use your own hands and mouth to raise the swain to heights of delight. But, what must you always remember?"

Agnes knew the answer already.

"To keep my knees together."

"Just so. To assure this, you must make sure your swains have devoured the atmagupta cake."

"Atmagupta cake?"

"Yes, dearie," Ouida explained. "For another piece of silver, I will provide you with atmagupta leaves that come from distant lands. You must mix minced atmagupta leaves with even parts of wheat or barley flour. Blend the mixture with enough honey and anisette to make a dough. You bake the fashioned dough into a tasty honey cake and offer it to your would-be lover. Your swain, after partaking of the lovecake, will be satisfied with the ministrations you offer him. But harken well. Make for yourself similar recipe, but without the leaves. You must never take even so much as a bite of the lovecakes, lest you succumb to the desire that will burst your precious flower. The lovecakes are only for the swain. You will be nibbling on the unlaced cake. Do you understand?"

Agnes had a second coin with her. She crossed the old lady's palm with it. When the coin had disappeared into the depths of the hag's skirts, Agnes received a small sack containing the promised leaves.

"Now," the sorcière hissed. "You need to learn and practice the arts of love. That is, learn how to please a male without suffering penetration to yourself."

Ouida dismissed Agnes with a flip of her fingers.

Agnes withdrew to the other side of the fire, clutching the bag of leaves.

Ouida motioned for Antoinette to approach.

"Your case is quite different, dearie," Antoinette was told when she had scooted herself beside the formidable old lady and had forfeited the necessary silver coin..

"You need not keep your treasure unruptured to achieve your destiny. But you must keep from bearing fruit from your erotic encounters. You can and will yield completely to the desires of your swains. But you will need a certain potion to forestall fertility. Cross my palm once more with silver."

When Antoinette delivered the coin, the sorcière cackled.

"Here, take this packet of mandragora. You must boil three pinches in a cupful of vinegar. Soak the concoction in a linen strip and insert it where it will kill off the seed of the male. You will not blossom into pregnancy if you follow that procedure. Do you understand?"

Antoinette understood completely.

She needed to prepare the potion as directed and get it up her cunt in a tiny piece of cloth. That would allow her to get fucked. But she would not get pregnant as long as she prepared herself ahead of time.

As the maids slunk away from the wheeled home of the beldam, they heard her evil laugh following them on their path back to the castle.

"What do you think?" Agnes asked her cousin.

"This time, I'm a believer, too," was her cousin's reluctant answer. "And, although the lovecakes are for your swain, I'd like my swain to have some, too."

"Of course you can have some if you want," Agnes assured her. "Can you get one of the servants to bake some cakes for us if we provide the dough with the atmagupta?"

"Of course," Antoinette replied. "Drusille, who works in the kitchen, is my friend. She'll bake some for us. She's been my friend all my life. I won't tell her about the atmagupta leaves. Just that the dough is for honeycakes. We'll give her a couple of the harmless ones."

"And your mandragora potion?"

"I can get it boiled up, too."

"What's next then?"

"I'll find François. And have him bring one of his friends for you. And we'll go learn the arts of love."

The girls went to the kitchen of Maignelay Castle where Drusille, the cook, helped them prepare the honey cakes and the contraceptive mixture.

The girls met François and his friend Joachim the next day at the hayloft of a barn that Joachim knew to be safe from prying eyes.

And, on a fine afternoon in the first week of May, Joachim, under the influence of the lovecake, was content to fondle Agnes' breasts while she jacked him off. He was satisfied if she kissed him and inserted her tongue in his mouth. Particularly if she would lower those lips and suck his cock until he was ready to come.

She wasn't yet ready to receive his jism into her mouth. But a few jerks with her hand gave him as much release as he felt he needed.

Agnes found that she was able to keep her knees together without argument from her swain.

And her cousin yielded herself to François, who, as it turned out, had never really had a full sexual relationship until that afternoon.

He was not the experienced lover he claimed to be. But he had taken care of the maidenhood thing for her. She was now no longer a virgin. And she knew she didn't have to fear pregnancy.

She discovered she *loved* fucking.

Agnes, wiser in the ways of males, returned to Crevecour with her mother on May 12.

As Jean Sorel met his wife and daughter upon their return, he was obviously in a jubilant mood.

"My dears, have you heard the news?"

Mother and daughter did not know what he was referring to.

"The Maid," he said. "The Maid, Joan of Arc, has just led the French forces to raise the siege of Orleans. The battle was successful. The Goddams have left the city in disarray. The tide of war has turned to the French cause, by the Grace of God."

There was no question who the Goddams were. That was the name the occupied French used to refer to the English occupiers.

"That is, indeed, reason for rejoicing," wife Catherine replied.

"And what is more, the Maid is leading Charles to Rheims, to be crowned there. Once properly anointed in Rheims, he will truly be Charles VII, Charles the Victorious. Glory be to God."

"Glory be to God," mother and daughter echoed.

Joan of Arc's victory was the happiest day for France in decades.

Chapter Two

The French were now on the way to winning the interminable war against the Goddams. They had a consecrated king, Charles the Victorious. True, the Maid, Joan of Arc, who had raised the siege of Orleans, had been captured by the Burgundians. She was handed over to the English, and burned at the stake in Rouen on May 30, 1430. But her martyrdom did not halt the new vigor that was inspiring the sons and daughters of France.

Agnes knew her destiny lay in France. She practiced her arts of love on many a swain, steadily perfecting the art of satisfaction without penetration. And that practice was directed towards her perceived destiny of "ruling a great nation."

In 1432, at Christmas time, life took a decided turn for Agnes. Her parents, at the dinner table, told her of their decision to send her south to Toulouse.

"Agnes," her father said, unsuccessfully attempting not to sound gruff. "It is now quite clear, after nearly a century of doubt, that our beloved Picardy is destined to be French, not English or Flemish."

"Yes, father," Agnes answered in the meek tones she reserved for communicating with the Lord of Crevecour."

"I have decided, that is, your mother and I have decided, that it is necessary for you to learn the ways of the French nobility. You will soon be nineteen. And we will never get you married off satisfactorily unless you receive the..."

Jean Sorel paused. His wife supplied the next word for him.

"Polish."

"Humph, yes...the polish that life at an elegant court in the South could provide."

Agnes' heart seemed to jump and then miss a beat. She knew she lacked some quality to meet her destiny. And that quality she now realized was... polish.

"Yes, father."

"Your godmother, Suzanne, has a very good friend who lives in Toulouse, a certain Madame..."

"Chassaing," wife Catherine interposed.

"Humph, yes...Chassaing. And this Madame's husband was a military companion of the Duke of Anjou, Duke..."

"René," Catherine said with a slight questioning tone.

"Yes, Duke René d'Anjou. And the wife of Duke René, Duchess..."

"Isabelle d'Anjou," was interjected by Agnes' mother.

"Yes, Duchess Isabelle let it be known she would be accepting a new maid-of-honor at this time."

Catherine Sorel, uncharacteristically, took up the narrative.

"You see, my dear. It has been arranged that you will be one of Duchess Isabelle's maids-of-honor, if she chooses you after proper examination. Next month, you will travel to Toulouse, to Narbonne Castle where the Duke and Duchess currently reside. I will accompany you there, of course, as will your brothers Charles and Jean. If the duchess agrees to accept you, after meeting, examining and questioning, you, you will remain to learn the ways of a great house."

"But papa, maman. How very kind of you to arrange such a wonderful education for me," Agnes enthused.

Catherine went on. "Of course, you scarcely have the right attire at present. There has been no need of it here in our province."

Jean added, "So at great expense, I have engaged a tailor to come here from Amiens. He is reputed to be up on the latest fashions of the court of Charles VII. So, what do you have to say?"

"Oh, Father," Agnes gushed. "You are the kindest, most generous, most loving papa any girl could ever have."

She would have hugged him, but knew he would be embarrassed. So she embraced her mother, while the lord of the castle looked on, pleased at his daughter, and at himself.

At last, the day dawned. A coach arrived that was well insulated against the winter cold with leather window covers outside and thick blankets and furs within. Agnes, her mother, and two of her brothers entered the carriage that would take them as far as Angers. The ride was far from comfortable. The cold weather intruded on the passengers, despite the leather, blankets, and furs. Mother Catherine complained constantly. But for Agnes, the voyage was a delight.

"Why, Maman, if Duke René is the Duke of Anjou, why is his palace not here in the duchy of Anjou?" Agnes asked when they arrived in Angers.

"One of the vicissitudes of this interminable war with the Goddams," Catherine explained to her daughter. "Life was not safe for the duke up here several years ago. The sovereign, Charles VII, granted him and his duchess a more secure place, Narbonne Palace, farther south in Toulouse. Narbonne was the palace of the counts of Toulouse, a property that passed to the House of Valois. You see, Duke René is also King of Sicily. Unfortunately, he is prevented by politics from going to Sicily to rule there as he is entitled to do. René is the brother of Queen Marie of France, Charles VII's wife.

"René and Marie, who is, as I mentioned, our beloved queen, were the children of Louis II of Anjou and his wife Yolande of Aragon. Now, it was Louis II and Duchess Yolande who really raised our king from the time he was affianced to their daughter Marie..."

Agnes was sorry she had asked. Her mother's answer was more than she wanted to know. She stopped listening, but continued smiling attentively.

The voyage from Angers to Toulouse lasted two weeks. The weather became warmer as they proceeded south, but there was still a chill in the air. The ever-changing countryside of the south of France was a delight to Agnes. As they stopped at the wayside inns in the evening, the sound of the spoken language merged gradually from Langue d'Oeil to Langue d'Oc. Agnes was versed, of course, in the two versions of the French language and delighted in being able to match the variations between the two dialects with the features of the countryside.

They passed through villages, towns, and cities. Each interesting in its own way. But nothing had prepared Agnes for Toulouse.

As they approached the city, Agnes burst out in smiles.

"Look, Maman! The city is rose colored. Have you ever seen a city so beautiful?"

"I have never been here before either, Daughter. It is lovely, isn't it?"

"And the houses, see? They have silver-tiled roofs. Have you ever...?"

"Very nice, Agnes. Look at that clock tower. It must be five stories tall. And it tells time on two different dials."

There were, indeed, bell towers, steeples, and immense naves. It was a beautiful city, embraced by the Garonne River. But when the coach approached Narbonne Castle, the mother and daughter were struck speechless.

The castle was topped by eight separate towers, each one flying a colorful pennant. It was a magnificent sight. The wooden drawbridge was permanently lowered. The horses' hooves clacked loudly as the carriage passed over the bridge and into the cobblestoned courtyard.

The arriving party was met by liveried footmen who escorted Agnes and her mother to the vestibule. Agnes' brothers were taken to the men's quarters.

Duchess Isabelle d'Anjou, attired in a violet velvet dress adorned with seed pearls descended the grand staircase to receive and greet Catherine and Agnes Sorel. Agnes was immediately in awe of the duchess. She was perhaps only two inches taller than Agnes' five foot two, but seemed to tower above her. She carried herself with a studied stateliness. Her red hair, worn in a gold, pearl-studded net, was highly coiffed. Her hostess smile showed a row of small, gleaming teeth that appeared nearly predatory to Agnes. But the overall impression Agnes had was that this woman was of an urbanity that would be becoming to a ruler of a great nation. The duchess was certainly one to be studied, and learned from.

After the customary bows and curtsies, Duchess Isabelle addressed her new guests. Her voice was deep-pitched, with rounded tones. It was a voice that radiated self-confidence and authority.

"I know that after your tiring journey here from Picardy, you will want to rest and refresh yourselves. But I did want to be the first to welcome you personally to Toulouse and Narbonne Castle. Our seneschal, Henri, will show you to your quarters. If there is anything at all we can do to make your stay comfortable, Henri stands ready to provide for your needs or even for your whims."

The ladies from Picardy expressed the appropriate responses, and followed Henri to quarters on the third floor.

The apartments provided for Catherine and Agnes were lavish by any definition. They had connecting rooms, very similarly furnished. The large, four poster, canopied beds were spacious enough to accommodate several people. A tall marble fireplace stood in the wall separating the two chambers in such a way that it heated both rooms. But, lavish as her room was, Agnes was most impressed by the windows. They were composed of little glass squares encased in lead. That luxury particularly appealed to Agnes.

One maid, Lucille, was in attendance to provide for the two of them.

"Would my ladies desire me to draw baths for them?"

The ladies did so desire. Servants then brought tin bathtubs into the rooms. Additional servants followed with buckets of hot water. Soaps, perfumes, oils, and lotions followed. After the baths, masseuses ministered to travel-weary muscles. The naps that followed the procedures were deep and gratifying.

In the evening, when they had dressed and re-coiffed themselves for dinner, mother and daughter descended to the grand dining room. The room was filled with knights, ladies, ladies-in-waiting, and maids-of-honor. Isabelle d'Anjou went to the foot of the stairs and greeted the new arrivals. First they were introduced to Duke René d'Anjou. He seemed the perfect mate for the duchess. René was somewhat shorter than his duchess, but seemed taller than he was due to his overwhelming presence. He was clear-eyed, had brown hair, and the build of a bull. His baritone voice expressed a prodigious appetite for life.

He first greeted Catherine, kissing her hand. When he caught full sight of Agnes, his appreciation for her stunning beauty was fully apparent in his fixed regard of her features.

As he fixated on her breasts, she could virtually feel his lips sucking on her nipples. As he ogled her groin, she could swear she saw his dick pulsating beneath his codpiece.

Agnes felt as if she had been publicly disrobed by the duke and violated right in front of all these people. Then she noticed that no one else had seemed to pay attention to the disrobing, and she relaxed.

She knew in her heart she could deal with this randy duke.

When Agnes returned to her chambers after the lavish dinner, she confided in her mother.

"Maman. I know I am going to like it here."

"I am happy for you, Agnes darling. You are going to fit right in here."

Agnes did not say it aloud. But to herself she said, "How very right you are, Maman. Not only will I fit in, I will learn how to rule here."

Catherine Sorel knew the protocol involved in her stay. At the end of three days, it was understood that she and her two sons would leave Toulouse to return to Beauvais and Crevecour. It was also clear to her and to her daughter that Agnes would return with them if Isabelle d'Anjou did not specifically invite her to stay on as a maid-of-honor. Officially, Agnes was at Narbonne castle merely as an invited guest for three days. During that time, of course, she would meet often with the duchess. And the duchess would determine in that period whether Agnes was suitable to remain on.

On the second day of her stay, Duchess Isabelle discussed music, literature, poetry and fashion with the young lady. Could Agnes play any musical instrument? She had learned to play the psaltery in Picardy. The duchess sent for a psaltery. It was a particularly lovely wood-and-ivory instrument, the finest Agnes had ever seen. Agnes played the popular "If I err when I love." The duchess had a fine clear voice, and joined her guest in a duet. The duchess was pleased. Did Agnes embroider? She just happened to have brought her latest with her. A servant was dispatched to fetch the handwork. A most exquisite piece indeed. The duchess was pleased.

One test after another. The young lady did, indeed, seem to have promise. But all her skills would prove to be worthless if she could not pass the essential test for a maid-of-honor. She must truly be a demoiselle. It was essential that she be *virgo intacta*. That she still have an unruptured cherry.

Agnes was summoned to the duchess' own private chambers. When she arrived two servants helped her undress. As she was being disrobed, the duchess entered and addressed her.

"Agnes, dear child. You told me you are a virgin."

"Yes Madame. I so told you. And did not lie."

"You are, of course, aware that, although I believe you to be honest, it would be unfair to all the other maids-of-honor if I were not to make the necessary investigation anyway."

"I understand, Your Grace," Agnes replied, as layer after layer of clothing was being removed by the two serving maids.

She had traced the path up her twat with an oiled finger often enough to have assured herself that the cherry still bloomed.

"Even the sainted Joan, the Maid of Orleans, had to be examined, you know," Isabel told Agnes. "She simply could not have been admitted to audience with my brother-in-law, the king, at Chinon, claiming to represent Our Lord and

His Saints if she were not a proven virgin."

"So I have heard, Madame."

"It was my mother-in-law, Duchess Yolande, who conducted the examination, with her own anointed hand."

Agnes nodded in understanding. Her last undergarment was removed and the serving maids retired from the room. Agnes stood in regal nudity before the Duchess d'Anjou.

"My, my, my, Agnes. How perfectly lovely you are," the duchess remarked. "Indeed, you are the most perfect specimen of feminine beauty I have ever observed. Those breasts — magnificent, divine.

"My, how my husband the duke would love to fondle them. You must not allow him to do so, you know. He is a very naughty duke. But if any of my maids-of-honor were to allow King René (he is the rightful king of Sicily, you know)…I say, if any of my maids-of-honor were to allow such intimacy with the Duke, she would have to be dispatched from my court in disgrace."

"Of course, Your Grace," Agnes assented.

"Your blond hair, truly a remarkable gold, complements your ivory skin in a way that can be appreciated only when seeing you totally unclothed. You will be a perfect adjunct to our court, if you are, indeed, unblemished in your maidenhood."

"You are very kind, Your Grace," Agnes replied modestly.

Isabelle anointed her right hand with a jasmine-scented ointment.

"Now come here, dear. You mustn't shy away from the examination."

Agnes approached, not in the least shy. Isabelle ran her aristocratic finger up Agnes' crack to check and see that the vital membrane was, indeed, not ruptured.

"Ah, wonderful, my dear. *Virgo intacta*. I will call the dressers back in to assist you into your habiliments. I will be pleased to inform your mother at dinner this evening that I have invited you to join our household."

"Thank you, Your Grace," Agnes replied.

As the duchess was leaving the room and the serving girls were entering, Isabelle shot one last statement back to Agnes.

"And of course, dear. I will be conducting this examination of your… flower…once a month. It is the custom in every well-regulated court in France."

"Of course, Duchess Isabelle. And thank you again," Agnes agreed, pleased that her pathway to power was clearly under way.

She would not object at all to having that slender finger run up her cunt whenever the duchess felt impelled to do so.

Two days later, Catherine Sorel bid a tearful, yet happy, farewell to her daughter. She felt assured that Agnes would learn the finer points of living a courtly life, and would thus attract a husband who would be an asset to the house of Sorel.

Agnes thoroughly enjoyed life at the Anjou court. She was the newest member of the carefully chosen ten maids-of honor of the duchess. At Narbonne Castle, Agnes was trained in the ways of elegance and courtliness that were absent in Picardy and Crevecour. She learned to dance the gaillard and the passepied. She already spoke High French, Flemish, and English, the three languages of Picardy. Her knowledge of the languages of Toulouse, Langue d'Oc and Provençale, were adequate but somewhat sketchy. She soon had mastered their finer points as well.

Agnes was often chosen to read aloud to the duchess and the maids from the extensive Narbonne library. Poetry, particularly the poems of the troubadours, was often preferred. But chivalric tales were quite the mode as well. And, of course, the immensely popular *Romance of the Rose* had to be read again and again.

At musical gatherings, Agnes and Isabelle d'Anjou often entertained with duets. Isabelle with her dulcimer and Agnes on the wood-and-ivory psaltery accompanied themselves in singing the popular rondos, joc partits, jovens, and pastorelas composed by the troubadours.

Her beauty, her talent, and her gay spirits made her a court favorite soon after her arrival. Agnes felt herself definitely on the road to fulfilling her destiny.

And she enjoyed the regular sallies of the duchess' finger up the koozie. It was a royal treat.

And it seemed clear to her that the duchess enjoyed the experience possibly even more than she herself did.

Chapter Three

Agnes felt she had to keep practicing the arts of love while at Narbonne Castle. There was always more to learn from the young men she seduced. She had brought six dozen atmagupta cakes and six un-laced honeycakes with her to Toulouse. She knew the lovecakes would retain their potency. She thus had plenty of time to find a sorcière in Languedoc to secure a fresh batch of leaves.

Life at the court of Duke René was more lively than anything she had previously experienced. There were feasts, parties, games, gallantries, even duels. The country was experiencing peace for the first time in a century. The French seemed to feel that pleasure and a lack of care should rule every minute.

Agnes spent the first full week at Narbonne in search of a swain or swains upon whom she could practice and from whom she could learn. She knew, of course that the knights and noblemen would be too risky to approach. It was safe to flirt with the courtiers, but not to engage in amorous pursuits. All the gentlemen played the chivalric flirtation game. And Agnes instinctively played it back with ease. Every man knew that if he were fortunate enough to win the game and bed the demoiselle, she would be dispatched from the premises in disgrace the next time the duchess examined her. But that was, after all, part of the game. It was the principle of the hunt, with the maiden the prey. It made the stakes more delightful for the hunter. And when one bagged a demoiselle, and she was banished, the duchess always managed to replace her with a new delightful morsel. And the dazzling blonde with the periwinkle eyes and the killing coy smile was by far the choicest game provided yet.

A gentleman could play the *fin'amors* (courtly love) game alone, or accompanied by a companion. The seductive exchange was always intended to be witty and allusive, never direct or vulgar.

One afternoon, Duke René was strolling down one of the corridors of the castle in company with a cousin, Thierry d'Aubusson. Agnes was walking nonchalantly in the same area when she was overtaken by the cousins.

"My word, Thierry. I am stunned," said the duke.

"I am not surprised. The magnificent beauty I spy just ahead seems to have quite blinded me as well," his cousin answered.

"Perhaps, *chevaliers*, you mistake the pale moon's glow for Phoebus' chariot," Agnes answered as she came to a stop and unleashed her smile on the two.

"René, I do not believe I have had the pleasure..." Thierry exclaimed.

"Oh, Thierry," René responded. "Apparently your temporary blindness has been remedied. May I introduce the duchess' newest maid-of-honor, the demoiselle from...Picardy I believe it is?"

"Agnes Sorel," she replied. "At the service of the two noble messires."

"Oh," said Duke René. "Let it be not so. It is I, rather, who would be honored to serve you."

"My lord the duke jests with his wife's least worthy maid-of-honor," Agnes said demurely.

"Not at all, my lovely," replied the duke. "I am a knight of the realm of our noble victorious sire. It is well known that a knight must, above all, serve beauty."

"And you, Messire," she addressed Count Thierry. "Do you agree with my lord the duke?"

"Demoiselle," Thierry responded. "I have been in such awe of your exquisite beauty that I hardly dared introduce myself, lest I stammer. I am Count Thierry d'Aubusson. And may I say, with all due respect, that I quite agree with my esteemed cousin? I, too, am a knight who offers himself at the disposal of beauty."

"It is apparent, Demoiselle Agnes," said René. "That the mere encounter with your radiance has caused two of the most dashing knights of the realm to fall and grovel at your feet."

"Behold, cousin," Thierry interjected. "A rose blush appears to be tinting the ravishing pure white skin of the demoiselle."

"By Saint John!" René exclaimed. "I do hope Demoiselle Sorel will continue to blush. The effect is quite intoxicating."

"My lords. How you do go on," Agnes responded coyly.

"But I must go on," the duke replied. "I have, I must admit, been aware of your loveliness from the moment you arrived in Toulouse. But I never would have guessed that shyness lurked behind those alabaster features."

"Shy, my lord?" Agnes shot back. "Why not a whit. It is just that the two of you have quite overwhelmed me. I see that I must call forth my reserves."

"Oh, attention, cousin," Duke René addressed the count. "This fortress appears to be defended with more forces than we had anticipated."

"But René," the count retorted. "The more difficult the taking, the more exciting the maneuvering."

The cousins bantered back and forth.

"The breastworks, my old friend, the breastworks," Thierry punned. "Have you ever seen the like?"

"Absolutely exquisite," Thierry agreed. "Particularly if constructed by Nature rather than by Artifice."

"I assure you, my lords. Entirely the work of Nature. And quite permanent," Agnes answered. "They have always proved themselves adequate guardians of the fort."

"Then, René," Thierry riposted. "they are ramparts, rather than breastworks, after all. But all the more admirable."

"The fortress, gentlemen, happens to be absolutely impregnable," Agnes shot back.

René volleyed:

"However, Demoiselle Agnes. You just might discover that surrender can be sweeter than defending in a siege."

"Yet, Messire," Agnes half whispered with a seductive glance that belied her words. "When Virtue and Wisdom are the vigilant defenders, be assured that the fortress shall not fall."

"Aha!" Count Thierry fairly shouted. "I should have known it. The demoiselle knows well the *Romance of the Rose*."

"As well she might," the duke responded. "It is, indeed, the very bible of the Doctrine of Love. *Gai saber* (poetic wit) and *fin'amors* (chivalric love), have been raised to the level of a rite by the romance. And at Narbonne Castle, love rules all."

"My lord obviously means to add that love rules, as long as it remains within the bounds of *gai saber*," Agnes laughed.

"That goes without saying, you most ineluctable of all beauties."

"I know not whom you are addressing, my lord, with such outlandish praise," Agnes demurred. "But to get back to the romance. You will recall that the rose is protected by a solid wall. You know, of course, of what that wall consists."

"Pray, tell us," answered the gentlemen.

"Of its virtues, my good lords. Of its virtues," Agnes responded.

"I seem to recall, however," Thierry answered, "That at the end, Bel Accueil (Welcome) allows the lover to...*pluck* the Rose."

"You are, of course, correct," Agnes agreed. "But anyone who would strive to enter the...*Garden of Delight*...must prove his honesty, his courtliness, and, above all his...generosity."

The two knights knew that by the rules of the game the first skirmish had been declared over. With deep bows, the men retreated a step.

"Allow me, fair lady, at this time, to render my sincere homage to Beauty," Duke René said.

Agnes answered: "I accept such homage in the name of your noble wife, my mistress, Duchess Isabelle."

Agnes felt she had won the skirmish hands down.

Fin'amors was all very well. Agnes was courted in the *gai saber* mode by nearly every male with even a trace of blue in his veins. But for Agnes, it was all a mind game, or, occasionally, an artistic game. But it could never lead to physical contact. Not until the moment Destiny had in wait for her.

To ploy her physical arts, the pages were what she needed. No page would dare attempt an intimacy, not even in eye contact or gesture, with one of the duchess' maids-of-honor. It was rumored that the duke himself would employ physical mutilation on any male who crossed class or caste lines upward. Oh, a young man could dream, all right. But he had better not evidence untoward interest in the aristocratic lasses for fear of having his balls cut off with a pair of scissors reputedly kept in the duke's private repository.

For pages, intimacy was confined to those of one's own class, or better yet, classes below one's station.

Agnes was vigilant. She planned to select a page and assure him that the great transgression would never be known. If he were to tell of any carnal contact with her, a member of the duchess' select maids, the result for him could be unthinkable.

Every page had a ghastly picture of the duke's reputed scissors in his imagination.

Therefore, Agnes was doubly prudent. She needed an additional weapon to assure secrecy on the part of the chosen swain. She knew she would be successful in finding that assurance.

Agnes spent many an hour sitting in the shadows, observing but unobserved. She saw the pages, the varlets, and the wenches about their assigned employments. She observed them at rest and at play. The lusty young bucks vied for the favors of the wenches. The wenches knew coquettery with every refinement practiced by their betters. Agnes had always been amused observing the human comedy. The manners of the comedy varied from class to class. The underlying roles of male and female, however, were uniform.

One young man particularly caught her eye. He was one of the taller pages, and of a muscular physique. He was the same age as herself, eighteen and of comely appearance. He had dark black hair and deep brown, long lashed, mischievous eyes. He was not in the least bashful about grabbing a wench to him as she passed. His attempts to place a kiss on the lips of the girl were met with much good-natured laughter, but never, as far as Agnes could tell, with a successful placement of lips on lips.

Agnes took to following the handsome lad's progress at various off moments of the day to discover a weakness of his that might play to her advantage. One afternoon, her watchfulness paid off.

Agnes, observing from the shadows, saw Guyot, for such was the young man's name, slipping into the room of a visiting knight, Sir Jauffre de Miraval. She waited. Scant minutes later, Guyot peered out the door, felt himself unobserved, and stepped briskly into the corridor. In his hand he held a silver dagger encased in a jeweled sheath. With his treasure, he scurried down the arched walkway and out of sight.

That evening, at dinner, Sir Jauffre informed the duke of his missing treasure. The guests were horrified. A theft at the court of the Duke of Anjou. Unthinkable! The culprit must be caught!

Questioning of all the servants, grooms, varlets, pages, even the squires, yielded no clues. The mystery was not solved. But Agnes knew who the guilty party was, and was ready to use the information.

Agnes now was ready to spring her trap.

One afternoon, when Guyot was sitting alone in the courtyard, Agnes stepped out of the shadows of the archway and appeared to have discovered a pebble in her shoe. She bent forward, reaching for her ankle. As her ankle was revealed in its perfection, her bodice slipped. Guyot was simultaneously made witness to both a perfect ankle and the most stunning breasts in France. As he gaped open-mouthed at the amazing spectacle, Agnes brazenly stared at him. He looked up and, drawing his eyes away from the enticing tits, gazed into a pair of coquettish periwinkle eyes.

The page blinked. He could not believe what his eyes revealed. The demoiselle returned his gaze, winked, and returned a fixed stare directly at him. Guyot was prepared to brave whatever might befall him. The invitation was too explicit to ignore.

Wearing the garb of the bourgeois classes, Agnes had explored every corner of the lovely pink city of Toulouse. On the outskirts, she discovered an inn that was fastidiously clean, and with a completely discrete innkeeper. It was called the Laughing Rooster (Au Coq qui Rit), and was exactly suitable to her purposes.

Guyot, dressed like a bourgeois himself, met her at the inn on a brisk Thursday afternoon. The fireplace in their room crackled in a lively manner, casting its heat over the snug yet adequate room.

The furnishings were sparse. A rude table with two chairs. An unpretentious but inviting bed. A pitcher of Provençale wine and two tankards rested on the table. The window was modestly draped with a thick leather curtain.

Agnes was already in the room when Guyot arrived. He came into the room rather timidly, and awkwardly. All the bluster he displayed in his constant pranks with the wenches at court was gone. Agnes thought the shyness of his new demeanor rather becoming.

"Come in. Sit down and relax, Guyot. Are you all right?"

"Yes, thank you, Demoiselle," he muttered, falling down heavily into one of the chairs.

"The host has provided us with some rather nice wine. I was about to enjoy a sip. May I pour some for you?" Agnes invited.

"That would be fine, Mademoiselle," Guyot stammered.

"And, to accompany the wine, I have brought along a couple of honey cakes for us to enjoy. Here's one for you. And here's one for me," Agnes offered.

Guyot's cake was laced with atmagupta. Agnes was careful to keep in mind which cake was destined for her playmate and which was for her.

"Thank you, Demoiselle," Guyot managed to say as he took a nibble of his cake and sipped a bit of wine.

He was so ill at ease that Agnes was beginning to wonder whether she had done well in choosing the youth after all. Well, time would tell.

As they sipped their wine, the couple exchanged glances. Agnes looked Guyot up and down, focusing on the sensual mouth and the broad chest. Guyot fidgeted in his chair. Although uncomfortable, he was enjoying this.

He was deeply aware that her glance kept dropping to his codpiece.

He, in turn, stared at her lovely mouth, and then at those unmatchable breasts. Agnes could see he was coming around. Some of the spunk and wantonness returned to his features. Everything was going to turn out just fine.

"I have noticed you trying to kiss the wenches back at court," Agnes said.

"They have been quite skilled in slipping away from me," Guyot answered, far less haltingly than he had been.

They both laughed.

"Have you ever succeeded in really kissing a girl? Truthfully now," Agnes teased.

Guyot blushed and hesitated.

"Come, come now, Guyot. You must tell me the truth. A real kiss? Ever?"

"I have to admit," Guyot acknowledged. "Never. But not from lack of trying."

"What if I told you that I think your lips are beautiful?" Agnes taunted. "And that I am mad to kiss them? What would you say?"

"I would rather not say. I would rather show you."

That was the pluckiness she was looking for.

Agnes rose from the chair and sauntered provocatively to the bedside. Guyot set his tankard down and followed her.

He was clearly unschooled in kissing. When she slipped her tongue into his mouth, he gave such a start it caused her to laugh. He stopped the laugh with a fresh assault on her lips that was more fierce than soft.

Bit by bit, by example, Agnes coached his mouth and tongue into soft, sweet, playful, gentle, loving sensuous kisses.

In the midst of a deep, passionate kiss, Agnes' hand grazed Guyot's codpiece. It was clearly an invitation.

Guyot showed himself unskilled at the art of removing a bodice and blouse to get his hands on the most inviting breasts in Europe. As he groped and struggled, Agnes very skillfully managed to remove his codpiece. As his pecker emerged into a valiant hardon, she caressed it gently.

She required him to sit quietly on the bed fully displaying a very attractive prick. Agnes felt she had chosen her swain well. When entirely disrobed herself, she approached the bedside. Guyot remained sitting on the edge, dumbstruck. She gave him a gentle push back into a lying position and joined him on the bed.

She kissed him on the neck, and then across his chest. She ran her tongue languidly across his nipples. That was invitation enough for him to do the same to her.

While, without coaching, he fixed his boyish lips on her awaiting nipples, Agnes gently fondled his throbbing dick.

Three caresses and he was a goner.

She had seduced enough young virgins to know they spurted their wad with very little stimulation.

She assured him that she thought his ejaculation was proof of his virility, and that she had a way to bring him to full harness in no time at all.

She urged him to finish his honey cake and sip a bit more wine.

He relaxed as he did so.

When she knew that the time was ripe, she urged him to lie spread-eagle on the bed.

When he seemed sufficiently relaxed, she bent over him and took his rising cock into her mouth.

The cock was what Agnes classified as medium sized. Which meant that she could take it entirely into her mouth and into her throat. The larger and thicker cocks of the youths she seduced got little more than the bulb at end swallowed.

She particularly enjoyed servicing the length and circumference of this young swain's cock.

Agnes continued to teach the young man love games that satisfied him while still protecting the forfended spot she had managed to keep inviolate.

When the love games started to play themselves out, much later in the afternoon, Guyot said to her:

"Mademoiselle, this has been the most wonderful day of my entire life."

"Of course," was her simple answer.

"And I wouldn't want you to think I'm complaining, because I'm happy and completely fulfilled."

"As am I."

"But...I was under the impression that the act of love involved..."

"Penetration?"

"That would be the word," Guyot agreed.

"Penetration of the cunt is reserved for the marriage bed," Agnes explained. "It is not essential for a completely amorous and erotic exchange such as we have enjoyed."

"I see, My Lady."

"One more thing you have to see, Master Guyot. You must never speak of our encounter to anyone."

The lad nodded agreement.

"Anyone at all. Friend, lover, master...priest...No one," Agnes insisted.

"Yes, Mademoiselle."

"On pain of severe consequences."

"Yes, Mademoiselle."

"If you were to spill even a hint," Agnes warned him. "It would surely seep back to the duke. And if word got to the duke, there would be two consequences."

Guyot could only continue to nod, open mouthed, in agreement.

"The first consequence would be that the duke would personally cut these manly balls off you with his special scissors."

She encircled his balls to focus his mind.

Her glance at his crotch was all that was needed in the way of explanation.

Guyot winced.

"The second consequence would be that I would have to inform the duke who stole the silver bodkin in the jeweled sheath."

Shock registered on the young man's face.

"The punishment for one of your humble class would be execution," Agnes explained precisely. "A slow, painful death, to be enacted before all your peers. As an example, you see."

Horrified, Guyot jumped out of bed and began fumblingly to clothe himself.

"And, of course, the execution would take place after, not before he had snipped off these balls with his famous shears."

She encircled his nuts again as she spoke.

"However," she purred. "If you are very discrete, and never mention our relationship here at the Laughing Rooster, life can be very sweet for you. For, in that case, we will meet here often."

Guyot's lips were absolutely sealed. He never mentioned Agnes to anyone, for as long as he lived. And, true to her word, Agnes met Guyot there often.

Chapter Four

Duke René made amorous pass after amorous pass at Agnes. She had no problem fending off his advances. She was as skilled as he at the game. And she did not intend to lose.

Conquests were one of René's chief forms of amusement. He was not, and never had been, faithful to his wife Isabelle. That fact was offset by her absolute unfaithfulness to him. Indeed, it was reported that Duchess Isabelle took on more lovers than the duke. And yet, the two were always discrete with each other, purposely turning blind eyes to the unlawful pleasures of their spouses.

There was no doubt that Duchess Isabelle loved the duke. Loved him dearly. And her intimates knew she loved one other as well. That "other" was Pierre de Breze. The rest of the men Isabelle bedded were flings, entertainments, whims, and frolics only. She loved the way each man made love in a different fashion. The permutations were infinite. But woe to the lover who repeated his techniques identically twice in a row. He was unlikely to be invited to the duchess' bed for many a month, if ever again. The duchess could not abide unimaginative lovers.

The duchess' love life never produced unfortunate embarrassing fruit. Like every knowledgeable lady of rank, Isabelle knew the power and uses of mandragora. It had never failed her. She chose her pregnancies with a constant eye on the succession of the House of Anjou. She and Duke René had great hopes for their daughter. Marguerite d'Anjou, though still a mere child, was very attractive and of aristocratic birth since Isabelle was also Duchess of Lorraine in her own right. And, of course, Marguerite was the niece of King Charles VII and Queen Marie of France.

On a snowy February day, Isabelle received a note from Pierre de Breze. Chills ran up and down her spine. Chills that had nothing to do with the wintery weather. The letter formally informed her that Breze planned to visit Narbonne Castle three days hence.

Charles VII had entrusted Narbonne Castle in Toulouse to his in-laws for the winter months. Their holdings in Anjou, were, of course, still left in their control as was their palace in Lorraine. In their absence from Anjou and Poitou, Breze as seneschal was overseer of their properties. He was not only Isabelle's servant, he was her favorite lover.

Pierre de Breze was the Seneschal of Poitou, a valiant knight, a heroic warrior, and an adept at *gai saber* and *fin'amors*. And, reportedly, he was a marvel in bed. In Isabelle's opinion, he was the most strikingly handsome man in France. She was not alone in that opinion. Breze had won more trophies in bed than on the battlefield.

Needless to say, Pierre de Breze dwelt in Isabelle d'Anjou's heart in a position equal to, or perhaps a trifle above, that of Duke René.

When Breze arrived in Toulouse, his eye immediately picked out Agnes Sorel for what she was. The most desirable creature in the realm. His interest was not unnoticed by his lover.

That night, before they snuggled into each other's arms, the duchess brought up the subject of Agnes Sorel to the seneschal.

"My dear, this is scarcely the moment to discuss one of your maids-of-honor," Breze complained.

"It is *exactly* the moment to discuss her," Isabelle retorted. "I saw the way your eyes lit up when you caught sight of her, you rascal. I will not allow one of my maids..."

"Isabelle, my mad little sweetmeat," Pierre capitulated. "You have caused my prick to arise with ardent expectations of being administered to by your hand, your mouth, your cunt, your ass, or even by a surprise body part. The moment is hardly right for foolish chatter.

"But, if we must discuss this matter at this most awkward moment, so be it. Yes, I found a mighty attraction towards the young lady. What man with blood in his veins would not? But I am not stupid enough to venture into that garden of loveliness known as your maids-of-honor to gratify my carnal lusts. It is another of my lusts that has been awakened by your Agnes Sorel."

"You are going to lie there with that prick of yours throbbing at me thunderously. And you have the nerve to tell me you have a lust more powerful than love?" the duchess laughed.

Looking down at his demanding dick, he replied, "No, my dear. Maybe not more powerful. But perhaps as powerful. It is an overwhelming craving I have observed in you as well, you gorgeous hussy."

"I cannot imagine to what you may be referring," Isabelle questioned.

"Power, my pumpkin squash," Pierre declared.

The duchess was intrigued. She knew it was true. Breze craved sexual gratification. But he also was mad for power. And it was true that she shared that craving.

Before she would allow her lover to proceed with the delights of the bed chamber, she forced him to divulge his plans for Agnes Sorel.

As a result, his hardon took a short vacation. He outlined his master plan for increasing his political power.

Having heard those plans, Isabel realized that if the plan was successful, it could increase her share of political power as well.

Although her hunger for more power was kindled by Breze's plan, there was now another craving to be satisfied forthwith. She could wait no longer to enjoy the seneschal's magnificent body.

She applied her aristocratic lips to Pierre's vacationing member. She did not have to wait long for amorous indulgence..

Three days later, Breze was back in Poitou. In the comfort of the castle's private dining room, he was entertaining Jacques Coeur and Etienne Chevalier. The three men had just finished feasting on a sumptuous repast, and were sipping after-dinner wine.

They constituted a most unlikely threesome. Breze was an aristocrat, Coeur a businessman, and Chevalier a clerk. Breze, seneschal of Poitou, was a warrior, tall, handsome, majestic. Coeur, the richest man in Europe, was a merchant and banker — rotund, bald, relaxed, and jolly. Chevalier, a scholarly clerk, was short, thin nearly to the point of emaciation, morose, and could be taken for a monk.

As different as the three men appeared, they shared one characteristic. All coveted power.

"An excellent repast, *Messire le seneschal*," Jacques Coeur exclaimed expansively. "May I particularly complement the array of wines you served?"

"All products of my beloved Poitou, Messire Jacquet," Breze answered, addressing Jacques Coeur by the nickname he preferred. "Since you financed most of the vintages yourself, I am delighted they please your palate as well as your purse."

Coeur laughed heartily, his face turning an even rosier red than usual.

Etienne Chevalier did not crack a smile. Jocularity was hardly in his stock of expressions.

"Did Messire de Breze call us together to discuss vintages?" Chevalier asked sourly. "I fear it is a subject with which I am not conversant."

It was difficult for the other two men not to laugh. The monkish little man was so dry and humorless. But, with a straight face, the seneschal answered.

"No, my friend. I did not really have vintages in mind for discussion when I sent you the invitation. Although, I will have to admit, I had vintages in mind to accompany the repast. But it was this period, after our dinner, that I looked forward to with great relish."

"Well, then, Messire Pierre," Jacquet chuckled. "We have imbibed. But, like our learned friend here, I must admit that I am curious about the post-prandial topics you had in mind."

"Nothing less, Messires, than the future of France," Pierre announced.

"Now you begin to intrigue me, Messire le Seneschal," Etienne answered. "A subject dear to all our hearts, I am sure."

The bookish little man smelled the underlying topic. Power. Somehow Pierre de Breze was aiming at a plan that would involve the three of them in obtaining more power in the king's court. Interest showed on his ordinarily dour face.

"I believe it has become quite clear that our country is involved in a transformation," Pierre de Breze began. "And that transformation begins to show in our sire, His Majesty the King."

Both his guests nodded in agreement.

Pierre continued: "The old ways can only impede the progress our poor land is striving for. The king must be helped to assist in that progress, lest we go not forward, but backward."

Coeur concurred: "Not only is France rejuvenated by our victories over the English, but the king is looking less doleful. Still melancholy in appearance, but with perhaps an incipient optimism. Have you noticed his bearing? More regal. Yes, I must agree, the king seems ready to imbibe some measure of happiness."

"Yet," Breze continued, "He does not seem to fully realize that he is restrained from exercising the kind of leadership needed in this new era. His council is made up exclusively of the old aristocracy that thinks old thoughts and has old values. These advisors are the very people who allowed France to be occupied by the Goddams for the past hundred years."

"Yes," Coeur chimed in. "If France is to grow, our industries must be revived. Trade that has been dominated by foreign lands must be regained by our merchants. Our finances must be revamped. In short, new blood must be pumped into the heart of our beautiful land."

"New blood," Etienne Chevalier said. "Yes, yes. Messire Coeur is exactly right. New blood. New people in power. People who see the world as it now is, and as it could be. Not those whose perspective is all in the past. I could not agree more."

"For five hundred or more years," Breze continued his theme, "Land was the basis of wealth in France. The aristocrats owned the land, the serfs worked it, and the bourgeois rested somewhere in between. That was the old order. In the new emerging world, trade is the basis of wealth. It is so in the Venetian Republic, in Tuscany, and even in England. But how much more apparent that fact is in France. Our friend here, Jacques Coeur, has the largest merchant fleet in the world. French wines, cereals, and other produce are sent by him to every port in the known world. And the treasures that come back to France are incalculable. Jacquet manages the king's property for him, yet does not share in royal power."

Jacques was born the son of a furrier. His business sense made him the owner of the most extensive warehouse in the land for jewels, clothing, luxury items, and, of course, furs. He knew the seneschal spoke truly, and merely smiled in agreement. There was no cause for false modesty.

"I understand the drift of what you are saying, Messire le Seneschal," the clerk, Chevalier, said. "You are indicating that Messire Coeur should be a voice on His Majesty's council. I would have to agree. Do I infer that you have called us together to promote his sphere of influence?"

"I am not thinking exclusively of Jacquet," Breze smiled.

"Of course not," the clerk said. "It is known far and wide that you are the finest speaker in France. You are a noted warrior and hero. There must be a plan for yourself in all this as well."

"Perhaps," Breze replied. "But there is a position as well for a fine scholar with fresh ideas. Someone who is highly lettered, fluent in all the languages of

Europe, plus Latin and Greek. The king's private secretary, who sits in the royal council, should possess such erudition. But he should also think with an eye to the future, rather than to the past."

For the first time in recent memory, an actual smile crossed the clerk's face. He understood now why the three of them were sitting together.

Knowing now what was on Breze's mind, it was Jacquet who moved matters right along.

"Pierre, I believe our esteemed scholar here and I understand what you are proposing as an end. What I do not see is the means you propose to that end."

"For France to take her place in the world, our sovereign must become the true master of his kingdom," Pierre explained. "The English are now in retreat. Burgundy clearly is preparing to leave the side of the Goddams and make peace with us. Charles VII can now pursue his true interests."

"Which are...?" Jacquet queried.

Breze elaborated: "We know His Majesty's ability on the tennis court, in the fencing match, and the hunt. He is very skilled in the use of the crossbow. But he is also interested in the arts. He loves music and plays the harp himself. Poetry is one of his passions. He enriches his library daily. A man of such sensitivity, as we know, is most attracted to that most precious of the arts."

"Which is?" Etienne asked.

"The art of love," Breze declared. "Practiced on a beautiful woman. Wouldn't you agree, Jacquet?"

Jacquet expressed his agreement by spreading his hands wide in acknowledgment.

"And so, our liege needs to have as a companion the most beautiful woman in the land, perhaps in the entire world. A woman who is beholden to us. One who will counsel him on the pillow with persuasions beneficial to us. And, of course, to France."

"Who is such a woman?" asked the two guests simultaneously.

"The young lady's name is Agnes Sorel."

"You know this person?" Etienne asked, a certain amount of distaste evident in his voice.

"I have seen her. She is a maid-of-honor in the household of René d'Anjou."

Jacquet chuckled good naturedly.

"Everyone in France knows that our eminent seneschal is as renowned for his victories in the bedchamber as for his glorious feats of valor on the battlefield. If, Pierre, you say this creature, this Demoiselle Agnes, is so fascinating, that is warrant enough in my mind for it to be so. And, I understand that you do have influence with the current tenants of Narbonne Castle. If you believe Demoiselle Agnes will benefit France by being our...ambassador...to our sovereign, I say, *vive la France.* I am willing to bank my future on your persuasive powers with the lady. I will not ask how you propose to get her first into the king's presence, and thence into his bed. I cannot even imagine the machinations necessary. But let me say, I am with you."

"And you, Messire Chevalier?" Breze asked.

"Messire, I am a patriot," the little clerk stated. "I see that your plan is best for France. I am with you."

Jacques Coeur, always a realist, added, "Not only what will benefit France the most, but what will surely benefit the three of us as well."

It was now up to Pierre de Breze.

Agnes and Isabelle d'Anjou were practicing a duet together, Agnes on the psaltery, Duchess Isabelle on the dulcimer. The duchess sang one line, Agnes the next. Back and forth they exchanged the lively words and music.

> *Amors vai com la belluja*
> *Que coa'l fuec en la suja*
> *Art lo fust e la festuja,*
> *— Escoutatz! —*
> *E non sap val qual part fuja*
> *Cel qui del fuec es gastatz.*

> *Love goes like the spark*
> *That feeds the flame in the embers.*
> *It consumes the wood and the tinder.*
> *— Listen! —*
> *He who doesn't know whither to flee,*
> *That man is burned by the fire.*

The comic intent of the song was not wasted on the two women. The song, however was not chosen at random. Duchess Isabelle selected it as an opening for a very important discussion she had planned with her most important maid-of-honor.

With a deep, rich laugh, the duchess addressed Agnes:

"A most amusing ditty, wouldn't you agree, my dear?"

"Most entertaining, Your Grace."

"Love!" the duchess declared. "It is a constant preoccupation in our songs. Well, indeed, in our dear France love is valued above everything. Doesn't it appear so? Our troubadours here in Languedoc, in Provence, have raised love to the status of a religion. *Fin'Amors*. It is all the rage."

"So I have observed, Madame," Agnes agreed.

"Carnal love. It is not really a sin, you know," the duchess continued her discourse. "Among the lower classes, of course, it is quite another matter. Their idea of love is so bestial. But I am sure that God approves of carnal love. When it is refined, of course."

"I am sure you're right, Your Grace," Agnes stated.

"Take the duke and me, for example," Isabelle elaborated. "The duke has not been what prigs would call 'faithful' to me since the end of our honeymoon. And me? Even during the honeymoon, I invited a scrumptious young squire to... Well, all I can say is that he was an even more tasty morsel than René, if you know what I mean."

"Your grace is most kind to share this information with me," Agnes replied.

"Then, I take it, Agnes, that you are not shocked by what I am telling you."

"Not in the least, my lady. I am not unaware of the sophisticated nature of the manners of the noblest classes of our land."

"Good," Isabelle explained. "I was quite sure you were not prudish. But I had to be even more certain before I introduced a certain subject to you."

"My attention is at your ladyship's disposal," Agnes replied demurely.

Agnes' nervousness was not apparent. But she was aware that Isabelle d'Anjou was leading up to an important proposition. Could it be that her Destiny was soon to burst into reality? Her anticipation was keen.

Isabelle led into her subject.

"My brother-in-law, the king, is a very lonely man, my dear. He always has been. When still a child, his father, the former king, became quite mad you know. Yes, raving mad. He became convinced that Charles was not his son at all.

"Well, Queen Isabelle, the mad king's wife, had views concerning the marriage bed that were the same as ours. But she was as careful about guarding the line of succession as I am. She certainly knew the efficacy of mandragora."

"I have heard rumors that there was unhappiness in our sovereign's youth," Agnes interjected.

"Then you know, of course," Isabelle continued, "that Mad King Charles VI, after the Battle of Agincourt, disowned his son, the Dauphin, and gave France to the Goddams."

"A sad moment for France, Your Grace," Agnes commiserated.

"Yes, quite," Isabelle agreed. "Our own poor sire was forced to be a king without a kingdom. All of our lands north of the Loire were controlled by England. Forces rallied to our king's cause, of course, to attempt to drive the English occupiers out of France. But Charles was very unsure of himself. Unsure, even, that he was actually the legitimate heir of Charles VI."

"Our family in Picardy always supported His Majesty's claim to the throne," Agnes said. "It was always our hope that France would be restored to the French."

"Your dear, dear mother informed me of that when she brought you here to Toulouse. Such a fine woman. Anyway, there were two astrologers who very much influenced Charles' past, and his present as well. One of them, Germain de Thibouville, who was court astrologer in the time of the former king, correctly predicted the deaths of Charles VI and of the English king, Henry V. He further predicted a Great Love would come to our Charles. A love that would consume him. King Charles has been waiting for that love all his life. Until now, he has never loved a woman with total passion. Then later, after Charles VI's death, a new court astrologer, Master Pierre de St.-Valerin, famous throughout Christendom, told Charles that France would be saved by two women: one who would love him spiritually and one who would love him carnally. Charles is still waiting to meet that second woman.

"You know of course who was the first of these women."

"Indeed," Agnes assented. "Joan of Arc, the Maid of Orleans."

"Yes. The Maid heard voices from Heaven above telling her to convince our Charles VII to lead his troops to victory, and then to conduct him to Rheims to be anointed and crowned the legitimate King of France."

"The most happy day of our lives at Crevecour Castle, Your Grace."

"Of course. In the heart of every true son and daughter of France there was rejoicing. You know how the Maid came to Chinon Castle, was examined for virginity, and identified Charles out of the crowd of courtiers."

"Yes, my lady."

Isabelle continued:

"The Maid told him that Heaven had informed her that he truly was the legitimate son of the House of Valois. Everyone knows that. And everyone knows that she also told him something no one at court knew but the king himself — something he shared only with the queen. That information, supposedly known but to Charles and Queen Marie. And God convinced him that the Maid spoke sooth. Do you know what that secret information was?"

"Of course not, Your Grace. No one does."

"The king knows, of course," Isabelle replied. "And his wife, the queen, my sister-in-law knows. And I am the only person she has shared the secret with."

"That is a heavy secret to hold, Your Ladyship."

"Look, Agnes," Isabelle confided. "This little discussion is not a matter of idle chatter between the two of us. Can you divine the direction in which I am leading?"

"I believe so, Your Grace."

"You are a clever girl. In this narrative, what have I left out?"

"The rest of Master Pierre's astrological reading?" Agnes suggested.

"Exactly. France was saved in the first instance, by the Maid who loved the king spiritually. The time seems right, my dear, for the second woman to appear on the scene."

Destiny knocked. Agnes heard the resounding advent.

"When do I meet His Majesty?" she asked.

Duchess Isabelle laughed aloud. How perspicacious the child was.

Isabelle told Agnes: "King Charles VII and his entire court are coming to Narbonne Castle next week. Narbonne will be the Court of France for as long as the sovereign remains here. The news is being broadcast throughout the land even as we speak."

"I am prepared to enhance the future of France, My Lady. You can count on me."

"I was sure of it, my dear."

"But I have one question," Agnes asked. "What was the secret the Maid revealed to our king?"

In a very confidential tone, the duchess said: "Her exact words were: 'The fleur-de-lys lies hidden beneath the Crown Jewels of France.'"

Agnes understood.

Duchess Isabelle had to add one more statement: "Before finishing our little chat, my dear, I want to remind you who is making this opportunity available to you."

"I am most grateful, Your Grace."

"Remember, I am a second mother to you," Isabelle declared. "No matter what happens, trust no one but me. No matter who attempts to secure your loyalty, your loyalty is due only to me. Do you understand?"

"Perfectly, Your Grace."

"Please call me Isabelle, dear," the duchess invited. "We now have a new intimate relationship, like daughter to mother."

"Again, I am grateful...Isabelle."

"Now, dear," Isabelle said in a chipper tone. "Let's get back to practicing that little ditty. How appropriate it sounds now, doesn't it?"

Amors vai com la belluja.

Chapter Five

Agnes was thrilled. She had never doubted the prediction of the provincial sorcière, Zèlde, about her destiny. Now she knew that a similar prediction had been forecast by two eminent soothsayers, Germain de Thibouville and Pierre de St.-Valerin. Both had been official astrologers to the kings of France. Could there be any doubt? She was destined to rule a great nation. It had been foretold. And she knew the moment was at hand when she would take her place among the mighty.

Duchess Isabelle arranged for Pierre de Breze to come to Narbonne Castle to interview Agnes.

"Agnes, dear," Isabelle said. "Last week we had a visitor here in Toulouse, a certain Pierre de Breze, seneschal of Poitou. Do you recall him?"

"Yes I do...Isabelle. He was not presented to us maids-of-honor, I recall, since it was said his business was urgent, and ceremonies would have to be omitted. But, yes, I do remember the occasion. And I was aware that he was observing the ladies of the court with an acute eye. We, of course, knew better than to stare back."

"Yes, Messire de Breze is very observant. Do you know anything about him, though, my dear?"

"Well, of course, we ladies gossiped about him. You know every visitor gets discussed by us. His visit caused some of the sillier girls — I won't mention any names — to giggle. They claimed Messire de Breze was the most handsome and most valiant knight in Christendom. That he was irresistible on the battlefield, and in the boudoir. Those who had seen him on his former visits declared him a beautiful specimen of masculinity. That's all."

"Not a bad description, as it happens," the duchess chuckled. "He *is* quite an eyeful. At any rate, he is visiting us tomorrow. Or, to be more exact, when I say us, I mean you and me. He is going to be here to discuss the little matter you and I conversed about...?"

Agnes understood perfectly well what the "little matter" was. This meeting with the seneschal appeared to be the next step on her way to power.

Isabelle wanted Agnes to appear at her most ravaging when she was to meet Pierre de Breze. To that end, she provided her maid-of-honor with a low-cut gown of periwinkle blue with gold trimmings.

The décolletage was tailored to show as panoramic a view of the dazzling tits as possible within the range of good taste. And the hemline fell at a point where an observant male could glimpse a perfectly turned ankle.

It was intended that the seneschal's libido get assaulted full bore.

The seneschal arrived the next afternoon. Seeing her natural beauty so stunningly attired pleased him immensely.

The effect of her loveliness at his groin assured him that this certainly was the woman who would excite King Charles.

If Breze was enticed by what he saw when Agnes entered the room, Agnes was bedazzled by the seneschal's appearance. He was superbly dressed in a deep purple velvet robe lined with marten. His strong masculine features with their piercing dark eyes set in the tanned, attractively weathered face, were compelling. He flashed a smile at her that revealed strikingly white teeth gleaming behind full sensual lips. For the first time in her life, Agnes was smitten by virile beauty.

"This is what love feels like," she whispered silently to her heart. "This is the man of my dreams. But if I allow myself to fall deeply in love with him, my destiny, which is to rule, will be jeopardized."

All this transpired in a split second. She could not dwell on this new emotion. It was too fresh, and too dangerous.

Isabelle saw the effect Breze had on Agnes. She turned her attention on Breze. Disaster! The seneschal, who had many a conquest to his credit, showed a very dangerous attraction to Agnes. Isabelle well knew the difference in a man's eyes between love and lust. She had no problem with lust for another woman in the eyes of her lovers. She expected it. But love! That was unacceptable. However, there was no time to deal with that now. Perhaps the lust for power in each of these two would submerge romantic love.

"I am enchanted, Demoiselle, to make your acquaintance." The seneschal expressed the customary words of courtesy with more warmth than pleased the duchess.

"The honor is mine, *Messire le Seneschal*." Yes, rote words. But with tones that did not please the duchess. Courts of Love were held in the south of France. They were a deep-seated ingredient of the customs of the age of chivalry. Isabelle d'Anjou had presided over many such a court. She had heard the tone of voice that revealed ardent passion. And she recognized it in the banal greetings her two companions expressed. *Well, time enough to deal with that later.*

"Agnes, my dear," Isabelle said. "*Messire le Seneschal* has been kind enough to visit us. He would like to discuss the future of France with you. I assured him it was a topic with which you have demonstrated a great deal of interest."

"The seneschal is too kind. I am sure that my modest capabilities hardly warrant his attention," Agnes replied modestly.

"Believe me, Demoiselle Agnes," Breze said, broadcasting his most devastating smile as his eyes flashed admiration at the cleavage confronting him. "I believe your capabilities are more than adequate to consider my poor observations on the state of our beloved kingdom."

"*Messire le Seneschal* has some insightful thoughts, I know," said the duchess. "He has been generous enough to share some of his thoughts with me on previous occasions. Would you care to elaborate for Demoiselle and me a synthesis of your insights, Messire?"

Breze leaned forward in his chair. The emotion he felt when he looked at Agnes was all too apparent. He realized that he would have to direct his dialog at Isabelle or he might lose his train of thought.

"It is a subject, Duchess, that consumes me. I will accept your offer to elaborate.

"Our French kingdom has suffered at the hands of the Goddams and the Burgundians for a hundred years now, and more. As a nation, we have forgotten how to laugh."

"Yes," Isabelle agreed. "You hear laughter in Italy all the time. Even the English court is said to be quite gay. My husband, the duke, is certainly as cheerful a man as any I know, and our court shows it. But I have observed that the court of my dear sister and brother-in-law can only be called dismal."

"Exactly," Breze chimed in. "If our beloved kingdom is to take its place in the family of nations, *la belle France* must learn to laugh again."

He turned his attention to Agnes. "And to love again."

Agnes had seldom in her life blushed. His words caused her to flush. Isabelle did not miss the reaction

Quickly returning his gaze to Isabelle, Pierre continued.

"To laugh again, our mother France must be ruled by a joyous king. There must be an antidote to the mournful souls who surround His Majesty. And I believe there is only one person who can provide that antidote."

The pregnant pause that followed that statement caused Agnes to want to squirm in her chair. By an effort of will she remained in attentive stillness.

When the pause became unbearable, Isabelle spoke up.

"I have told my dear Agnes here about the predictions of the two court astrologers. That two women would influence the sovereign's successes and victories. One of those prophecies has already been fulfilled. France awaits the next. The one of whom it was foretold would be Charles VII's consuming love."

Agnes heard the footsteps of her destiny descending on the scene. The feeling she had was more of relief than anything else.

Breze felt Agnes' assent to his proposal. He knew she was ready to win the king's heart.

He also knew she would have to become aware of the dynamics actually present at court. So he launched into phase two of his discourse.

"Not that the road leading to the rejuvenation of our France is a path strewn with roses. There are briars in the path. Briars about which the second female savior of the kingdom must be aware."

"Yes," Agnes thought. "This is what I was waiting for. To find out what the real impediments in the process are."

"Like the Maid of Orleans," Breze continued, "the second liberator of the soul of France must have courage. The Goddams and the Burgundians were not the only enemies of the realm. In the direct line of succession to the crown, there is a danger that constantly hovers."

"You refer to His Royal Highness, Messire?" Isabelle asked, as though unaware of the answer.

"Yes, Duchess, the Dauphin. I hate to have to say it to you, Your Grace, but your husband's nephew is a viper in the heart of France."

"*Messire le Seneschal,*" Isabelle scolded. "I don't believe I wish to hear evil spoken of my husband's kinsman. Perhaps dear Agnes has some questions she would care to pose."

Isabelle and Pierre turned their attention in Agnes' direction.

"Messire and Madame," Agnes confessed. "I must admit that I find your premise interesting. That is, the idea that there is a woman with whom our sovereign is fated to fall desperately in love. And that that woman will exert such a beneficial influence on France. I'm sure I cannot imagine where such a creature might come from. But there appears to me to be an insurmountable impediment to the possibility of there being such a lover for our sire, the king."

"Yes...?"

"His Majesty is already in love. Certainly Queen Marie is the woman who fulfills the prophecy. What need has the king for another love?"

"Aha," Breze smiled. "A question that has often been raised by those who know the astrologers' forecasts.

"It is true that Charles VII loves Queen Marie. They were raised together, like brother and sister. They were betrothed to each other as young children. They lived as playmates, practically like brother and sister in Countess Yolande's care. The affection between them is as thick as porridge. But, although Charles loves Marie, he has never been 'in love' with her. Do you catch the difference?"

Agnes nodded. It was answer enough.

Breze explained further: "As king, as the father of the nation, as Charles VII the Victorious, it is His Majesty's duty to sow the seeds of the House of Valois into the royal womb of the woman tied to him by the Church. Duty, not passion, reigns over the royal marriage bed. And...the seed does germinate, that is true. Yet the fruit of that union, time after time, produces not life, but death."

Agnes knew, as did every person living in France, that Marie's pregnancies ended up, time and time again, in miscarriage, stillborns, and sickly infants who died within the first year of their life.

"And yet," Agnes insisted. "There are surviving children."

"You refer, of course, to the Dauphin," Breze assented. "But we have agreed not to mention the duchess' husband's nephew at present."

"Thank you, Messire," said the Duchess.

"So let us return to Her Majesty the Queen," Breze continued.

"Every night when she is not in flux, Queen Marie invites her royal spouse to share her bed. And on that occasion, the royal couple performs the sacred and political rite of coupling. A state occasion which we all applaud.

"But the king is a man of flesh and blood. A man whose vigor and virility require a more passionate outlet. He is a great lover of beauty. And feminine beauty is a constant pursuit of his. And we are grateful for His Majesty's healthful pursuits in that regard.

"The king's known bastards are seven in number. Of those, three had mothers of the petty nobility and four had commoner mothers. The royal treasury pays for the care of the children in accordance with the mother's status. The four boys were guaranteed preferment at the age of maturity. Two of them are at present officers in His Majesty's service and lead battalions. The girls are guaranteed handsome dowries. The king is quite fond of them all. The Dauphin, of course, the legitimate fruit of the royal bed, loathes all his bastard brothers and sisters.

"But that," he said, with a sidelong glance at the duchess, "Is another story."

"It seems our sovereign well deserves the title 'Sire'," Agnes proffered dryly.

The seneschal chuckled. The duchess smiled wryly.

"That does not necessarily account for all the king's bastards, of course," Breze continued. "It is most likely that other bastards have been engendered on women who never realized they had been bedded by royalty. After all, King Charles did not wear his crown while coupling."

All three smiled at the seneschal's witticism.

"Well, my dear. There you have it," the duchess added. "The worthy seneschal has told you much that you need to know. We would not want you to be blind to the situation at the royal court."

"You are, indeed, most kind, My Lady," Agnes said. "I thank you both most heartily."

"Knowing there would be problems to surmount, are you willing to become the most important woman in France?" Pierre de Breze asked directly.

"Me, Messire?" Agnes replied with a wicked smile. "I hardly imagined you had me in mind."

All three laughed. The comic irony was not wasted on her audience. Agnes did not have to say more. Everything was understood.

That afternoon, Agnes retired to her chambers. The new rooms had been offered to her just a few days previously. Unlike the quarters of the other maids-of-honor, Agnes' bedroom was quite private. It was carpeted with rugs imported at great expense from the Orient by Jacques Coeur. Rich tapestries adorned the walls. The chamber was dominated by a huge four-poster bed, as large as that in the duchess' chambers. And she was provided with a private servant, Nini.

Agnes disrobed and stretched out on her luxurious bed. Her thoughts dwelt on the handsome seneschal. So this was what love felt like. Love or at least infatuation. No, she decided. Not infatuation. Love.

Agnes considered her physical infatuation with Pierre de Breze. She knew a love affair with Pierre was a forbidden romance. It should never consummate with any actual physical contact. Virtual lovemaking was all that should be possible. Corporeal lovemaking should be limited to the man Destiny was calling to her bed.

She would have to be content with fantasizing.

Lying on the enormous bed, she allowed her right hand to slip up her thigh and find a resting place on her cunt.

Her left hand easily slipped into the revealing bodice.

She pictured the virile seneschal. The hands intimately exploring her tits and twat were not her own. In her fancy they belonged to Pierre de Breze.

When she came, the orgasm was elicited by the man with whom she had just fallen in love.

Later that afternoon, Agnes was taking the afternoon air in a cloistered area of the castle. Her heart skipped a beat. The man of her dreams and fantasies was approaching her. He was garbed in a different suit from the one he wore that morning. But it was made of the same deep purple velvet. He totally disarmed her with his gleaming smile.

"Surely the seneschal is here to declare his love for me," Agnes thought. "I'm not sure how I should respond. Not physically, of course. We could be observed."

"Demoiselle Agnes," Pierre de Breze said. "I was so hoping I would see you like this. In private."

"Charmed," she replied simply.

"I have something important to say to you. Something I could not say within the duchess' hearing."

Agnes blushed and gulped. This appeared to be the moment she both hoped for and dreaded.

"Yes, Messire?"

"It is to warn you about the dauphin," Pierre said bluntly. "His Highness is known in court, behind his back, as the 'universal spider.' He hates his father and constantly plots against him. He is vicious to his enemies, and anyone who is close to the sovereign he sees as an enemy."

This was a disappointment. A tremendous letdown. No hint of romantic badinage. No *gai saber*. Agnes was utterly taken aback, but willed herself not to show it.

Agnes answered in calm, measured tones.

"If I should ever be in a position to be, as you say, close to the sovereign, I will certainly remember your words. My most gracious thanks for sharing this information with me."

"There," she thought. "I hope I didn't sound as cold as I feel."

"Ah, but Demoiselle," Pierre said, again with that winning smile. "There really was another reason I wanted to see you before I leave for Poitou."

"This is it, then," Agnes thought hopefully. "First get the business taken care of, and then the unburdening of his heart."

"I am attentive, Messire."

"When the prognostications of the court astrologers are fulfilled," Breze declared, "it is important that you trust no one other than me. Remember that it is I, and I alone, who prepared the way for the lady who is to save France. I trust she will not forget to whom she owes her loyalty."

So that was it. A self-serving farewell.

Agnes wished she did not love this man so much.

But love him she did.

Chapter Six

Charles d'Anjou, the Count of Maine, and known as Messire Charles, was the brother of Duke René and Queen Marie. He, René, Marie, and King Charles had all been playmates and companions in the Anjou palaces when they were young. Charles d'Anjou was a close companion of the king. In matters of discretion, particularly those concerning the pursuit of feminine flesh, Charles was the king's most trusted go-between. Indeed, it was rumored that the king's brother-in-law was also his pander. Harsh words for the attractive, blond man. Court gossip could often turn malicious.

Charles VII was in Bergerac where he had been holding court just short of a month. He had been persuaded by René and Isabelle d'Anjou to bring the court to Toulouse, and he was delighted to do so.

Pierre de Breze had come to Bergerac to confer with the king and with Messire Charles.

Both Breze and Messire Charles were in earnest conversation with the king a week prior to the royal visit to Toulouse. It was Messire Charles who was addressing the sovereign at the moment.

"My brother René is delighted, Your Majesty, that you are bringing the Court to Toulouse next week."

"Toulouse is such a delightful city," Charles VII replied. "And I do miss my old friend René very much. I look forward to seeing him and Isabelle again."

It was true that for many years, René was the king's favorite companion when hunting, carousing, and wenching.

The king smiled as he considered heading for Toulouse.

"I'm sure René and Isabelle's court is the gayest in the realm."

"So it is," Breze agreed. "Life in Narbonne Castle scarcely lacks liveliness. Parties and gallantries are ever the order of the day. Your Majesty's spirits will certainly revive there. It is exactly the locale in which to put behind the royal court the outrages visited upon our land by the Goddams."

"My dear Seneschal," Charles VII replied. "You are as observant as ever. I truly am ready to shed this cloak of gloom that has clung to me for so long. Narbonne Castle may be exactly the medicine I need. The incessant wars of liberation are coming to an end. I do seek a quickening of the spirits."

Messire Charles, who sized up feminine beauty for the king, spoke up. "I believe Your Majesty will discover a surprise in Toulouse that will inspire the gaiety you are looking for. My sister-in-law Isabelle has among her maids-of-honor a demoiselle who is unparalleled in beauty. The last time I visited René's court, I was astounded by what I saw."

"You have the most cultivated taste in France, my friend, when it comes to appraising the fair sex. Is it not so, Breze?"

"I totally concur with you, Majesty," Pierre affirmed. "And in this case, my own observations confirm Messire Charles' statement. I recently had matters of state to attend to in Toulouse, and while there, I was dazzled by the appearance of a young lady whose beauty was beyond compare. She sets a tone of loveliness that causes the court of the Duke and Duchess of Anjou to glitter. I believe she may just prove to be the centerpiece of your visit."

"Come, come now, my old companions," the king laughed. "Do not hold out on me. Who is this demoiselle you rave about so?"

"Her name," Breze answered. "Is Agnes Sorel. She is a native of Picardy and is a true flower of that province. Hair of the blondest gold, my liege. And eyes? Of an indescribable blue. What would you say of her eyes, Messire Charles?"

"Like the reflection of the bluest, clearest sky, on a placid lake, on a glorious summer's day, my dear Breze. But, no. More striking still."

"And a complexion, Your Majesty, of the warmest alabaster. Her neck is a wonder of nature."

"Hips of such inviting curves, Sire, as to drive a sybarite mad."

"But her ankle, my companions. Superbly turned."

"And her breast?" the king asked.

"Divine!" the other two exclaimed in unison.

Breze felt impelled to expand.

"The last time I was at Narbonne Castle," he divulged, "I was privileged to sit in a parlor with her and the duchess' other maids-of-honor. The blouse this Agnes wore was so designed that I caught glimpses, from time to time, of her tits.

"My God, Majesty! My prick practically knocked my codpiece right off. I was alarmed lest that violent uprising expose my immodest staff to fly out into the room and alarm the ladies seated around."

"I am sure the sight would cause them to swoon," Messire Charles jested.

"I assure you, it could happen," Breze joked back. "It has happened before, with the result of a roomful of demoiselles breathless and expired on the floor."

Charles VII had been conducting his court through Languedoc. He believed the time had come to proceed on to Toulouse. He now felt sure he would find a most delightful cure for his melancholy there.

"Agnes, my love," Duchess Isabelle announced. "A herald has just informed me that the sovereign is less than a league from Narbonne Castle. Wouldn't you like to come with me to see the procession approaching?"

"How thrilling, Your Grace...Isabelle. It's as though the skies cleared just for the occasion. It is the loveliest day we've had this month. Where will we go to get the best view?"

"Let's go up into the barbican," Duchess Isabelle suggested. "We'll have the best view of the pageant from there."

As the two ladies were walking across the great hall on the way to the barbican, Agnes remarked to the duchess:

"I recall one of Count René's young pages — I believe his name is Guyot. I haven't seen him around court for a while."

Duchess Isabelle smiled wryly. "Guyot...Guyot? Oh, that rather fresh acting, half-insolent, good-looking young man?"

"I think that would describe him," Agnes remarked. "He used to observe me in what I would consider a rude, forward manner. I've been relieved at not seeing him around lately. I was just wondering...?"

"Wonder no further, my dear," Isabelle assured her. "I am very observant also, you know. I have searching eyes everywhere. An accident befell one of the pages of our good friend, the Baron de Perpignan. I suggested to René that this Guyot individual be sent down South to take the place of the unfortunate young man. Perhaps Guyot's insolence will not be as noticeable down there. The Perpignan court is rather lax in these matters you know."

Agnes realized that the duchess was more aware of happenings at Narbonne than she had thought possible. She sighed with relief. Guyot could possibly have been an annoyance as her big moment approached.

When they got to the appearance window of the tower, the royal procession was just coming into view down the road.

In front, on foot, were squires bearing standards. At the head of those standards was the black and gold Oriflamme of France, emblazoned with three fleurs-de-lys. Behind the standards, riding a black horse, was the royal verger, his rod of office held high.

Following the verger, on a large white destrier, was Charles VII the Victorious, wearing a green plumed hat, a green doublet and trousers, and a black cloak decorated with three fleurs-de-lys. In the distance, he was an imposing sight. Riding palfreys to the left and right of the sovereign were the dauphin and the Constable of France, General Poton de Xantrailles.

Next in line was Queen Marie in a gilded litter, with Princess Marguerite at her side.

The procession following them consisted first of the royal guard, then the great lords and ladies of France, mounted, in carriages, and in litters. Foot soldiers, pages, squires, baggage handlers...the procession reached as far back as eye could see.

Crowds lined the pathway, waving, shouting exuberantly, hailing the king who had driven most of the occupiers out of the realm, and who was continuing to rid France of the last of their kind.

"Long live the king."

"Victory! Hail to Charles the Victorious."

"Death to the Goddams!"

"Noël, Noël."

Christmas was five days behind. But the shouts of "Noel" were simply expressions of joy at the arrival of the now well-beloved sovereign.

The wooden drawbridge was lowered over the moat to the flurry of trumpets.

The standard-bearers marched proudly over the moat. Agnes and Isabelle could see their shining faces.

The verger rode across on his magnificent horse.

Then, on foot, Count René d'Anjou passed under the portcullis and onto the drawbridge to another blast of trumpets. He removed his elegant felt hat, and bowed deeply before the approaching king, the master of the castle paying homage to his liege lord.

Now Agnes could see the king quite clearly.

Before the king's destrier reached the drawbridge, an extraordinary thing happened.

"Why is the king dismounting, Isabelle? I would think he would want to ride into the courtyard."

"One of our sovereign's peculiarities, my dear," the duchess replied. "He does not ride his horse across bridges."

"A royal custom I was not aware of?"

"The custom is unique to Charles VII," Isabelle told her. "And it is a new occurrence. You know of the Battle of Montereau?"

"Of course," Agnes affirmed. "One of our sovereign's more recent victories over the Bugundians. I've heard it said that as a result, Burgundy may be forsaking the English cause to conclude a treaty with France."

"You have heard correctly, Agnes," Isabelle assured her. "Perhaps what you did not hear, because it was not widely broadcast here in France, is that as our king was crossing the river in Montereau, the wooden bridge collapsed. Charles was in full armor, fell into the river, and came very close to drowning. We very nearly lost him, right there and then. A very near tragedy for France."

"My word! I didn't know," Agnes exclaimed.

"Since then," Isabelle continued, "our king has not been able to bring himself to ride a horse across a bridge. He experiences vertigo whenever he crosses water when mounted. But look. He is walking across now, and is greeting René with such warmth of affection. What a lovely sight."

"Yes, but, Isabelle," Agnes wondered. "A king afraid to cross a bridge?"

"Remember, child," the duchess informed Agnes, "Charles is a very brave king. A valiant and victorious warrior. He is a hero to his people, to us. He does harbor that one intense fear. Perhaps there is someone in France who can help him attain that one last ounce of courage?"

Isabelle gave Agnes a very knowing look.

Yes, perhaps there was such a woman. The lover the king waited for, the one foretold years ago. Perhaps.

"But Isabelle. His Majesty does not have a particularly imposing appearance," Agnes observed.

Agnes was comparing the king's impact on her with the physical attractiveness of Pierre de Breze. She believed that all men would forever have to be compared to the one with whom she had fallen in love. This great monarch had narrow shoulders, a thin chest, and spindly legs. The elaborate costume he wore did not conceal his frame. He was over twice her age. And the years of self-doubt, wavering, and defeat that had preceded his recent glorious victories had taken their toll on his features.

Isabelle patted the young lady's cheek.

"My dear. You must learn to appreciate others by what they *are*, not by how they look. If you cannot learn that, you are not the woman I took you for."

"Oh, I know you're right, Isabelle," Agnes agreed. "But look at that nose."

"A noble nose never disfigures a face. Not in France, anyway," Isabelle smiled.

"But those lips."

"Those, my dear, are the lips of a sensualist," Isabelle assured her. "If the king were not highly sensual, the second great woman in his life would scarcely be successful. Would she?"

Agnes understood. And hoped she would learn to love this man.

The formal presentation of the duchess' maids-of-honor was to take place that evening before the ball that was arranged by Duke René in honor of the arrival of the court of France.

Nini, Agnes' handmaid, fluttered about the chambers like a distraught butterfly. It was certainly the most exciting day in her simple life. Her madcap gaiety did not distress Agnes, who felt somewhat giddy herself.

The duchess had provided the complete attire for Agnes. Isabelle d'Anjou was considered one of the major arbiters of style in the kingdom. Her couturiers were all Italian and were steeped in the latest fashions reigning in Venice, Tuscany, and Genoa. Agnes had learned everything she knew about fashion from the duchess. So she was aware of how perfect this gown was for the occasion.

Agnes had already plucked her eyebrows and was patting her hair that was carefully piled up under a hairnet.

"Oh, stop flitting about like a mad wren," Agnes chided Nini good-naturedly.

"I can't help it, Demoiselle," Nini chirped.

Agnes smiled at how appropriately the wren designation seemed to fit her handmaid at the moment.

"Oh, Demoiselle," Nini went on. "Just imagine. Our king right here in our castle. Charles the Victorious. And guess what, Demoiselle? *Madame la Duchesse* told me I might peek through the curtains and catch a glimpse of His Majesty, if I were very quiet and discrete. Isn't it too exciting?"

"You'll be peeking no farther than the privy room if you don't get over here and help me into this dress," Agnes scolded. "You're no use at all in the state you're in."

The chiding was gentle, but effective. Nini fluttered over to Agnes' side.

The gown Agnes was wearing was emerald green in color, a shade that accentuated the ivory tones of her skin. It was a very modish simple sheath that clung to her shape in a way that left no need for imagination to fathom the sleek curves of her body. A marten lined cape draped down her back, coming to an end above the buttocks so as to lead the eye to the lovely round protuberances of her exquisite ass. The bodice had a lace inset that allowed ample view of the cleavage between the fair, white boobs. Around her slim waist she had Nini encircle a thin satin sash adorned with seed pearls.

"Now, Nini," Agnes ordered. "Very careful with the hennin."

The hennin was a stylish conical headdress with sable tufts that accentuated the cream-like tones of Agnes' perfect forehead.

Thus attired, the beauty from Picardy descended the stairs and joined the other maids-of-honor awaiting the presentation.

Duchess Isabelle placed Agnes fourth in line of the maids-of-honor so the king would spot her after meeting three demoiselles, and have her in his mind as six more were presented to him. A very calculated placement.

Agnes' moment was at hand. Destiny opened the door on her future, and, in the company of the duchess' other demoiselles, she glided into the Great Hall.

Chapter Seven

The room was crowded with elegant people dressed in their finery. Knights and dames stood about exchanging witticisms. Lords and ladies were discussing affairs of state or gossiping about affairs of the heart. The king of France was seated on a dais observing the crowd. It was his fate to attract a crowd wherever he was. Often it seemed to him a mob rather than a crowd. That was one of the burdens of being the sovereign. Queen Marie was seated some distance away, surrounded by ladies. She was many months into another pregnancy, and was engaged in a discussion about the impending birth.

For the occasion, the king had ordered that the castle of the previous counts of Toulouse be modified to reflect the new spirit he envisioned now for France. Count René was given free access to the royal treasury to transform the Great Hall. René ordered elaborate tapestries for the walls, silk and wool carpeting for the floor, and rose-perfumed candles by the hundreds. Jacques Coeur was happy to provide for every need. For a price, of course.

The monarch was seated on a great, heavily brocaded, gilded chair. Charles d'Anjou, Messire Charles, was standing to the right of the throne. A green velvet robe, sable lined, covered the king's angular body. On his head he wore a hood. His cape was festooned with fleurs-de-lys. For him, this was a joyful day.

King Charles was pleased with the festive appearance of the hall. He was ready to discard the dour, frugal days of the past and fully embrace beauty, luxury, pleasure, and love.

"Charles," he said. "The room is splendidly appointed. And a delightful scent permeates everything. It is not a scent I associate with winter."

"You are correct, Sire. It is indeed reminiscent of summer. For the occasion, Count René appears to have selected candles scented quite rarely. I believe he told me the perfume was rose. 'Roses of Picardy' to be exact."

"I see," the king responded with a pleased, knowing smile. "Let the duchess begin the presentations. The appearance of her lovely maids-of-honor promises to be delightful."

When Duchess Isabelle approached the king, every lip fell silent. It was known that the maids-of-honor were about to be presented. Duchess Isabelle curtsied deeply before her sovereign, then took a position to the left of the throne.

The congregation was largely made up of courtiers who had come with the monarch from Bergerac. For most of them, the sight of the duchess' demoiselles would be a novelty. To most of the gentlemen, the presentation of the duchess' young ladies was like a luscious buffet for the eyes. And the ladies of the court were always interested in the fashions that would be displayed under Duchess Isabelle's direction.

The maids-of-honor entered the Great Hall in a cluster, and then lined up. Individually, they approached the dais.

"Your Majesty, may I present Demoiselle Suzanne?"

"Your Majesty." Curtsy.

"Enchanted, Demoiselle."

One at a time, the formula was repeated.

As the fourth of the demoiselles approached the king, electricity seemed to fill the air. Every eye was focused with fascination on the demoiselle.

Agnes stepped forward with that erect posture that caused her to appear more regal than royalty. She lifted her skirt at each step, revealing the finely turned ankles that drove every male to distraction.

"Stunning."

"Oh-la!"

"Shocking. The bosom is scarcely covered."

"Look at those splendid..."

"Such décolletage may be all very well in Italy, but in France...?"

"Where has the duchess kept her hidden..."

"Disgusting display of..."

The silence was rustled with whispers, asides, and sighs.

"Your Majesty. May I present Demoiselle Agnes?"

"Your Majesty."

"Enchanted, Demoiselle."

The smile that graced the demoiselle's lips was echoed by a royal return.

The king's eyes lit up with a vivid intensity. Agnes lowered her eyelids and proceeded directly to pay her respects to Queen Marie.

Demoiselle Yvonne, who was to be presented to the king next, held back, seeing that there was a discussion among the people on the dais. The whispering and fluttering of the courtiers suddenly ceased. *What is the king saying? Is it possible to catch even a word? It seems the king has learned the virtue of a truly muted whisper.*

"Isn't that the demoiselle you told me about, Messire Charles?"

"Indeed it is, Sire," Messire Charles replied. "Her name is Agnes Sorel. She's the girl from Picardy I tried to describe to you."

The monarch said, "I didn't think such a beauty existed on this earthly plain. No. I didn't think it possible."

The king's facial expression was immediately readable to those who knew him.

Pierre de Breze was standing aloof in the crowd. He smiled wryly. He knew the king had swallowed the bait. His path to power now seemed assured.

The presentation of the remaining six maids-of-honor seemed anticlimactic. They were charming, beautiful young ladies, but the star had obviously appeared, and they could only play the part of supernumeraries.

René d'Anjou, as master of revels, had planned a ball to follow the presentations. He signaled to the musicians, and couples began to form on the dance floor.

The rebecs, violes, lutes, and gitterns tuned up. The pipe, tabor, shawm and tambourine players took their places. The most noble courtiers, dukes, counts, and barons, led similarly ranked ladies, duchesses, countesses, and baronesses, out onto the floor for the opening passepied. One by one, the maids-of-honor of the duchess and of the queen were invited by the lower nobility present to join them on the floor.

The eye of every male, from the dauphin down to the members of the honor guard, fell on the young lady who had so obviously caught the king's eye. Would it be a case of *lèse majesté* to ask the beauty to dance? Perhaps. But then, possibly worth the chance.

Poton de Xantrailles was not intimidated. He had sized up the situation and decided that it would be a service to his liege to deflect attention from the encounter that perhaps already had tongues wagging.

Poton was an accomplished general of His Majesty's Cavalry. He was Constable of France and Master of the Royal Stables. He was a professional military man above suspicion or rebuke. And he appeared to be the oldest man present who still expressed an interest in dancing.

"May I have the honor, Demoiselle?"

"I would be delighted."

Poton offered Agnes his arm and escorted her into the line of dancers.

"Demoiselle," he whispered. "There is much jealousy and suspicion lurking in His Majesty's court. But, I assure you, I am blindly loyal to our sire. And I hope you will know that you can trust my discretion implicitly."

Agnes knew instinctively that this elder cavalier did, indeed, intend to be her friend. She intuited, somehow, that he could be trusted. She felt he was the only person she could trust outside of the three who had collaborated in bringing her to the king's attention.

Even though General Poton was near her own father's age, he danced like a dream. With him as her partner, she fully felt the freedom, the grace, and the exhilaration of the dance. Her body curved, her leg pointed, and her foot glided, revealing that ankle that could drive men mad.

The king was grateful to his old comrade in arms. As Agnes' dancing partner, the general enhanced the loveliness of the beauty's fluid motion.

Agnes even pretended to flirt with Poton. Poton played the part of the mature rake to a tee. He knew the game. Agnes knew it. And, most importantly, Charles VII understood it and was both grateful and amused. He knew Poton to have integrity beyond dispute. Back when the king was a boy, as dauphin, rejected and reviled by his father, Charles VI, Poton de Xantrailles was loyal to him. That loyalty and integrity had never wavered through the dark years, and now through this period of the re-awakening of France.

Once the old general had broken the ice, other courtiers took the chance of dancing with the belle of the evening.

As Pierre de Breze approached her, dressed, as always, in his deep purple habiliments, she feared she might swoon. Why did he have to be so very attractive? He had come to ask her for a dance. Agnes was quite excited to dance with this man of her dreams. She discovered that he danced well, but not superbly. He had grace and good looks, but his dancing legs were not his best feature.

Messire Charles danced with her. He was a fine dancer, but not the equal of the old general who had led her on the first round of the evening.

Arnaut de Greuze, a member of the court she did not know, led her on the most delightful dance of the evening. His grace was nearly equal to her own. None of the other men at the ball that evening, not even General Poton, had the grace of this good looking, blondish young man.

At the last dance of the evening, it was René d'Anjou, the gallant master of revels, who danced with Agnes. He did not, on this occasion, make untoward advances. He was perfectly behaved. Perhaps René saw that his preferment with his relative the king probably depended on having this dance partner a friend rather than a conquest.

When the ball was over, the king was excited as he thought of the lady with the perfect tits, the transparent skin, and the golden hair. He knew that his current favorite, Josephine d'Auxerre, would be waiting for him in her quarters after the ball. He could not bring himself to seek carnal refuge with her. The vision of Agnes haunted his entire being too much.

To visit the queen's chamber and joylessly perform his royal duty there was equally unthinkable this evening. And anyway he had always honored Marie's pregnancies by not intruding on her person.

So, thus resigned, he went off to his own chambers. His favorite chamberlain, André de Villequier, undressed him. His current *mignon*, Arnaud de Greuze, who slept in the royal bed every night, was waiting for his king. Perhaps there would be some kind of relief for the monarch after all.

Nini was all a-twitter.

"Demoiselle. There is a very handsome gentleman at the door who says he requests the honor of an audience."

"Tell me, Nini. Does this messire happen to have a name?"

"What he actually said, Demoiselle, is 'Messire Charles requests the honor...'"

"Yes, yes. I know the rest, Nini. You may tell the count that I would be most happy to receive him at three o'clock this afternoon."

"Of course, Demoiselle."

When Nini told the count what Agnes had said, he took his leave. Before departing, he said, "Thank the Lady of Beauty for allowing me an audience. I will return at three."

When Nini reported back to Agnes, Agnes said to her: "Excellent, Nini. Now go to Messire Guirant, the sommelier, and advise him that I will require a pitcher of an afternoon dessert wine and a few pastries by early afternoon. Inform him that I will be entertaining Count Charles d'Anjou. Messire Guirant will know exactly what wine and what kind of cakes are pleasing to His Grace. Hurry along now. I can take care of brushing my hair by myself while you are off on your errand."

"Yes, demoiselle. Thank you very much," Nini said as she hurried off on her exciting errand.

Messire Charles was punctual in arriving at the door of Agnes' quarters at three that afternoon.

"Demoiselle Agnes," Messire Charles said with an elegant, courteous bow. "Thank you for according me the honor of attending you this afternoon."

"The honor is mine, Your Grace. Won't you be seated?"

"Most kind."

"I have taken the liberty to order some light refreshment," Agnes told the count. "Would you care for a glass of Château Vorey?"

"How kind. It is my favorite," Messire Charles smiled.

"So I had been told. Nini! You may serve the wine and cakes."

"Very good, Demoiselle Agnes," Nini replied, nearly tripping herself as she rushed from the room to fetch the refreshments.

Agnes and the count discussed matters completely inconsequential, as was appropriate between a man and a woman on such a visit. The topics lightly touched on were the decorations at the previous evening's ball, the attire of both ladies and gentlemen, the quality of the musicians, and the popularity of the dance steps imported from Italy. They talked about which dances were really suitable to the current French tastes. The passepied, estampie, rondeau, and carole had become standard dances, at least in the south of France. There was no difference of opinion between the demoiselle and the count about that. Agnes was partial to the newer Italian imports, the ductia, nota, salterella, piva, bassadanza, and quatermaria. Charles d'Anjou was of the opinion that the newer forms needed to be adapted, or, as he put it, 'Frenchified' before being accepted wholeheartedly.

"As has already occurred especially with the estampie," he opined.

The conversation was excessively stilted and polite. As, again, intended.

At length, Charles d'Anjou coughed politely, cleared his throat, and removed a small blue velvet bag from his sleeve pocket.

"Demoiselle Agnes," he began.

"Your Grace."

"I have very much enjoyed our pleasant conversation. I find your comments enlightening and witty."

"How kind of you to say so," Agnes replied politely.

"However," Messire Charles went on. "I must admit that I had an ulterior motive in requesting this audience."

"Really, Messire," Agnes responded. "I would never have guessed. I was of the opinion that I was being paid a social call."

"Let me hasten to inform you that my object was, and is, social," the count hastened to add. "The pleasure of your company was certainly sufficient motive for my intrusion on your time. However, it is possible for a courtier to have more than one reason for paying a visit to a demoiselle. Is that not so?"

"Quite, Your Grace. Please proceed."

Agnes knew that the big moment had come. She had suspected that it would be Count Charles d'Anjou who would be entrusted with the office of go-between. She smiled to herself that she had guessed correctly.

"I have been charged with telling you that your beauty has quite overwhelmed a person of great distinction."

"I am most honored to hear so, Your Grace. I am sure I am not worthy," Agnes replied.

"The personage who sent me would surely beg to differ with that, Demoiselle. And may I say that I heartily agree with him."

"Thank you, *Messire le compte*."

"The one who sent me asks that you receive this gift as a token of his devotion." Charles d'Anjou said as he extended the pouch to Agnes.

Agnes accepted the proffered bag. She opened it to discover a gold ring with a fleur-de-lys in tiny diamonds and rubies patterned on the bezel.

"It is indeed a lovely ring, Your Grace," Agnes protested. "But I am not sure I should accept it."

"Believe me, Demoiselle. It is a gift that carries no obligation whatsoever on your part. It is a token of esteem. A statement of admiration."

"I am still not sure that I should."

Agnes knew the game. Two refusals were mandatory if she were to play this out to her advantage.

"I assure you that you should accept. I insist that it is not given in exchange for anything. It is purely an expression of wonderment that such beauty as yours exists on this earth," was the count's courtly response.

Agnes slipped the gift on her right ring finger. It fit perfectly.

"Then please inform the person who sent you here with it that I am humbly grateful. Will you carry my profound thanks to him for his generosity?"

"Enchanted, Demoiselle," Messire Charles said with a bow. "Moreover, there is an additional item I would mention to you. You are aware that His Majesty is hosting a dinner this evening?"

"Indeed, Messire. I received an invitation earlier this afternoon."

"I understand that General Poton de Xantrailles will be escorting you to the banquet," Count Charles told her.

"He has been kind enough to offer to do so."

"The banquet will be a somewhat intimate affair," the count said. "There will only be some thirty or forty diners present. It is a dinner dedicated to Beauty. A subject dear to His Majesty's heart.

"The one who sent me asked me to inform you that he will be greeting every lady and demoiselle personally. Should he see this ring upon your finger at that time, he would be most gratified."

"I see," Agnes said concomitantly. "I will take into consideration what you have said. Perhaps I shall wear the ring this evening. Perhaps not."

"As you wish, of course, Demoiselle," Charles d'Anjou said, having fulfilled his role. "But look. I have already taken up too much of your time with my presence. I will be at the dinner this evening myself. I look forward to the pleasure of seeing you at that time."

"Enchanted, *Messire le compte*. Thank you for your visit."

"The pleasure was mine," said the count, retiring from Agnes' chambers.

"Aha!" Agnes said aloud when the door had closed on the count. "With this ring, my reign begins. France, be prepared for a new sun to break over the horizon."

Nini could not fathom what in the world her mistress was talking about.

Chapter Eight

The courtly general arrived at eight o'clock, in a splendid uniform, to escort Agnes to the state dining hall.

For the occasion, Agnes had decided on a demure, black, loose fitting gown trimmed in miniver. She did not wear a headdress, but piled her long hair high on her head. The coiffure was held in place by five bodkins. An unmistakable touch of cleavage was revealed at the bodice. The gown did not quite reach the floor, so her silk-sandaled feet were visible. Her intent was to look virginal, but not excessively so.

"This evening, we will be joined at table by the dauphine, Demoiselle," Poton explained as he escorted Agnes through the tapestry draped corridors of Narbonne Castle. "Have you made the acquaintance of Her Highness yet?"

"I met her briefly when I was presented to the queen last night," Agnes answered. "But I have not yet had the pleasure of conversing with her.

"You say, General, the dauphine will be with us. Will she not be with her husband, the dauphin, as well?"

Poton's brow wrinkled:

"His Highness, the dauphin, is, I regret to say, negligent in his office of husband," Poton told Agnes. "He will not attend this evening's festivities, leaving the dauphine unattended. He is derelict as well, if I may be so blunt as to say so, in never visiting Her Highness' bed chamber. The dauphin not only neglects his wife by shunning her bed. He insults and reviles her in public."

Agnes had been informed by Breze that Dauphin Louis was cruel and unsavory. She had not heard that he was unkind and distant to his wife, Marguerite of Scotland.

"I was not aware of the rift between the prince and the princess," Agnes said.

"It is a matter of great concern to Their Majesties as well," Poton went on. "Both the king and the queen are very fond of Dauphine Marguerite. The king, especially, dotes on her."

"Is it possible that the dauphine is at fault in the matter of her marriage?" Agnes asked.

"Only to the extent that she has not provided an heir for Louis," Poton explained. "Of course, she is unlikely to do so since the dauphin does not deign to join her in her solitary bed. But, she is, indeed, a very frail young woman who, back when she was still visited by her husband, did not bear his child. The prince blames her for barrenness, and expresses that blame openly, to everyone, in her presence."

"Shocking," Agnes said. "You have heard him do this yourself?"

"Many times," Poton said wearily. "You see, I was Princess Marguerite's champion and supporter before anyone at court had even met her. When our sire contracted the betrothal with King James of Scotland for Louis and Marguerite, there was great rejoicing in both courts. Both France and Scotland have been at war with the Goddams for decades. The joining of the two houses by marriage of our prince with the Scottish princess was immensely popular in both lands. Our king was gracious enough to send me personally to Scotland to escort Princess Marguerite to our shores."

"So, as you say, you knew her even before the king, queen, or dauphin had seen her," Agnes commented.

"Not only did I make her acquaintance. I was, and am, captivated by her. She was the loveliest, the gentlest and the most cultivated lady I had yet met. That is," Poton hastened to add, "Before Picardy sent us its loveliest rose."

"What a gallant you are, General Poton," Agnes laughed.

They had arrived at the dining hall at that point. Poton patted Agnes' hand in an avuncular way, and smiled at her.

"Demoiselle Agnes. I am an old man," he said. "And I am a great admirer of beauty — beauty of person and of character. When I declare my admiration for the dauphine and for you, it is truly the admiration of an ancient connoisseur. Believe my devotion to both of you. It is akin to my devotion and loyalty to our liege lord. Come. I see that the dauphine is already at the table reserved for us. I am anxious to introduce you to her."

Agnes recognized the dauphine, of course. And Marguerite of

Scotland recognized her in return. They embraced without requiring Poton's introduction.

Marguerite had skin as fair as Agnes'. But it had a definite pallor that bespoke frailty. Agnes wondered whether Marguerite's freckles appeared as unattractive across the channel in Scotland as they did in France. She hoped not. In France, freckles were not fashionable.

Marguerite's hair was of a redness seldom seen in France, particularly in Languedoc and Provence. It was attention-getting, but not modish. Back in Picardy, though, it might have been considered vaguely acceptable.

The dauphine was short, tiny boned, and astonishingly flat-chested. The thin face, with its high cheekbones, was classically attractive. If one could forget the freckles.

Agnes, Marguerite, and Poton sat down at the table. No sooner were they seated than René d'Anjou entered the room. He stood very erect and with stentorian voice announced:

"Messires, Mesdames. His Majesty, Charles VII the Victorious."

Three trumpeters blasted on their silver instruments and the king made his entrance. The forty diners arose, the men bowing, the women curtsying.

"Pray be seated, my subjects," the king said. "I wish to greet each of you individually, and would not have you all remaining standing on ceremony. Let the wine be served as I make my way around the tables. I would not have any of my beloved subjects perish of thirst due to my leisurely progression."

Laughter filled the hall at the king's joviality. Serving men streamed into the room carrying pitchers of wine while serving wenches provided goblets and tankards.

When everyone had a filled goblet, Duke René held his glass aloft and shouted out, "To the health of our Sire!" The toast was echoed by everyone.

"To France!"

"To Toulouse!"

"Victory over the Goddams!"

It was the king who proposed the final toast.

"TO BEAUTY!" The king cast a sly look at Agnes. Many observed the glance.

Agnes hoped she was the only one who caught the significance.

Agnes, Marguerite, and Poton resumed their seats and began sipping the wine after the final toast.

"I see the king is attired in green," Agnes said. "It seems that every time

I see him, he is wearing that color. Is it truly his favorite?"

Poton told his two lovely table companions the story of why the king was so often garbed in green.

"It began a while back. Our sire was at Chinon Castle when Joan of Arc arrived. She had to undergo several trials before being allowed access to His Majesty. First, the king's confessor asked the Maid numerous questions concerning her faith. It had to be established that she had no heretical leanings. She was found to be a good Catholic Christian and it was established that the voices she heard were not inspired by Satan. Then Countess Yolande examined her for virginity, to make sure she truly was a maid as she claimed.

"While Her Grace was conducting that examination in the ladies' quarters, our sire devised one additional test for the Maid. There were some thirty courtiers, including myself, in the Throne Room. The king was wearing a suit of deep blue velvet, the family colors of the House of Valois. I was wearing a green uniform, green being the colors of the regiment under my command at the time.

"King Charles asked me to exchange clothes with him. 'Poton,' he said. 'When the Maid enters the room, seeing you in royal garb, she will take you to be the king. That is, unless her voices direct her to me. Let us see if she be truly inspired by Heaven.'"

"A clever ruse, on the part of the king," Marguerite exclaimed.

"I felt so as well," Poton continued. "So I donned the royal vestments, and Charles clothed himself in my green uniform. When the Maid entered the room, we were all milling about. I stepped forward to greet her, playing the part of the king. She looked at me, then glanced over the crowd. The king was in a far corner of the room. Joan of Arc ignored me, walked straight through the crowd, right up to the king, and knelt before him.

"'You, My Lord, are the true king of France,'" she proclaimed. "'Heaven has revealed to me that France's enemies must be driven from our soil and that you must be crowned at Rheims.'

"Charles took her aside to talk. In that sequestered conversation, as final proof, the Maid told him something that convinced him that she was, indeed, sent to him by Divine mandate. He yielded to her request that she be allowed to lead my battalion to raise the siege of Orleans.

"In honor of the moment he met the Maid, King Charles has chosen to wear green even more often than his royal blue."

Agnes asked, "What was it that the Maid told our king in private that finally convinced him to accept her advice and requests?"

"That, my dear, no one knows, but the king." Poton paused for a moment. "Or, perhaps, his queen. I believe His Majesty confides everything to her. But, aside from those two, no one knows. When she was captured by the Burgundians and sold to the Goddams, the Maid was tortured by our enemies in an attempt to find an answer to that question. She never revealed a word of what she told the king back there in Chinon."

While Poton was telling his story, the king had visited most of the tables. He had not only greeted each couple. He engaged in a short personal conversation with each one. Before moving to the next table, he bowed to the gentleman and took each lady's hand in his own.

The table occupied by the two ladies and Poton would be the last one on the king's progression. He was holding a discussion just three tables away when Poton turned his attention to Agnes.

"I understand, Demoiselle, that you have an interest in poetry."

"You have been informed correctly, Messire. Since I have come to this land of the troubadours, I have become enchanted with Provençale and Languedoc poetry. At the court of Duke René and Duchess Isabelle, the art of poetry flourishes."

"Yes," Poton agreed. "All the arts are kept alive by Their Graces. Did you know, Demoiselle, that Her Highness here is a poetess in her own right?"

Marguerite blushed.

"But, how marvelous," Agnes exclaimed. "What kind of poetry do you like, Your Highness?"

"My talents in composing poetry in Langue d'Oc are, I fear, limited," the princess replied. "Back in Scotland, my father the king is a great patron of our Celtic bards and minstrels. I learned to love poetry practically in the cradle. The poetry here in France is quite different from our Celtic poems. It is more sensual. Even, if I may say so, a bit shocking. But I have grown very fond of it."

The king was just finishing his discussion at the next table, and approached the table where the two young ladies and Poton were holding their discussion. The three stood as the king approached. The ladies curtsied and Poton bowed.

Charles VII took Marguerite's hand in both of his.

"My dear," he said. "I fear the queen is indisposed this evening. I was hoping you would serve as hostess for the banquet."

"I would be honored, Your Majesty."

"Ah, Demoiselle Agnes," Charles said as he turned towards her. "It is a pleasure to see you here."

"An honor for me, Your Majesty."

The king took her hand in his. He looked fixedly at the ring on her finger. His eyes lit up.

He shifted his gaze from the fleur-de-lys ring to her vivacious blue eyes, and smiled. He felt an electric twinge of pleasure in what he privately called the "Crown Jewels of France." They happened to be held within the royal scrotum that hung below the "Royal Scepter."

Agnes returned his smile, and coyly lowered her eyes.

She had divined from what Duchess Isabelle had recently told her what was meant by "the Crown Jewels of France." She intended to have them cradled in her hands before long.

A silent message had been conveyed. Each felt a flush of excitement. An entire romantic episode had been played out in front of a roomful of people. Yet no one but the two of them was aware that a pregnant moment had just elapsed before their unknowing eyes.

The king then addressed Poton, commenting on the current favorable negotiations with the court of Burgundy. Then all four sat down.

Duke René approached their table.

"Sire. Shall the banquet begin?"

"My lord of Anjou," the king answered. "Her Highness the Dauphine will be serving as hostess this evening. Pray ask her."

The Dauphine requested that the banquet be served. At a nod from René, servers entered the hall with the first course, steaming platters of eel boiled in a broth spiced with cinnamon and coriander.

As they began their repast, Poton addressed the king.

"Your Majesty," he said. "As you were approaching our table, the lovely ladies here were discussing their love of poetry. It appears that it is a shared passion of theirs."

"We are certainly in the right environment for poetry lovers," the king said, relaxing into the conversation. "Toulouse has been the center of our troubadour tradition for over a hundred years. While our wars with the English and the Burgundians have been devastating our lands, the poetic fire of Languedoc was never quenched. I believe that as long as that spirit of *gai saber* lives, France will always prevail in the end."

René d'Anjou was passing by the table, and overheard the sovereign's remark.

"Your Majesty is certainly a patron of all things beautiful." He gave a knowing glance at Agnes. "Perhaps to celebrate your stay in Toulouse, we might hold a *joc floral*."

Festivals of music and poetry called *jocs florals* were an ancient tradition in Toulouse. These contests were competitions among the troubadours, and as entertainments were as popular as jousts.

"Splendid idea, René," the king enthused. "Can you organize one on short notice?"

"Since Your Majesty will only be gracing us with your presence for a short time, I doubt that we can gather together many troubadours before your departure. But I will contact the Consistory to see if there are a few readily available."

"Even two or three would please me," Charles said.

Addressing Agnes and Marguerite he asked, "What would you two ladies think of a small scale *joc floral* here at Narbonne Castle?"

"I cannot think of anything I would enjoy more," Marguerite answered.

"I concur with Her Highness," Agnes said, discharging her most stunning smile on the king.

René was just the man to organize such an event.

The banquet was a very regal affair. Following the conger eel, the courses included chopped sparrow, roast swan redressed in its own feathers, venison, and carp. Wine, beer, and mead flowed in abundance.

"I find the food here at Narbonne Castle unparalled anywhere in the realm," the king remarked.

"Yes," Agnes agreed. "I have been impressed by the care Duchess Isabelle gives to the food preparation."

"You are interested in cuisine, Demoiselle?" Marguerite asked surprised.

"Yes, Your Highness," Agnes answered. "In my home province, Picardy, it is the custom for the chatelaine to be very much involved in the workings of the kitchen. And here at Narbonne Castle, the duchess has been kind enough to allow me to work with the kitchen staff. Food preparation is a source of infinite amusement to me."

"How interesting," the dauphine replied. "In Scotland it would be unthinkable for the nobility to be so engaged. I find your interest admirable. I truly envy you."

"It is not all that unusual here in France," the king added. "Food preparation comes close to being a religion with us. And some of our finest dishes have their origins in Picardy."

"And what is your favorite dish?" Marguerite asked Agnes, genuinely interested and impressed.

"I make a cheese and carp timbale that is much admired," Agnes said. Then she added, looking coyly at the king. "Yet my honey cakes are my real specialty."

A wicked grin passed over the king's mouth as he said, "I hope someday I may have the pleasure of enjoying your...honey cake."

The stirring within the "Crown Jewels" was intensely pleasurable.

Agnes nodded her head. The exchange went completely over the dauphine's head.

The feast of edibles pleased the king greatly. Yet, for Charles VII the real feast was that devoured by his eyes. He felt he had never found any experience more enjoyable than taking in the beauty of the blonde demoiselle from Picardy. He did, indeed, look forward to sampling her honey cakes.

Chapter Nine

Back in her chambers, Agnes played over in her mind the banquet she had left a couple of hours previously. The splendor of the room, the endless order of courses, the music, the jugglers, the festive garb of the knights, ladies, and courtiers. But the thing that most occupied her recollections was the king's apparent devotion to herself.

As she was thus reminiscing, Nini approached her.

"Demoiselle Agnes. There is a page at the door who claims to have a very special message for you."

"A page? How extraordinary. Whom does he represent?"

"I don't know, Demoiselle. He is very handsome. The most handsome..."

"I didn't ask if he was good looking or ugly," Agnes responded petulantly. "I asked whom he represents."

"As I said, Demoiselle, I don't know. I only know what he said."

Agnes was growing more irritated at her maid with every word.

"All right, Nini. What did the lad say?"

"He said, and here are his exact words, Mademoiselle, he said, 'I have been sent by my master, who is Demoiselle Agnes' most ardent admirer, to deliver a very special message to her.'"

"Most ardent admirer," Agnes thought to herself. "Oh, if it could only be a protestation of love from Pierre de Breze... Or, of course, the king." Her heart hoped it was Breze's message. Her mind desired it to be the king's.

"What color is the livery of this handsome young page, pray?":

If green, he would be from the sovereign. If deep purple...

"A beautiful emerald green, that looks so fine on him..."

Agnes didn't let her serving maid go on. Her heart despaired. Her mind quickened.

"Go, go, go, Nini. Let the young man in."

Nini was all aflutter as she trotted back to the door.

"Demoiselle will grant you an audience."

As the page stepped past her, Nini's eyes followed him with devotion. The young man was eighteen years old, with olive skin, black curly hair, and large brown eyes. Nini fell in love for the first time in her young life.

Agnes was seated in a chair with her back to the messenger. He entered her room and waited to be acknowledged. Agnes stood as Nini fluttered over to swivel the chair around. As Agnes re-sat, the page went down on one knee and extended a wooden box towards her.

"Demoiselle, my master bade me present to you this token of his high esteem."

"I am sure your master is most kind and generous, young man," Agnes answered.

As she leaned forward, the page placed the elaborately carved rosewood case into her extended hand.

"Agnes opened the box and removed a bracelet composed of an array of sapphires and emeralds set in a band of intertwined gold and silver filaments.

Sapphires, the blue of the House of Valois. Emeralds, the green of Charles' reign. The king's signature in precious stones.

"Lovely!" Agnes exclaimed. "Please express my thanks to your master."

"I will do so, Demoiselle. However, my master bade me ask you for some tangible token in return for the gift. A token that would reveal to him what sentiments you hold in your heart."

"I understand," Agnes replied. And she did, indeed, understand. It was the moment for her to declare to the king whether she would accept his amorous intentions. It was time to declare a clear "yes" or "no."

"Nini," Agnes commanded. "Fetch me my silver scissors, my wax, and my seal. And make sure the wax is heated."

Nini hastened off to obey her mistress. When she returned with the items she could not resist fluttering her eyes at the page. He rapidly glanced away from Agnes and smiled at the maid. Agnes was secretly amused.

"Remove the bodkins from my hair," she directed Nini. The rich blond hair cascaded nearly to the floor.

Agnes measured off a length and told Nini to cut off a lock. Agnes twisted the strands together. With her seal, she bound the two ends forming a circlet and motioned for the page to rise. She placed the box in his hands and deposited the lock of hair within.

"Your master will understand my response, I am sure."

"Thank you, Demoiselle," the messenger said.

Agnes was keenly aware of Nini's infatuation with the youth. For her benefit she asked:

"What might your name be, lad?"

"Guilhem Raimbaut, your servant, Demoiselle."

"And your master sends this lovely gift to me through your offices rather than those of Charles d'Anjou?"

"I am, Demoiselle, though young and of mean birth, my master's most loyal and trusted messenger. An honor that is more important to me than my own life."

"Then here, Raimbaut," Agnes offered. "Please accept these coins for your service."

Agnes motioned to Nini to bring her purse.

"My lady," Raimbaut stated. "I am much obliged and thankful. But if it would not offend you, I would prefer nothing in exchange. My service to my master is the sole reward I desire."

"Then God go with you, Raimbaut," Agnes replied in dismissing him.

Nini rushed to the door to show the page out. Love lit her eyes. A knowing smile crossed the page's lips.

Agnes had very definite ideas for a celebration of her own following the joc floral. She busied herself immediately in preparation for the late night festivities.

She repaired to the castle kitchen accompanied by Nini. The kitchen staff knew her well, and welcomed her with bows and smiles.

They bustled about gathering the woodcock, the fish, the cheese, the herbs, spices and condiments for the timbale and the ramier. The sommelier brought forth the exact wines Agnes wanted. The baker measured out the portions for Agnes' special honey cakes. Agnes, herself, mixed in herbs and spices for the timbale. Then she added the atmagupta to the honey cakes for her guest's dessert. Nini was left in the kitchen to gather the preparations and bring the results to Agnes' quarters. Agnes herself needed to seek out Duke René.

"Your Grace," Agnes said when she found him. "Among the musicians you will have at the joc floral, will there, by any chance, be a psaltery player?"

René smiled. He immediately divined the reason for her question.

"I fear not," he said. "I have engaged the same musicians who played at the ball."

Agnes appeared dismayed.

"However, my dear," René continued. "I will see to it that the psaltery we have in the music room will be in the festival hall tonight. It will be among the instruments at the disposal of the court musicians. It would cause my heart to overflow with joy to see your sensual fingers erotically plucking those strings."

"Your Grace understands the subtleties of music more than any man in France," Agnes responded.

"I trust, Demoiselle Agnes, that you will pluck more than a psaltery string tonight."

"It is my intent," Agnes answered.

Both Agnes and the Duke felt quite sure that the king would be Agnes' instrument before the night was over.

And he would, indeed, get plucked.

Agnes felt sure it would be a more memorable plucking than any he had received from any woman heretofore.

Agnes next went in search of the duchess. As she guessed, Isabelle was in the music room practicing a pastorella.

"Will you be performing this evening at the joc floral, Your Gr...Isabelle?" Agnes asked.

Isabelle replied: "I would like to perform Marcabru's delightful and naughty *L'autrie jost'una sebrissa* (the other day beside a hedge). It always makes me laugh. But I need someone to play the part of the shepherdess while I play the role of the knight."

Agnes knew this was a strong invitation to perform with the duchess that evening.

By way of increasing the force of the invitation, the duchess sang the line, "Your beauty would be doubled if you would lie down under me."

Agnes sang back the shepherdess' reply. "Gape, you fool, for your come-on is hopeless, at least in the middle of the day."

The two of them laughed. That was agreement enough that they would sing the duet at the joc floral.

"Isabelle," Agnes said. "I am in such distress."

"Why, my dear? Whatever in the world is wrong?"

"I plan to wear an emerald and sapphire bracelet to the joc floral tonight."

"Really? Emerald and sapphire? Interesting! A gift from an admirer?"

"Why, Your Grace. You just might cause me to blush."

They laughed at that, knowing Agnes was not very likely to blush. They both knew the drama that was unfolding between her and the king.

Agnes continued. "As you know, I have a lovely emerald velvet gown, but no blue scarf to go with it. And what is equally distressing, I would love to drape my green hennin with a blue chiffon. But I haven't one to my name."

"Oh, my lovely," the duchess countered. "Do not shed even a tiny tear. I happen to have both items in my wardrobe. Do send Nini to see my Manon. She will find both items for you."

With Nini's assistance, it took Agnes two hours to complete her toilette and get dressed. After Nini draped the scarf around her mistress' shoulders, Agnes arranged it to show off her swanlike neck to its best advantage. Nini placed the conical hennin on Agnes' head, with the chiffon draped down to meet the scarf at nearly the right angle. Agnes gave it a slight re-adjustment.

Agnes applied attar of roses to her cheeks and breast area. Then, washing her hands in rose water, she sallied out into the corridors leading to the festival hall. When she was satisfied that everyone but the royal family was inside, she made her entrance.

As Agnes entered the hall, a hush fell over the assembly. Since the ball and the dinner, she had become the talk of Toulouse. She stepped in and paused dramatically. Languidly, she observed her surroundings. A joc floral required that the hall be heavily decorated with flowers. But even this far south in France, there were no flowers readily available this time of year. However Jacques Coeur had provided Duke René with enough imitation roses of imported silk to overwhelm the room. The candles scented with attar of roses completed the floral illusion.

While the attendees were busy ogling Agnes, she allowed her eyes to wander lingeringly and luxuriously over the crowd. The multi-colored merry-makers were attired in heavy velvet and shimmering silks. There was the shimmer of hennaed hair and the appearance of three-cornered hats and extensive, feather-festooned berets. The fashion was more outrageous than ever previously displayed. As she made her way through the crowd, whispers, babbling, laughter, and sotto-voce conversation resumed. Mixed with the scent of expensive perfumes there lingered a strong odor of garlic and sweating flesh. The bracelet Agnes wore did not pass unnoticed. It elicited whispers, gossip, and frowns.

Duke René gave a signal to the orchestra, which played a flourish. Silence descended on the hall.

"Ladies and Gentlemen, their Majesties and Royal Highnesses."

Every eye turned to the enormous entry door as it was opened by the liveried footmen. The king, queen, dauphin, and dauphine entered to stately music. The men all went down on one knee. The women curtsied. The king and queen appeared in a festive mood. They stopped occasionally to address someone in the assembly. The dauphine wore an anxious smile.

The dauphin, thin, dark, aloof, with a bored expression did not deign to speak to anyone.

By an exchange of glances, surprise was shown that His Highness had even agreed to come at all. It was well known that the dauphin detested music and poetry.

The royals proceeded at a stately pace to the thrones set up for them on the dais. As they sat, the crowd began to buzz a bit.

René stepped up onto the dais.

"Your Majesties, Your Highnesses. Honored guests.

"Toulouse has been the site of jocs florals for well over one hundred years, since 1323. The festivals are always held in May, and are celebrations not only of the glorious springtimes enjoyed in Languedoc, but of the flowering of troubadour song and poetry with which this beautiful province has regaled the entire world.

"His Majesty, Charles the Victorious, has brought peace and security to our beloved land. A peace we had not known for five generations. So, when he requested a joc floral in January, by royal edict, we have brought Spring to Toulouse three months prematurely."

Polite laughter swept through the crowd.

"At this rapidly improvised joc, we could not assemble the customary dozens of troubadours. However, we were able to bring to Narbonne Castle the two most preeminent troubadours in the world, Masters Peire Cardenal and

Guilhem de Montanhagol. They will regale us with their rich poetry and song for the first portion of the joc. Then, following a pause for refreshments, members of the royal court and of the court of Anjou will perform with renditions of the troubadour tradition."

While René spoke on and on, the king's eyes skimmed over the adorned and beautifully coiffed heads of his subjects. His glance sought, discovered, and rested upon the glorious bosom of the one person he was interested in. Then, as if indifferent, he continued his visual sweep over the crowd.

When René finally came to the end of his speech, the king thanked him. And then went on to say,

"My Lord of Anjou. Prior to the introduction of our honored and esteemed troubadours, the royal family would like to circulate among our beloved subjects to greet personally many of those we were unable to address during our progress to our thrones."

The crowd applauded the statement.

The king, queen, and dauphine descended from their thrones and began mixing with the crowd. The dauphin remained seated, and was approached and surrounded by a group of his devotees and toadies.

The king made his way slowly through the crowd, much as he had at the previous evening's dinner.

When he reached Agnes, she curtsied.

"The green and blue becomes your complexion," he said, indicating the colors of Agnes' outfit. She reached out to kiss the king's hand, and he looked at the bracelet and the ring that he had given to her. He raised his eyebrows. She nodded her head. A clear understanding was reached.

"Do you enjoy the music of the troubadours of Languedoc, Demoiselle?" the king asked.

"Yes, rather," Agnes smiled graciously. "I have been enchanted with their music ever since I came South. The troubadours' language, Langue d'Oc, is more sonorous and melodious than our High French. It accommodates itself to the music so well. It quite carries me away."

"True," the king replied. "It seems that the isolation of this part of France has managed to preserve the originality of its poets."

"I do hope this evening comes up to Your Majesty's expectations." Agnes expressed, with innuendo that could not possibly be misunderstood by the king.

"I feel sure it will," the king replied with notable emphasis that was pregnant with amorous intimation.

He continued:

"But, first, the joc floral. With your permission, Demoiselle."

And with that, the king returned to the dais to indicate to his brother-in-law, Count René that the festival could begin.

Chapter Ten

At René's signal, Peire Cardenal stepped forward, bowed to the royals, stepped to the side of the dais so his back would not be to the king, and strummed an introduction.

His first song dealt with carnal love, with the theme that lust has an overwhelming power over kings, princes, and dukes, causing them to listen to their penises rather than to reason. Everyone looked at the king so see whether he took offense. Was this a case of *lèse majesté*? There was general relief when it was seen that the king laughed very heartily, signaling that the audience could take the verses in the spirit of the lusty troubadour tradition and laugh as well.

For the next forty minutes, Peire continued to amuse his audience with his witty verses that employed vernacular words for the bodily parts of both males and females.

Since His Majesty took no offense, neither did his subjects.

When Guilhem de Montanhagol followed Peire with his lute, his songs were in much the same spirit as his predecessor. However, as he performed, he walked among the crowd and sang each song to first one lady, and then to another, to the great delight of his audience.

For his last song, he bent on one knee before Agnes, addressing her directly:

> *Be'us dic que mielhs cereire deuria*
> *Que sa beutatz desus del cel partis,*
> *Que tan sembla obra de paradis*
> *Qu'a penas par terrenals sa conhidia.*

"I declare that I am quite sure that her beauty descended from Heaven, for she clearly appears to be a creation from Paradise since her grace appears hardly to be of this world."

The audience was stunned. Agnes, though, stood regally through the recital with lowered eyes and a coy smile on her full, luscious lips.

Dauphine Marguerite descended from the dais to award the prize. She declared for Montanhogol and presented him with a ruby encrusted lily. Her choice was greeted with cheers.

Duke René declared an intermission and footmen and pages coursed into the room with goblets of local wine and barley cakes.

The dauphine remained on the floor, talking to Agnes.

Provençale poetry was a subject dear to both of them. None of the others present chose to interrupt their discussion.

After a half hour had elapsed, René d'Anjou beckoned to the orchestra, which played a short flourish. The goblets were spirited away by the servants, and the second part of the joc floral was about to begin.

Duke René invited the dauphine to lead off the second part of the program. She did not rise from her throne, but recited a poem by Raimon de Miraval. She did not sing it, but in her soft voice, with its Scottish accent, spoke the words with exquisite feeling.

Chanssos, vai me dir al rei...

"Song, go tell the king for me that all is well..."

While his wife was reciting, the dauphin glowered and slumped in his throne.

Following the dauphine, the Count of St.-Pol sang a song while a friend accompanied him on the lute. Arnaud de Greuze sang an ironic, erotic poem, *Compahno, tant ai gutz d'avols conres*, composed by Guilhem IX of Aquitaine some two hundred years before. He sang it in a rich counter tenor voice that quite surprised Agnes.

René, as master of the revels, mounted the dais to announce that his charming wife and one of her maids-of-honor had a surprise duet. The psaltery and dulcimer were brought forth by one of the court musicians. Duchess Isabelle and Agnes ascended the dais, curtsied to the royals, and faced the crowd. The audience received them enthusiastically. They sang *L'autrie jost'una sebrissa*. The raucous laughter that followed the last line, sung by Agnes, proved the performance an enormous hit. The duchess herself announced that the duet would be followed by a solo performance by Agnes.

Agnes played a short introduction, and then launched into the song she had chosen for the occasion.

> *Quecx auzel quez a votz sana*
> *De chantar s'atilha,*
> *E s'esforsa si la rana*
> *Lonc la fontanilha,*
> *E'l chauans ab sa chauana*
> *S'als non pot, grondilha.*
>
> *Sesta creatura vana*
> *D'amor s'aparilha,*
> *Lur joys sec la via plana*
> *E l nostre bruzilha;*
> *Quar nos, qui plus pot enguana,*
> *Per qu'usquecx buzilha.*
>
> *"Each bird with healthy voice*
> *Prepares to sing.*
> *And the frog tries likewise*
> *Beside the spring.*
> *And the owl with his lover,*
> *If he cannot do otherwise, grumbles.*
>
> *"These simple creatures*
> *Approach each other through love.*
> *Their joy follows a smooth road.*
> *Yet ours wavers;*
> *Because we must dissemble at present*
> *And so cannot come together openly."*

The message was clear enough to Charles VII. It was quite well understood by the duke and duchess of Anjou and by Pierre de Breze. A sardonic, wily look spread over the dauphin's face. But, apparently, most of the revelers simply took the performance as a simple entertainment, and expressed their enjoyment of a pretty song performed by a beautiful lady with an enchanting voice.

Agnes' was the final performance for the evening of the joc floral. Each performer was invited to come to the thrones on the dais to receive thanks from the king and a silk rose from the queen.

As the king took Agnes' hand, ostensibly to compliment her on her performance, he whispered:

"My dear. I understood your song so well. 'Because we must dissemble at present, we cannot come together openly.' I must see you."

"I would be honored if Your Majesty would join me for a little supper in my chambers later this evening," Agnes answered in a soft, sultry voice.

"You have aroused my appetite, Woman of Beauty," Charles told her. "People are watching and trying to listen. I will send Raimbaut to see you."

Agnes curtsied and went on to present herself to the queen, where she received the silk rose. She then went on to converse with the dauphine.

"It was absolutely lovely, wasn't it, Your Highness?" Agnes asked.

"Oh, yes," the princess gushed. "It was the loveliest evening I can remember. I absolutely love the poetry and song of Languedoc. And your rendition of *Quecx auzel quez a votz sana* was absolutely exquisite."

"And your recitation of *Chanssos, vai me dir al rei* was truly lovely," Agnes replied.

Agnes mixed with the other maids-of-honor, each of whom complimented her on her singing. Poton approached and went so far as to kiss her hand and then her cheek. The duchess and the seneschal were the last of her well-wishers.

"I believe your performance went very well indeed," Pierre de Breze said, with a meaningful wry smile.

"So it would seem," Agnes answered.

"Seem, nothing," the duchess insisted. "It is clear that you have won the prize."

Duchess Isabelle was not referring to the silk rose Agnes carried in her left hand.

When Agnes returned to her chambers, Nini was ready and excited to assist her mistress with a change of costume. When the scarf and robe were removed, Agnes was in her silken, lacy undergarment. When the hennin and bodkins were removed, Agnes' hair tumbled down her shoulders and clustered about her mid-back in golden curls. Nini removed Agnes' undergarment and replaced it with pink silken deshabille. The silk robe revealed much more than it concealed.

The ladies did not have to wait long for the discrete knock on the door. Nini, in a twitter, hastened to the door. She returned to Agnes' chamber.

"Mademoiselle. Joven Raimbaut brings word from his master."

"Allow entry to the page, if you please," Agnes directed.

Raimbaut entered and sank to one knee.

Nini fluttered a fan at one side of the room. One would think she wanted to arouse the attention of the young man.

Raimbaut's shiny handsome young face looked up at Agnes with devotion.

"Demoiselle Agnes. My master has been given to understand that you have extended an invitation for him to sup with you."

"Your master is well-informed, Joven."

"He begs to know the hour when he might be expected."

"The supper is already prepared," Agnes informed the youth. "I await his arrival at his convenience."

"Thank you, Demoiselle. I will so inform him."

Nini scampered behind the page as he left the quarters.

It was scant minutes later that there was another discrete knock on the door. Nini's excitement knew no bounds.

When she opened the door to the king, her legs nearly gave way beneath her. The curtsy was occasioned not only by respect for the king but by her own trembling knees.

As Agnes greeted the king, Nini made the last minute arrangements in the adjoining bedroom, where the table was set up. When Agnes led Charles VII into the bedroom, Nini had withdrawn.

The enamored couple was, at last, truly alone.

Agnes poured the muscadet into the goblets.

"May we drink to our beloved France, Your Majesty?"

They sipped.

"And, Demoiselle Agnes," Charles countered. "I would propose a toast to beauty and pleasure."

Agnes acknowledged the complement with a smile and sipped.

"I prepared a timbale *à la picardienne* and *ramier salmi*, an it please Your Majesty."

"With your own skillful, snow-white hands?"

"I do hope Your Majesty will find my hands to have been skillful, My

Lord."

"And, hopefully," the king insinuated, "perhaps, skillful in other endeavors?"

"As it may please Your Majesty." Agnes responded with a winsome smile.

She knew she would have the "Crown Jewels" in her alabaster hands before long.

Charles VII was very observant of every graceful move Agnes made as she served the supper she had prepared. She artfully moved in such a way that the silken sheath exposed her rosy nipples and the outline of her golden bush to her guest's discriminating eyes.

The conversation was polite, but nearly every sentence carried a double meaning. Both Agnes and Charles were quite skilled in the language of *fin'amors* and *gai saber*. Indeed, the king was more accomplished at the courtly repartee than any of the courtiers who had engaged in the sport with Agnes.

The supper terminated with the partaking of the honey cakes with the last of the wine. Agnes suggested they sit on the cushioned settee facing the fireplace to enjoy dessert. The king carried both his own goblet and Agnes' with him. She brought the cakes on two separate platters. When he had seated himself, Agnes sat close enough that their bodies touched. The king's well-laced cake began to take effect nearly immediately. Although Agnes had noticed that the movement of her body likewise had affected her supper companion.

His left hand grazed the curve of her ass. Once that purchase was made, it slipped around and performed traceries on her thigh.

When they had finished the delicacies Agnes turned her eyes toward those of the king.

"Your Majesty does not appear totally at ease in his doublet," Agnes observed. "May I be allowed to remove it for your comfort?"

Charles did, indeed, allow it. Nor did he resist as her skillful fingers removed, very slowly and deliberately, all his outer garments. He was now in a greater state of deshabille than her.

"Would you object to a kiss, Demoiselle?" the king asked gallantly.

"I would be honored, My Liege."

The king's sensuous lips did, indeed, know how to kiss. Agnes was aware that he would be an extremely skillful lover.

She coaxed his tongue into playful contact with her own. And, despite herself, she could not help but imagine that it was the tongue and lips of Pierre de Breze she was embracing. And with that thought, she fully submitted to the vibrant sensations she was experiencing.

Chapter Eleven

Charles VII had been sexually active since the age of thirteen, when he was still the dauphin. His sexual experiences with the starry-eyed nymphets and experienced courtesans who were at his beck and call were actively encouraged by his mother, the queen, Isabella of Bavaria. Her sexual appetite was legendary. Indeed, it was her promiscuity that prompted her husband, the mad King Charles VI, to disinherit the dauphin, claiming he was not his legitimate heir.

Mother Isabella often even chose the companions for her teen-aged son's bed. And Dauphin Charles, having inherited his mother's taste for sexuality and luxuriousness, was an avid pursuer of all things amatory. He learned sexual technique from some of the most sophisticated women in Europe. At a young age, he was a very accomplished lover.

When he was ten, Charles was betrothed to Marie d'Anjou. And when he was fourteen, he was sent to Anjou to be raised by his future mother-in-law Yolande of Aragon. He was a precocious lad, and continued his course of libidinous studies at the Court of Anjou. However, he did not extend his lusty endeavors to his betrothed, Marie, who not only was closely watched by her ever-present mother, but was not endowed with the libido of her future husband. Marie simply found no interest in anything of a sexual nature. Though they loved each other as if brother and sister both before and after their marriage, Charles and Marie never had sex with each other for other than dynastic and ritualistic purposes.

Charles VII had wider experience than Agnes in the practice of lovemaking, and was not adverse to helping her extend her knowledge in that department. Agnes had honed her own skills, and had a few things to teach to His Majesty as well.

Following the arousal kiss, the couple took each other by the hand and proceeded directly to the silk sheets that adorned the bed.

As they sat next to each other on the edge of the bed, Agnes instinctively cupped her hand behind the king's neck to draw him into an embrace.

"Wait, my love," Charles whispered with a soothing tone of voice she had not previously heard from his lips.

She looked at him with wondering eyes.

"Before we relax into each other's embrace, I want you to know that I am aware you are a virgin."

"I have saved myself for you, my lord," Agnes sighed. "I am, indeed, a virgin."

"It would have been all right with me if you weren't, you know," Charles continued. "My sister-in-law, Isabelle, told me you were *virgo intacta*. Yes, I did ask her. I hope you don't mind."

"I am honored that you inquired about me at all, Sire."

"As you are aware, when either lover is still flowered, it behooves the other to take that into account. So I will not hurry our night of love. You will find that I can be very gentle. So I hope you will not be tense."

"I understand, Your Majesty," Agnes assented. "I assure you, I am quite at ease in your presence."

Charles felt this was the time to clarify how he would like his lover to address him.

"Outside these doors, it is right and proper for you to call me 'Your Majesty' or by any of my other titles. Within the walls of your chamber, the titles feel a bit...stilted. Wouldn't you say so?"

Agnes could only nod her head. Sitting on the side of a bed, next to a naked monarch, and discussing how he should be called, was outside the pale of what she had considered an imaginable situation.

"And likewise," Charles continued. "Outside that door, in that other world we inhabit, I will, of course, continue to address you as Demoiselle Agnes. But here in our privacy, I would prefer to call you Beauté. Would that be satisfactory?"

Agnes regained the use of her voice.

"Yes, that would be pleasing to me. But then you must tell me how you would like to be addressed, here in our privacy."

"Very few even know the pet name I am called by my intimates," the king informed her. "I would like you to know that name and call me by it in our intimate moments. The name is Chatz. My mother was Bavarian, you know. And she always called me that as a term of endearment."

"The name is already dear to me, Chatz," Agnes said, and encircled his neck once more, drawing him into a lingering kiss. As they kissed, she softly brushed her fingers across his naked chest, having learned from practice that such a stroke was pleasing to the male body.

"If you would please me now, Beauté," Chatz told her, "you will rest languidly stretched out on the bed as I become acquainted with you by feel and by word."

Surprised again, Agnes stretched out as directed. She realized that her previous experiences and experimentations had not prepared her for a skillful royal lover. Up to this point, the awkward young men she had seduced were clumsily groping for her breasts. This lover could not be said to grope at all.

Chatz had spotted the cup of unscented oil that had been placed on a table next to the bed. He smiled. The beauty was not altogether naive concerning a night of love. He dipped his fingers into the oil, and began to very, very lightly and gently touch her skin, starting with her face. The gentle touches, around the cheeks, on the earlobes, behind the ears, over the lips, under the chin, and around the neck induced a sexual sensation totally new to her.

Charles was gentle, caring, and, above all, loving as he engaged Beauté in the pleasures of love.

Agnes could not lie still. Her hands caressed her lover's flowing hair. She grew so excited she gave a fierce pull to his hair. She tugged his head up to her lips, and they engaged in a kiss so passionate that both were left gasping.

Satisfied that he had given her preliminary pleasure, Chatz engaged himself with her gorgeous feet. Enraptured, he kissed each foot, sucking each toe, then licking the soles.

The king had been master of the engagement until then. But Agnes knew that if she were to be this man's mistress, she must begin to take charge herself

At her prompting, his head came even with hers for a full mouth-to-mouth kiss.

"Chatz," she said soothingly. "You have regaled me...royally. If you would give me more pleasure, do so by lying docile while I enjoy the mysteries of your body."

"As you wish, my *dame de beauté*. From the flavor of your honey cakes, and my reaction to them, I am aware that they were redolent of atmagupta. So it is unlikely that I will arrive at my *épiphanie* prematurely. I invite you to explore at will. France is at your mercy."

Encouraged by his assurance of staying power, Agnes began at his ears with the *lavage doux* that she had practiced scores of times on her swains. Her tongue traced a path from behind his ears to his neck region. He reached out to caress her breasts as she did so. Her tongue continued its pilgrimage southward, missing not an inch of the king's sensitive skin surface.

She breathed softly under his chin. She licked circles around his nipples. She rubbed her tits around his abdomen. She thrust her tongue into his bellybutton, then sucked on it gently.

The king's hardon was intense. But she mercilessly ran her tongue up and down the shaft to intensify the pleasure while not yet permitting orgasm.

Before taking the royal scepter into her mouth, she encircled his balls with her lips as she ran an oiled finger slowly, gently, up his ass and ever so lightly massaged his prostate.

As experienced as he was, this love-maneuver was new to the king. He knew that were it not for the atmagupta he had ingested, he would not be able to withhold his orgasm. With the drug, he was able to sustain an exquisite sense that imitated coming, but without ejaculation.

Agnes released his balls from her oral grasp and lifted his scrotum to look beneath the regal nuts.

As she had previously divined, on the Valois perineum was a scarlet birthmark. And that mark was in the form of a fleur-de-lys.

Before her eyes was confirmation of what she had intuited the meaning of Joan of Arc's secret revelation to the king to have been.

There was, *indeed,* a fleur-de-lys hidden beneath the crown jewels of France. That fact had been revealed to the Maid, Joan of Arc. She had revealed her knowledge of that hidden fact to the king as final proof that she was chosen by God and the Virgin to drive out the English.

The knowledge of that fleur-de-lys had been a secret hitherto known only to Charles' most intimate family.

After her confirmation of what she had previously intuited, Agnes continued her ministrations to the king's body.

He had bedded many a woman, but had never experienced such ecstasy. His body spasmed with delight.

When he recovered, he embraced her lovingly.

"Are you all right?" Agnes asked.

"Better than all right," Chatz replied. "I have died and been reborn a new man."

And although he had not yet come, it was true. So it was time to continue with the royal intimacies.

This time, the couple engaged in a basic act of love, fucking.

They came simultaneously, with deep sighs from both of them.

And with those sighs, Agnes yielded to her king that which she had preserved and reserved for this moment ordained by Destiny.

Her maidenhead yielded to the pressure of the prick Destiny had held in store for her. And the royal seed erupted through it into her awaiting womb.

Agnes was now positive she *would* rule a great nation. It would take time for her to achieve it. But the losing of her cherry was the first step on the road.

The simultaneous *épiphanies* had delighted them enormously.

The *nuit d'amour* continued on, hour after hour. The king was inexhaustible. As was his lover.

At one point during the night, Agnes whispered into Chatz's ear, "The fleur-de-lys lies hidden beneath the crown jewels of France."

The king realized at that moment that this was the second woman who had come into his life to save both France and himself. The night of love was an experience to remember. But the words of the Maid of Orleans uttered by the most beautiful woman in the world was more than an experience to remember. It was a signal to the king that Agnes' life was meant by Destiny to be entwined with his own.

The date of their coupling was February 14, 1434. Valentine's Day.

That day was held sacred by Agnes and Chatz for the rest of their lives.

Chapter Twelve

Following that night of love, Charles was totally besotted with Agnes Sorel. Previous to bedding Agnes, the king had been content to enjoy sex twice a day. He visited Queen Marie's bed daily as an affair of state except when she was in flux or pregnant. And in addition he had at least one carnal relationship with a favorite, a concubine, or an attractive woman of any class. Now, however, with the queen quite pregnant, Charles required a hearty fuck with Agnes a minimum of twice a day, and often three or four times.

It soon became apparent to the court that the king's new favorite was distracting him from the affairs of state. And chief among those concerned was the queen herself.

Charles VII decided to move the court to Poitiers. He came to the queen's chambers to discuss the move. Charles was fond of the time each evening when he and his beloved Marie sat and conversed.

As they were coming to the end of the discussion of the court's move to Poitou, Queen Marie said:

"My love. You know my fondness for Poitou, and Poitiers in particular. What wonderful memories I have of you, me, and my brothers Charles and René, playing there as children. Those were happy times, weren't they?"

"Some of my very happiest memories, Marie," Charles agreed.

"And my mother, how she loved all four of us," Marie reminisced. "It's been a year now since she died, Dear. And yet, I can't bring myself to believe we will never see her again."

"She lives on, and will live on, forever, in our memories, my love," Charles sympathized.

"How kind of you to take the court to Poitiers at just this time," Marie said. "I really want to be delivered of our next child there. One life has passed on from Poitiers, and another will be born there. I find comfort in that."

"As do I," Charles replied.

"It makes me so glad to see you happy again, Chatz," Marie told him. "The terrible years of rejection by your father, banishment from a large part of your kingdom, all your doubts and denials. They are behind. You are a new man, my sweet."

"It does show, doesn't it?" Chatz agreed.

"Yes, it does. And part of the new you, Chatz, is the woman from Picardy. I can tell."

"Does that hurt you, Love?"

"No, Chatz, it doesn't," the queen told him truthfully. "We have often before talked about your physical needs that I cannot really respond to. I have never begrudged you your liaisons with the women you attract and need. I have always understood your needs in that direction. And in the case of Demoiselle Sorel, I am particularly happy for you. I believe her case is different from the others. Previously, I have felt that you had merely carnal attractions. But this demoiselle seems to carry another dimension."

"She does, Marie. How good of you to perceive this and accept it with such grace."

"No," Marie informed him. "Not necessarily good of me at all. Your happiness has always been very dear to me. This woman means a lot to you, doesn't she?"

"I'm quite captivated by her. She's quite remarkable. She knew the Maid's revelation to me."

"About the crown jewels?" Marie asked, surprised. "Passing strange."

"Yes it is," the king agreed.

The royal couple sat, hand-in-hand, observing the lively flames in the fireplace.

"I believe it would be beneficial to the whole court, and to me in particular, if you were to make your relationship to this lady official," the queen opined.

"Official?" Charles said, somewhat startled.

"Yes, my dear. Official. With your previous women, there was always some element of stealth involved. Oh, you and I were always quite open about your carnal needs. And the courtiers were always aware of what they considered your escapades. But if you were to somehow openly sanction your relationship..."

"Hmm," the king pondered. "It would never have occurred to me. After all, there has never before been an official..."

"These are new times, Chatz. Royal affairs have been around as long as there has been..."

"Royalty," Chatz suggested.

"Yes," Marie replied. "As long as there has been royalty. The Bible is quite clear about concubines in Solomon's court. And there are King David's infatuations. God does not seem to have blushed at those situations."

"My dear!" Chatz laughed. "What a thing for my pious little Marie to say."

"Well," Marie insisted. "It's time, isn't it? We are quite aware of the extra-marital affairs of the other rulers of Europe. Court gossip is full of it. I say, let's squelch gossip about you, and acknowledge reality."

"But, my dear," Charles objected. "Other rulers are one thing. And what happened thousands of years ago in ancient Israel, well, that's...past history. But me? I'm a direct descendant of Saint Louis. What would people say?"

"More or less what they have been saying all your life," his queen affirmed. "Except that they would not have anything to gossip about. All hypocrisy would have to dissipate."

The royal couple sat observing the crackling fire quietly as they cogitated on the revolutionary idea.

"I believe you have something there, my dear," the king said at length. "We do exist in new times. Ours may be the first reign in European history to banish hypocrisy from an act as normal to sovereigns as breathing itself. But we don't have any title by which to call a lady who is official mistress to a king."

Charles VII pondered a bit.

"What would you think of 'Royal mistress' (Maîtresse royale)?" he asked.

"Your Agnes would not really be royal, of course," Marie answered. "I believe that would be confusing. And in my own mind, I had already dismissed reigning mistress (maîtresse regnante). That would elevate her too much."

"I agree," Charles replied. "I couldn't abide granting the title *regnante* to anyone but you, my dear."

Queen Marie suggested a different title: "'Declared mistress' (Maîtresse declarée)? Or perhaps 'Titled mistress'. (Maîtresse en titre). Doesn't that really say it all?"

"Yes, yes, my dear Marie. It does. I will, of course, discuss the concept with the lady. And if she is in agreement, we will announce the new title to the court and to the world."

"Not quite so fast, Chatz," Marie stopped him. "You are quite right that you should discuss the matter with Lady Agnes. She would have to agree to being publicly acknowledged as your mistress. But, following that, I believe you should wait before declaring the new status to the world."

"Oh?" the king wondered. "Why do you suggest the wait?"

"My pregnancy would be a hindrance at the present time. I do not believe the court would be sympathetic to the situation of an official mistress while the queen is carrying your heir. The concept will be shocking enough at first, when I am not pregnant. I think under the present situation, you should wait until I have delivered our child. Otherwise, many would be sure to take offense."

"You are right as always, Marie dearest," the king agreed. "It shall be as you say."

"You realize, Chatz, that there is a certain danger to the lady involved. There are court intrigues and jealousies that are bound to occur. I do hope you will appoint someone to guard her against any mischief."

"A good point, Marie," Charles said. "I believe my page Raimbaut would be just the person for such a post. If Agnes agrees to being named *maîtresse en titre*, she will have a guard to protect her from those who might want to do her harm."

The royal couple kissed chastely. They had just conceived an idea that changed European thought for centuries about the legitimacy of the sovereign's lover.

When Charles saw Agnes later that evening, they made love for several hours, as usual.

With the help of atmagupta, Chatz maintained a royal hardon for hours. And, in addition, had four or five orgasms during those sessions.

And he was able to give great pleasure to Agnes. With the many youths she had seduced, she actually never was sexually fulfilled.

The king was an unselfish lover who gained great pleasure from employing the erotic tactics he had learned from the hundreds of women he had fucked.

When they had both had their temporary fill of passion, they lay in each other's arms, the king's hand on the most beautiful breast in Europe.

"Will you regret leaving Toulouse for Poitiers?" Chatz asked.

Agnes' mind flashed rapidly on the knowledge that Pierre de Breze would be in Poitou. She attempted to erase that image from her mind.

"I look forward to the move, dear," Agnes told Chatz. "Toulouse will always occupy a very special place in my mind, of course. It was here that we fell in love and truly got to know one another. But I also know it is time to move on to a new level."

"Move on to a new level. Yes," the king agreed.

He then launched into the subject he wished to pursue.

"Agnes, my dear," he continued. "I detest how we have to meet surreptitiously."

"Surreptitiously, yes Chatz," Agnes agreed. "But yet our meetings are, I believe, known to everyone in court."

"Exactly," Charles replied. "The hypocrisy is what bothers me. I would like to acknowledge our relationship openly."

"How would that be possible?"

"If you do not object," the king told her. "I would like to declare to the court that you are my mistress, officially."

"I don't understand, Chatz. There is no such thing as an official mistress."

The king disclosed to her everything the queen and he had discussed. Agnes was thrilled. She had not really envisioned how she could be the king's lover and yet be truly in a position of power. The plan devised by the sovereign's own wife, the queen, was the solution to a problem that had concerned her for quite a while. Agnes was delighted, and showed her gratitude by engaging her lover in a new round of loving embraces that exceeded anything they had enjoyed previously that evening.

The beginning of the relationship between Agnes and Charles VII was simultaneous with the beginning of spring-like weather in Toulouse. That concurrence did not seem coincidental to the lovers. As Languedoc bloomed all around them, they felt that Nature herself was blessing their love.

And as the court headed north from Toulouse to Poitiers, the route burst into a garden of flowers and leafing trees and bushes. The cortege was over a mile in length, with the verger and advance guard at the head and the carts of baggage and rear guard at the back. Song broke out in different sections of the procession. The court musicians, traveling in an open wagon, played music much of the time. And since Spring was in the air, the songs tended to be mainly love songs.

Birdsong was abundant along the way as well. Villagers thronged the sides of the highway, hailing the king and court with huzzahs and often with song.

Charles VII rode his white destrier behind the royal guard. He wore a green gown and a blue velvet cape decorated with fleurs-de-lys. His horse was caparisoned in green. He waved at his subjects who were justly proud of their king who was victorious over the occupying Goddams.

Protocol would have placed the dauphin next to or just following his father. However, the prince had remained behind in Toulouse preparing to lead a regiment against a troublesome band of Goddams who were causing problems in Dieppe far to the north.

It was suggested by some that the real reason for the dauphin staying behind in Toulouse was that he was newly smitten by a pretty boy. Whatever the reason, few in the court really missed his dour presence.

Following the king were the lords of the land, richly garbed as well, and astride beautifully caparisoned palfreys.

The queen's golden coach followed the procession of the lords.

Directly behind the queen's carriage was that of the dauphine, which, in turn, was followed by that of Isabelle of Anjou. Most of the ladies-in-waiting and maids-of-honor rode palfreys. Only those who were physically unable to ride were in the secondary coaches.

Pages, clerks, doctors, and even clergymen followed along, some on horseback, others astride mules. Musicians, jugglers, and other entertainers were in a wagon pulled by mules. The heavy wagons and teamsters were, of course, followed by the rear guard.

The cortege moved by easy stages. Agnes rode with Duchess Isabelle's ladies. But whenever the procession stopped for the night at the larger castles, she was privately quartered where the king was able to join her surreptitiously for the night. Raimbaut was relieved of his position of page and made a member of the Royal Guard. And it was he who guarded the privacy of his liege lord and his lord's favorite.

Agnes was relieved that Raimbaut did not have to guard her against the possible machinations of the dauphin on this route. Whatever the prince was still doing down in Toulouse or on his way to Dieppe, he was not a current threat. Eventually, he would find out how intense his father's infatuation was with this beautiful young woman, who was closer in age to the dauphin than to the king. And when that happened, Raimbaut would have to be extremely alert. The dauphin was nearly certain to go into a rage, and attempt to do harm to the favorite. And when Agnes would become *maîtresse en titre* the dauphin was sure to become extremely vicious.

The route to Poitiers led the procession through Perigueux and the Limousin. The court remained for a full week in Limoges, where it was entertained sumptuously by Count Cyrille du Limousin with jousts, feasts, balls, and minstrelsy.

"The court here in the Limousin is nearly as gay as the one in Toulouse, is it not, Chatz?" Agnes commented as she relaxed in the king's arms their last night in Limoges.

"Whether here, or in Langedoc, or, indeed, at the meanest village in between, your presence makes any location sweet to me, my dear." the king answered.

"How gallant of you to say so, Chatz."

"No, Beauté. I'm not speaking chivalric blather. No *gai saber* involved in my utterance. The truth is that you have brought more happiness into my life since I have known you than I experienced in all the previous decades."

"And your happiness is my happiness as well," Agnes responded.

"I just wish I could demonstrate to you the depth of my love," the king continued.

"The jewelry you have showered on me seems demonstration enough."

"Jewelry! It is just...things. Isn't there something special, something non-tangible that I could do for you?"

Agnes knew what she had wanted to ask for weeks. But the circumstance hadn't been right until now. She hesitated as though thinking of an answer. Then she told Charles:

"Well, yes. There is something I would like, if you could arrange it."

"The chances are that I can do whatever it is you have in mind," the king chuckled.

"I have a cousin, Antoinette, who lives in Maignelay, in Picardy," Agnes told him. "She was my best friend, and she is very dear to me. And I miss her company..."

"You need say no more, my dear," was the immediate answer. "I will inform my sister-in-law Isabelle that she is in need of one additional maid-of-honor. Your playmate Antoinette will soon find herself in that position. And speaking of positions..."

The lovers settled into several positions that they found most agreeable.

The king returned to his own chambers and bed many hours later. His new mignon, Antoine de Chabannes had not waited up for the him, but was not asleep, either, when Charles returned. Charles curled up next to his mignon and dozed off. Chabannes was one of the very few members of the court who completely understood the relationship between Charles VII and Agnes Sorel.

Chapter Thirteen

As the royal cortege progressed from Limoges towards Poitiers, the countryside seemed awash with the pink and white blossoms of the cherry and almond trees. The pink and white motif of their surroundings created the illusion that the lovers were in a romantic wonderland.

The queen's condition was such that she had to travel the remainder of the journey in a special litter and in a sedan chair. Her advanced pregnancy had made travel in the gilded carriage extremely uncomfortable. The royal birth would take place in Poitiers. Queen Marie was anxious to arrive there, but progress was slow since her means of travel was now at a walking pace. In consideration of her sister-in-law's changed mode of transportation, Isabelle of Anjou rode in a sedan chair next to Queen Marie. Agnes and Dauphine Marguerite rode together in the carriage abandoned by the queen.

As the procession halted for preparation of the noontime meal near Bellac, a table was set up for the queen, the dauphine, the duchess, and Agnes, in the midst of a cherry orchard. Cherry petals covered the tablecloth, giving not only a delightful sight but a lovely scent. The four ladies were seated, sipping wine and conversing animatedly. Charles VII rode up to the table and dismounted.

"All this beauty in one place," the king observed. "May one refresh one's eyes here?"

"With the arrival of Your Majesty on the scene, glory is certainly added to beauty," Isabelle said.

"Beauty, Glory, Wine, Conversation, and Sunshine," the king enumerated. "It seems all we lack is music."

"We need not lack even that, if Your Majesty would enjoy a tune,"

Agnes said. "Manon over there has a lute. Manon, would you be so kind as to accompany me?"

Agnes and Manon conferred on the song they would render.

Manon strummed a few chords. Then Agnes began the song:

Ab la dochor del temps novel
Foillo li bose, e li aucel
Chanton chascus en lor lati
Segon lo vers del novel chan;
Adonc esta ben c'om s'aisi
D'acho don hom a plus talan.

La nostr'amor vai enaissi
Com la branca de l'albespi
Qu'esta sobre l'arbre tremblan
La nuoit, a la ploja ez al gel,
Tro l'endeman, que'l sols s'espan
Per las fueillas verz e'l ramel.

Qu'eu non ai soing d'estraig lati
Que'm parta de mon Bon Vezi,
Qu'eu sai de paraulas com van
Ab un breu sermon que s'espel,
Que tal se van d'amor gaban,
Nos n'avem la pessa e'l coutel.

"With the sweetness of the new season the woods leaf and the birds sing, each one according to its own voice. Now it is time for a man to approach what he most desires.

"Our love behaves like the hawthorn branch which trembles at night on its tree, in rain and frost, until the next day when the sun spreads its warmth through the leaves and branches.

"I care not about nasty talk that could separate me from my neighbor, because I know how gossip spreads. Those people who spout about love do so in vain. We are the ones with the bread of love and the knife to cut into it."

It certainly was not by blind chance that Agnes had chosen a song that reflected the season in which their love had bloomed and that dealt with the gossip that undoubtedly had started concerning their romance. No one understood the nuances of the song better than Charles.

"Agnes, my dear. You have interpreted that song in the most delightful way. And we are most grateful for it," said Isabelle of Anjou. "My Lord, would you like our Agnes to sing us another?"

"Thank you, dear lady, but I cannot remain longer," said the sovereign. "I must return to the head of the cortege. But it is with great reluctance that I do so."

The king waved, sent a look full of ardor towards Agnes, remounted, and withdrew.

Agnes felt the romantic warmth of the moment. To hold so much power over such a man! If he hadn't stayed to hear a second song, it was because he couldn't remain near her without betraying the truth of his love to the world. She observed this in his eyes, somber and sparkling at the same time. She felt the desire hidden behind his eyes, the trembling of his lips. Yes, within her hands she held the heart and body of the King of France. He was at her mercy. At the same time, she felt an immense intoxication.

And yet, there was a troubling thought as well. Just days away, they would be in Poitiers. Pierre de Breze would surely be there. And the romantic feelings that stirred within her for Breze conflicted with the warmth she felt for the king. For a moment, a shadow of worry passed over her. Then, joining in the conversation of her tablemates, she settled back into the present.

When the court finally arrived in Poitiers, the queen was exhausted. Yet, she remained in good health and was very happy to be in her beloved city. She kept to her own lavish quarters, surrounded by relatives, physicians, midwives, ladies-in-waiting, maids-of-honor, and caring servants.

The king took delight in introducing Agnes to this city. Lying in the enormous bed in her new chambers, Agnes was telling Charles about her previous visit to Poitiers.

"On our way to Toulouse from Picardy, my mother and I passed through Poitiers. But I scarcely had time to enjoy its beauties. And, of course, the weather was hardly as perfect then."

"So you like what you've seen?" the king asked with a smile.

"It is truly lovely." Agnes told him.

"I can't tell you how pleased I am that you like it, my Beauté. I lived here for a very long time, you know. Back when the only title I held that meant anything to the world was Count of Poitiers. The Goddams occupied most of our country, including Paris. So this was my capital, and my domain. It was not a happy time for me. But at least this city was mine. I loved it. And, indeed, I still do."

"It must have been a very trying time for you, Chatz," Agnes sympathized.

"It was nineteen years of great difficulty," Chatz admitted. "I was betrayed by my own father, repudiated by those who should have been my allies, pursued by our country's enemies, and discouraged most of the time."

"Yet, you overcame all that adversity, my dear. You kept France alive in your heart, established your court here, even founded a university. And you succeeded in winning the soil of France back to its people. Charles the Victorious."

"Yet," Charles declared, "here in your chambers, I know my greatest victory is the one over your heart."

"In that also, my dear Chatz, you are Charles the Victorious."

"Do I win a kiss from that most delectable of mouths?" the king asked.

"With deepest humility, pride, and pleasure, Agnes replied"

As he had done before, Charles sang to her in his true tenor voice. Since poetry and song were so dear to Agnes, he used his own love and appreciation for troubadour song as a gift to his love that seemed to please her as much as rubies and pearls.

The song he chose was composed, as was the song she had last sung to him, by Guilhem IX of Aquitaine.

> *Pus hom gensor no'n ot trobar*
> *Ni huelhs vezer ni boca dir,*
> *A mos ops la vuelh retinir*
> *Per lo cor dedins refrescar*
> *E per la carn renovellar,*
> *Que no puesca envellezir.*

"Since a man cannot find a more gracious lady, and eyes cannot see or the mouth tell, I wish to keep her for my very own, to refresh my heart and rejuvenate my flesh that it may not grow old."

"That is very naughty of you, you know, Chatz," Agnes said playfully. "Your attack on my fortress used a double flank strategy."

"How so, my dear?"

"You attack me with lovely verse, and are sure to follow up with those amatory skills that quite devastate me."

"Like...this?" the king suggested.

The next thing she knew, Agnes was covered with kisses. And bit by bit, nibble by nibble, the fortress was won and the treasure taken anew.

He felt he had achieved a sweet victory as his tongue entered his mistress' cunt.

After the mock battle of their love-making, the lovers lay in each others' arms in languorous desuetude.

"To think, my Beauté, that now, at the most gratifying period of my life, you are mine, and mine alone."

"Yes," Agnes agreed. "completely yours, my lord."

"My rivals for your affections must feel as helpless now as I did during my years of despair."

"Rivals, you silly dear?" Agnes answered, somewhat alarmed. "What rivals? You have none."

"Oh, but I do," the king answered. "And it pleases me that I have. There are many of my subjects who covet me your affections. And appropriately so."

"How you do talk, Chatz."

"You don't believe me? Let me choose one of my rivals at random. Let me see? Hmm. All right, for example...How about Pierre de Breze?"

Agnes' blood ran cold. What had the king divined? She willed herself not to blush or show any reaction. She was not sure whether any sign betrayed her feelings.

Coolly, she merely said, "De Breze? The seneschal? Surely, Chatz..."

"Exactly, the seneschal of Poitou. He gazes at you with such longing that it is quite clear he is madly in love with you."

Agnes started to protest, but Charles cut her off.

"Breze is a great warrior. And a very virile knight. If he did not respond to your beauty, I would have no use for him whatsoever. I need men who are real men, lusty, priapic, and lubricious. Men who are stirred to the bottom of their souls, or rather of their codpieces, by the astounding attractiveness of your breasts."

"My lord, I assure you..."

"You need assure me of nothing. My mignon, Chabannes, has noted how you size up the valiant de Breze when I am not looking. How you turn a lustful eye on his manly physique."

"I protest..."

"Hush, dear," the king said gently. "I told Chabannes quite clearly that I would disdain a lover who doesn't have an eye for masculine beauty. The woman I would love must have hearty carnal desires, like me.

"If you didn't occasionally fantasize welcoming his cock into your twat, you would be a cold lover indeed.

"For my part, I would not want anything to do with a lover who did not appreciate the attraction of a lusty handsome man.

"The truth is, Breze is attracted to you and you to him. But he is a true and chivalrous knight, and would never betray his liege lord. And you are as pure an example of womanhood, in your way, as the Maid of Orleans was in hers. As I trusted Joan of Arc, I trust you and Pierre de Breze."

Agnes felt quite uncomfortable. She wasn't at all that sure of Breze's virtue. Or of her own, for that matter.

"To take another example," Charles continued. Agnes was not eager to hear another example, but dared not interrupt.

"There is Etienne Chevalier."

"Chevalier?" Agnes responded, unable to choke down her amazement.

"Yes, that monkish little man who has been accompanying the seneschal recently. His appearance would belie passion of any kind. His bookish ways mark him out as an ascetic anchorite who would spurn so much as a glance at your well-turned ankle. Chabannes and I have had many a chuckle exchanging our glimpses at his lubricious ogling of your charms."

Agnes shuddered. Etienne Chevalier, indeed. That mousy appearing scholar.

"But it is Chevalier's covetousness that commends him to me," the king continued. "I can trust men who know they are men and display manly appetites. I only wish it were so with my heir." Charles looked despondent as he said this last.

"The dauphin, my lord?...Chatz."

"God has seen fit to endow my son with a preference for pretty boys over beautiful women. Louis is my legitimate son, and the divine heir to the throne of France. That cannot be disputed. It seems that he is impatient to wear my crown. My sources inform me regularly of his plans to depose me or to dispose of my unfortunate insistence on staying alive. Since I despised my own father, I suppose I cannot fault him for this.

"The marriage I arranged for him with the Scottish princess has not gone well. She clearly is barren. And her bed does not entice him anyway. If boys could become impregnated, perhaps I would not be as concerned as I am for the continuance of the House of Valois as the..."

Charles stopped his narrative abruptly, and looked at Agnes with surprise. He saw the tear in her eye.

"But, my dear. I must apologize. I have rattled on here about matters that are scarcely your concern. And I have caused you anguish. Let me wipe away that tear."

Agnes felt a deep tenderness for this man on whose shoulders lay the weight of France. His concerns about his son touched her deeply. She took him to her bosom and his concerns melted as his prick slid into the warmth of his lover's moist cunt.

It was two weeks later, as the warm weather presaged the advent of a particularly hot summer that Charles informed Agnes that he would soon be leaving for Switzerland.

"Is France going to war with Switzerland?" Agnes asked naively.

"No, my Beauté. This has to do with a bloodless war. At least, we hope it will be bloodless. The battle is between factions within the Church."

"Another schism?" Agnes asked, horrified.

"Yes, my dear. There have been over ten antipopes up to now. So this isn't exactly a new crisis for the Church. But the cardinals are split on which pope to recognize. So this time, the monarchs of Christianity must intervene. The crisis is as great as our war with the Goddams in many ways. After all, we kings derive our authority from God. If the Church were to crumble, chaos would break out everywhere."

"So you will be off to settle the matter of who is to be our pope?" Agnes asked.

"I fear so," the king replied. "The Council of Basel is in session. Eugene IV, the pope we have always supported, has been challenged by an antipope, Felix IV."

"How long will you be gone, Chatz? After all, there are still pockets of occupation here in France. Your people need you...I need you."

"You know how much I need you too, Beauté. Basel isn't that far from our borders, though. And I will write you every day."

"It may be difficult for you...physically, Chatz."

"Oh, I will have my *mignon* with me, Antoine de Chabannes. He will share my bed."

"This will be the first time since we met that you have needed a *mignon*."

"I will have you on my mind all the time, Beauté."

"I'll be anxious to get your letters, of course. But that doesn't answer my question. How long will you be gone?"

"Only God knows," Charles responded.

There was nothing more that could be said on the subject. Three days later, the king with a retinue of two hundred knights set out for Switzerland.

Chapter Fourteen

Soon after Charles VII had set out for Basel, Duke René announced that the Court of Anjou would be leaving Poitiers for Saumur. Queen Marie would remain on in Poitiers, awaiting the birth of the royal child. Duchess Isabelle wanted to remain behind in Poitiers with her sister-in-law for the birth, but reluctantly set out with her train of ladies and maids for Saumur. Agnes left with the duchess. As did Raimbaut, who would accompany her wherever she was. Nini was ecstatic that Raimbaut would be in the train. For she and Raimbaut were lovers, and it was possible, she thought, that she was carrying his child.

The procession to Saumur was accomplished in three days. The voyage through Poitou to Anjou was a sheer delight to Agnes. She wondered whether her pleasure stemmed from the burgeoning countryside or from the words that played over and over through her mind.

"I will come to you in Saumur."

Those were the words. Whispered words. Stealthily spoken in a shadowy corridor in Poitiers by the most handsome man she had ever encountered. Pierre de Breze.

Breze knew the king was her lover. Indeed, he had orchestrated the relationship. And he was aware that the king would be off to Basel for...who knew how long? The hushed tone. The furtiveness of the occasion. The love light in the seneschal's eyes. It seemed the fulfillment of a dream. Of a madcap dream. Of a dangerous dream. Decidedly of a forbidden dream.

Agnes was concerned that the other members of the Anjou court would read her constant smiles. She could not control her radiance. Pierre de Breze had sworn he would come to her. She saw his virile, manly figure in her mind, at every turn in the road. Sheer joy!

The other maids-of-honor complained incessantly about the muggy summer weather. To Agnes, it was heavily, erotically intoxicating.

From Thouars the caravan approached the Loire River. When the highway descended towards Saumur, Agnes was delighted. Like a jewel, Saumur Castle rested on an island perched in the lazily flowing river. It was the current ducal seat of Duke René. And was lovely beyond description.

The summer haze masked the wooden bridges that connected the island to each shore. The appearance, then, was of a fantasy castle floating above a shimmering cloud. The sun illuminated the fanciful towers. These towers were crowned by stone fleurs-de-lys. The roof was resplendent with a profusion of weathercocks. And the many chimneys rose to dizzying points.

And as the cortege approached the banks of the river, the drawbridges appeared out of the haze as if by magic. The south bridge was lowered so the procession could pass over it. The north bridge was raised so the brightly colored boats could float past, carrying passengers, baggage, and abundant produce as they proceeded up and down the glorious river.

The lawn on the south shore of the island was planted with a grove of pear trees. Geraniums lined the path to the castle door. In the middle of a hedged garden there was a bubbling fountain.

So this was Saumur! This was where the man who had conquered her heart would come to her. What an enchanting spot!

Agnes was given a private suite of rooms. She had a sitting room, a private bedroom, and two additional bedrooms, one for Nini and one for Raimbaut. She knew the couple needed only one bedroom, but did not comment on the fact. It seemed a waste to her to occupy such lavish space. The king was off in distant places. And when her lover-to-be, Pierre de Breze, would at last come to Saumur, she hardly dared entertain him in her quarters. She wondered how in the world they would manage to rendezvous privately.

Every few days, a courier arrived at Saumur with a packet for Duke René. After the packet was delivered, the courier repaired to the kitchen for hearty refreshments. Nini always found him in the kitchen, where he delivered sealed letters for her mistress.

In the evening, Agnes stretched out on her bed and read the king's letters. They were rife with poetical turns of phrase. They were intensely erotic, describing in detail what he would be doing with her were he at Saumur.

As Agnes read his billets-doux the images in her mind shifted from effigies of her lover-king to... Yes, it was no longer the king of France who filled her fantasies but the seneschal of Poitou.

Within a few weeks of arriving in Anjou, a courier brought a message to Duchess Isabelle that the queen was entering confinement. With just one of her ladies-in-waiting, Marie de Belleville, two swordsmen, and two archers, Isabelle headed for Poitiers to attend the birth.

Ten days later, she returned to Saumur, announcing to the court that the queen had given birth to a son, whom she had named Charles. There was a grand feast that evening in honor of the event.

It was the next day, as a group of the ladies was sitting on the river bank fashioning hats out of the flowers from the garden that Marie de Belleville could tell about her stay in Poitiers.

"The birth was not an easy one. Even after all the pregnancies the queen has endured, each birth is excruciatingly painful for her. She stifled her screams of agony by biting on a towel soaked in wine and poppy juice. It wrung my heart the whole time."

"Then you were in the birthing room?" Agnes asked.

"Yes. The duchess and I scarcely left her side. At length, after hours of writhing and gagged screaming, the child appeared. A miserable little red glob of a thing. A boy it was. The bishop appeared soon after the prince's appearance to baptize him."

"Baptize him? Right then?"

"Yes. The queen's children have all died very young. Except the dauphin, of course. The queen's children tend to be weak and scrawny, and to survive only days after birth. Of course, many are stillborn. And those who appear healthy at first often die in mysterious ways."

"Mysterious?" Agnes prompted.

"Many say, poisoned," Marie responded.

"But who...?"

Marie whispered into Agnes' ear the suspect for the poisoned princes and princesses.

Out loud, to the others, she declared, "I will not say his name. Only that he is currently reported to be in Dieppe."

Agnes whispered the ghastly news to one of her companions. The suspect's identity spread throughout the group only by whispers.

"And does the infant have adequate protection now?" one of the maids asked.

"General Poton has placed a watch over him," was all Marie could say.

Later, when Agnes was alone with Marie, she asked what the source of the rumors was.

"A servant confessed to poisoning several of the royal children. Under torture."

"Why did he poison them?" Agnes asked.

"He claimed the dauphin had paid him to do it."

"What happened to the servant?" Agnes asked.

"He was hanged."

No more was said on the subject. Agnes knew she needed a defense against the king's son. She trusted that Raimbaut was up to the task.

Soon after the royal birth, Agnes' cousin, Antoinette de Maignelay, arrived at Saumur. The cousins were delighted to be reunited. And they had so much to discuss.

Agnes confessed to Antoinette that she was the king's mistress.

"Really!" Antoinette gasped. "The prediction, Agnes. It has come true!"

"Well, not exactly," Agnes had to admit. "I do not yet rule a great country." She hesitated. Then she blurted out, "But I soon will. Now that the queen has born her child, Chatz...Charles VII...has said he will name me as royal mistress (*maîtresse en titre*). When he does, well, my Destiny seems to have revealed itself."

Antoinette was astounded, and delighted to know about her cousin's fortune. And to be so close to where such exciting things were happening.

"But tell me about yourself, Antoinette. Have you been doing...you know what..like the sorcière said you would?"

"I have had so many...romantic experiences, I've lost count," Antoinette admitted. "Fortunately, mandragora has prevented any unwanted outcomes. My activities have not yet yielded me a king..."

"Zèlde said you would comfort a monarch one day."

"I don't know about that," Antoinette laughed. "But I certainly have comforted many a swain. And, you know what? I love doing it."

Both girls laughed.

"So tell me, Agnes," Antoinette continued. "Did you really keep *it* intact?"

"My...maidenhead?" Agnes prompted.

Both the young ladies whooped with laughter. It seemed that word would always have a hilarious effect on them.

Agnes nodded her head in reply, invoking another round of laughter that had them clasping each other with tears running down their cheeks. They both knew that after her encounter with the king, "it" was no longer intact.

That evening the cousins shared the same bed – Agnes'.

Not since they were young ladies in Picardy had either of them kissed another female on the mouth.

Once settled, nude, into the large bed, they agreed to "practice" kissing as they did in their youth.

The kissing led to fondling. The fondling led to caressing. Caressing led to tit sucking, which, in turn, led to cunt licking.

The cousins had not previously gone so far in their intimacies.

"It's not like being with a man," Antoinette admitted.

"But it is a lot better than lying in bed alone and fluffing yourself off," Agnes said.

That set off an orgy of laughing and giggling. Which led to a renewed party of sexual exploration.

The cousins did not get to sleep until way past midnight.

It wasn't until the following evening, when the two friends were sipping wine in Agnes' sitting room, that Antoinette told Agnes of her most remarkable discovery.

"I had gone to Malo for a week to take the waters," she began. "Surprisingly, the weather up there was nice and warm, much as it has been here today. There was a great deal of gaiety, and I found myself, as usual, in the swirl. And in the course of the revels, I became involved with a beautiful olive-skinned sailor who had come from Constantinople."

"A heathen?" Agnes asked.

"No. He was a Christian. But a different kind of Christian."

"Not a heretic?" Agnes gasped.

"That's not even part of the story, silly. How should I know? His religious beliefs had nothing to do with anything."

"I'm sorry. So go on," Agnes apologized. "There was lots of partying, and you met this..."

"Michael. His name was Michael."

"Like in Michel?"

"Yes, Agnes. Like in Michel. Do you want to hear what I'm trying to tell you or not?"

"I'm sorry. It just all sounds so exotic and interesting."

"Well, the best part is coming," Antoinette continued. "If you'll ever let me get to it. So, I thought I had learned every possible way a man and a woman could...get engaged with each other. But after I had exhausted every trick in my repertoire with him, he told me there was still one more way I could learn to satisfy myself and my swain.

"He told me that the hetaerae in Constantinople..."

"What are hetaerae, for Heaven's sake?" Agnes asked.

"They're, like prostitutes. Only not common. Women with special skills that... Oh, Agnes. What difference does it make? Do you want to hear this or not?"

"All right. I get the idea," Agnes relented. "Your Michael said he had a new technique..."

"Not new, Dearie. Ancient. But one that he said we Westerners did not know about. So he taught me. He translated the name from Greek into French and called it *pompoir*. And it is the most amazing thing. Sensations like I never felt before. And for the male... It drives them crazy. I tell you Agnes, you try it out on your king and he'll never wander off to another woman."

"What is it?" Agnes asked.

"It's a thing you do with your koozie," Antoinette told her. "The best way to describe it is to have you get the feeling yourself. Are you ready?"

Agnes was ready to do whatever Antoinette said in order to get a feel for what this new/old technique was.

"Put a finger in your mouth," Antoinette directed.

"Which finger?" Agnes asked.

"I don't care," Antoinette giggled. "You choose a finger and put it in your mouth.

Agnes chose the index finger of her right hand and inserted it into her mouth.

"Now what?" she asked.

"Suck your finger," her cousin told her. "Really suck deep."

Agnes complied.

"Now, suppose that finger is Michael's cock."

Agnes took her finger out of her mouth.

"I don't know anything about your Michael's cock," she complained.

"That's good," Antoinette laughed. "Since your finger is a *lot* smaller than Michael's cock. But that's how he taught me. He taught me to suck my finger until I could tell how to pleasure it by tightening my lips around it and sucking sexily. Then I practiced on his cock to get the same clenching, sucking sensation."

"I'll bet he liked that, didn't he?" Agnes asked

The two burst into laughter.

"Now," Antoinette said when she stopped laughing. "Now stick your wet finger up your cunt. See if you can get the same sensation using your cunt lips and the muscles up in your love track as you did with your lips and mouth."

Agnes tried and couldn't get any real sensation.

"Now," Antoinette invited. "Slip that same finger up my twat."

Agnes did. And to her amazement, her cousin's cunt grabbed hold of her finger and squeezed it with its lip sphincters and sucked it up and down with her vaginal muscles as skillfully as if it was a deep, deep mouth.

"How do you do that?" Agnes asked.

"Any female can do it," she was told. "All you have to do is concentrate and practice and practice and practice. After Michael introduced me to pompoir I spent hours every day concentrating and practicing with my finger up my twat. In a week I could do it not only to my finger, but to his cock as well. And then I did it to every young stud I took to bed, no matter the size or shape of his thing."

In the absence of the king, and in anticipation of Pierre's arrival, Agnes practiced alone and with Antoinette. She practiced with her finger up her own twat and in her cousin's. Antoinette coached her by having her own finger up Agnes' cunt as well.

Agnes was determined to learn the technique and practiced assiduously every chance she got.

And within two weeks, she was an adept. She was a particularly adept, gifted, and a motivated learner. She could hardly wait for Breze to come to Saumur so she could pleasure him as she was sure no woman had ever pleasured him before.

It wasn't until the next day that Antoinette had her audience with the duchess. She delighted Isabelle. Antoinette frankly acknowledged that she was not a virgin, and was willing to return to Picardy if that were a requirement.

"My dear," the duchess informed her. "Virginity is a rigid requirement to be one of my maids-of-honor. And I cannot waive that requirement. However, my brother-in-law, the king, very much wants you here as a companion to his dear friend Agnes.

"So you can remain here as a guest. Virginity is not a requirement to be a guest at our court. If it were, I fear we would have very few visitors indeed. Therefore, here's what we will do. There is a guest room in the east wing of the castle. You may remain there as a personal guest of our noble sire."

Isabelle pondered a moment.

"No, no," she decided. "That would not seem proper at all. You will be *my* personal guest. No scandal involved there. And you may remain here as my guest for an extended period. But you won't have any official position. Do you understand?"

Antoinette had no need to be a maid-of-honor or lady-in-waiting, or anything else. As guest in this lively court, she could enjoy all the pleasures it had to offer. And could then return home, or travel, when she tired of Anjou.

"I accept Your Grace's invitation," Antoinette said. "I promise I won't be a boring guest. Or take advantage of Your Grace's kindness."

"I feel sure you will be the most delightful guest we have entertained in a long time," Isabelle said with a little pat to Antoinette's hand. Agnes would now have a good and faithful friend near-by.

Chapter Fifteen

Agnes, Antoinette, and a group of the maids and ladies were sitting in the solar working on their needlework and gossiping. Duchess Isabelle came swooping in, clearly ready to spread some news.

"Ladies, we are going to have a visitor next week."

"A visitor," said Madeleine. "Is it to be a visitor of the male variety or of the female variety, Your Grace?"

"It is Pierre de Breze, the seneschal of Poitou, who will be our guest," Isabelle replied.

"Oh, very definitely male," Madeleine exclaimed with a giggle. A number of other giggles burst out among the ladies.

"What are you laughing about?" Antoinette asked.

She had obviously never heard of Breze.

"It's only that he is the handsomest, the most virile, the bravest and the strongest knight in the world," Madeleine told her.

This elicited another round of giggles.

Agnes did not join in the laughter or the giggles. Her would-be lover was coming to see her. Just as he had said he would. She was thrilled and terror-stricken at the same time. Her body craved him so. Her caution warned her that a physical liaison with him could jeopardize her relationship with the king.

"What is planned to entertain the knight?" Margot asked.

"He will only be with us for two days," the duchess answered. "The first evening, Friday, we will have a grand feast. The second evening, Saturday, a ball."

"And how will the seneschal occupy himself during the daytime?"

Madeleine twittered.

"As always when he visits our court," Isabelle said stiffly. "He, Duke René, and the knights and noblemen in residence will go hunting."

Disappointment was shown by the groans and "Ohs" that followed that intelligence.

When Isabelle left the solar, none of the ladies continued with their needlework. They broke up into little chatter groups. Agnes, Antoinette, and Madeleine formed one such group.

"Tell me more about this luscious knight who's coming to Saumur," Antoinette asked. "Why all the twittering and giggling?"

"It is common knowledge," Madeleine said, "that the seneschal de Breze comes regularly to visit whenever and wherever the Duke of Anjou is holding court. But it is said that it is not the company of the duke he seeks."

"Meaning?" Agnes inquired. She wasn't sure she wanted to know the answer, but had to ask nonetheless.

"Meaning the duchess' bed is occupied by the most famous knight in Christendom when he is here. People whisper that he is a lover beyond compare. And that the duchess is one of the few women in France who can hold his devotion. Many, many have tried. But he is notoriously fickle."

Agnes didn't feel that she wanted to hear any more.

"Excuse me, Antoinette and Madeleine," she said. "I fear I indulged in too much of the garlic sauce at our noonday meal. I believe I'll go to my chambers and rest."

"Me, too," Antoinette said. "I have gas enough to give me the vapors. I believe I will retire as well."

As Agnes and Antoinette were wending their way back to the living quarters, Antoinette asked:

"What is it, Agnes? I could see that what Madeleine was saying was affecting you strongly Come on. Tell me all."

"It's nothing, 'Toinette. It's just the garlic."

"I smell something here," Antoinette said. "And what I smell is definitely not garlic."

Agnes felt uncomfortable. She was determined not to share her interest in Breze with anyone at all. Not even with her best friend and cousin.

When Breze came riding over the wooden bridge that led to Saumur Island, nearly all the ladies swarmed to the battlements to watch him arrive. He arrived rather early, about two hours after dawn.

Breze was a sight to behold as he rode his midnight black destrier over the drawbridge. He was attired in his purple velvet doublet and tights. His codpiece and cape were gold. He wore his knight's helmet with a gold feather attached on the very summit. Tall, muscular, knightly. The sighs of the ladies were audible down to the ground level where he proudly rode. Behind him rode a rather thin emaciated page, in remarkably drab garb.

René and Isabelle presided over the presentations. Breze greeted each of the ladies, making no more fuss over Agnes than any of the others. He joked with his fellow knights. His hearty laughter resounded off the walls. His page melted into the kitchen and thence to the servants' quarters.

Agnes was disappointed that he showed no sign of interest in her. But she realized it was essential that no one suspect there was anything between them. She did not remain long in the Great Hall, but retired to her chambers to ponder.

When she got there, Nini was waiting for her impatiently.

"Whatever are you so wrought up about, Nini?"

"This!" Nini exclaimed, holding a sealed letter out to Agnes.

"Where on earth did *this* come from?"

"The page who came with the knight, Demoiselle? He came to the kitchen. Raimbaut was at the kitchen door keeping watch over you. And I was keeping watch over Raimbaut."

"Yes. And...?"

"The page asked where Demoiselle Agnes' personal maid might be found. Raimbaut asked why he wanted to know. The page said he had a secret letter for her from the king. Raimbaut grabbed the letter from him and gave it to me. That is it, Demoiselle."

Agnes looked at the seal. It did, indeed, appear to be that of the king. She wondered why Breze would be acting as courier for the sovereign. But felt the explanation might be in the letter.

She took the missive to her bedroom and opened it with great interest. The writing was not that of Charles at all.

"What might this be?" she wondered.

"My most beautiful and esteemed Demoiselle Agnes" the letter read. "I am so enchanted thinking of your astounding beauty that I can scarcely hold this quill.

"I felt from the moment we met that there exists an attraction between

125

us that neither can deny. May I hope that we might meet in private?

"I will arrange to go out hunting with Duke René after the noontime meal. There will be a number of gentlemen in the hunting party, but I will manage to get separated from them. It is a trick I have often employed.

"I will head for the modest cottage of a shepherd on the north bank of the river.

"Find a pretext to go to the north shore by yourself. There is a dirt path leading off the highway to the right about one hundred fifty paces from the shore. Follow that path for a short while and you will come to a mud and wattle thatch-roofed cottage. The door will be unlocked. No one will be home. Go inside and await my arrival.

"If I don't find you there, my heart will be broken.

"DESTROY THIS LETTER COMPLETELY.

"With love in my heart,

"B"

Agnes believed this might just be the happiest moment in her life.

There was no fire in her fireplace, so she went to the kitchen and shoved the letter into the oven when no one was looking.

She was rummaging through the shelves when the head cook, Yves, noticed her.

"You were looking for something special, Demoiselle?"

"Yes, Yves." Agnes replied. "I was hoping there might be some fresh sweet marjoram on the shelves. I thought I might have some with my eggs at breakfast tomorrow."

"Dried leaves we have, Demoiselle. Right here."

Agnes had her answer ready:

"I recently spotted a marjoram plant in the forest on the north bank. I believe I could find it again. I will go looking for it myself later today. The fresh leaves are so much more fragrant than the dried. Wouldn't you agree?"

"Absolutely, Demoiselle," the cook agreed.

Agnes knew that word would spread from the notoriously gabby chef to enough people to explain her absence that afternoon. While in the kitchen, she boiled some mandragora with vinegar, and soaked a linen cloth with it. It would never do for the king's favorite to bear a child displaying the features of Pierre de Breze. She was prepared for an afternoon of love.

As she left Saumur Castle with an herb-gathering basket in hand, her heart beat so that she feared it could be heard far away in the donjon. She knew that Raimbaut and Nini were frolicking together in Nini's room, so she had no fear of her guardian following to protect her. She scarcely desired protection from Breze. She believed she needed protection from being discovered with him.

Once her foot traversed the bridge and landed on the sand of the north shore, her knees trembled so that she was afraid she might fall. But so far, no one had questioned her about her excursion.

She measured her steps as she followed the highway and found the narrow footpath Breze had described. The way up the path seemed interminable. But at length the shepherd's cottage was in full view in a small clearing.

First, she knocked timidly on the door. What if there were someone home? What would she say? What would she do?

There was no answer, and she entered. The room was a combination livingroom, kitchen, and bedroom. The bed in that room was clearly intended for a child.

She looked into the adjoining room. It contained a wooden bed with a straw mattress, a rough hewn chair, and a chamber pot. There was no window in the room which had a rather fetid odor. She was anxious to return to the main room again, which although not pleasant smelling, it did have a window that let in some air. Even so, it was stifling.

She cheered herself up thinking of the treat she would have to offer this lover. She would regale him with her newly developed skill of *pompoir*. This would be an experience Pierre would truly relish. He would certainly cherish her as the one woman he had ever met who could provide him with such exquisite sensations.

Her wait seemed to drag on forever. She wondered whether Breze had managed to get surreptitiously away from the hunting party. She even wondered if he wanted to. She considered that perhaps she was the brunt of a cruel joke. The longer she waited the more depressing the overly warm room became. And the more she wondered if she hadn't been very foolish to come there at all.

The surroundings were tawdry and comfortless. Sitting in such surroundings for an illicit lover made her feel uncomfortably degraded and wanton.

She wondered what kind of man would arrange to meet her in such vulgar surroundings. In what repute would he hold any female who would agree to meet him for dalliance in such a wretched hovel?

The realization swept over her that she would never again feel clean or wholesome if she were to engage in a liaison with any man under such conditions. She conjured up Pierre de Breze's image and observed not a desirable knight but a lecherous womanizer.

She envisioned herself in carnal embrace with such a knave, and saw herself as a trollop.

She needed fresh air. As she stood to exit the hovel, she rose to her full height. She was Agnes Sorel. She was destined to rule a great country. She had a royal lover who treated her with love and respect.

Agnes sallied out the door into the open air and started up the path that led to the Saumur road.

What if Breze should come riding down that path on his way to the pesthole where he had arranged to meet her? She did not want him to know she had even gone there, and made her way back to the main road off the path and through the wilderness.

Agnes had a serious discussion with herself as she marched back to the highway.

"Pierre de Breze only sees me as an easy lay. Or worse. He might see me only as a means to get next to the king.

"Well, *Messire le sénéchal*, from this moment on, I, not you, am in charge of what I decide and what I do. I will make the decisions that you will obey when I allow you access to the king's ear.

"I now know who I love. And I love him with all my heart. The King of France is my only lover. And I am his sole mistress. So help me God!"

On her slow trek back to the castle, she remembered to pick some marjoram leaves for her basket. But she returned with far more than a few herbs. She was suddenly the possessor of new wisdom and determination. Destiny was on her side, and the world had better beware.

Before she reached the river, she saw Raimbaut walking towards her.

"Demoiselle Agnes. I was concerned about you," Raimbaut called out. "They told me you had headed off into the forest in search of leaves. Are you all right?"

"Thank you for your concern, Raimbaut," Agnes responded. "I am fine. I found what I needed to find. Let us return to the castle."

Chapter Sixteen

The next morning, as Agnes was enjoying her eggs flavored with fresh sweet marjoram, Madeleine entered with a plate of bread and cheese. Madeleine sat next to Agnes, bursting with news to relate. But, before she could begin, Antoinette entered, too, with a shank of mutton and a tankard of white wine.

"Listen, ladies," Madeleine said while spreading cheese on her bread. "You'll be happy to know you have a friend with sharp ears."

Agnes was hardly in any mood to hear silly gossip. For from Madeleine's expression and enthusiasm, gossip it was sure to be. So she addressed her attention to her eggs and attempted to shut out the world.

But Antoinette was much inclined to hear whatever the latest was, and encouraged Madeleine to spill out the dirt.

"Last night," Madeleine went on. "I had difficulty getting to sleep. So I got up, put on my peignoir, and headed towards the kitchen to see if I could find any poppy seeds.

"And as I was passing the door of the duchess' chamber, the hallway was empty. Not a soul around. So, being a curious kind of girl, I put my ear to the door. And what do you suppose I heard?"

"Sounds of passion, I would wager," Antoinette fairly squealed.

"Yes, my dear. The virile seneschal was very actively entertaining Her Grace. Not only were her love-shrieks quite audible. His groans of ecstasy made a real duet with hers. It was most exciting.

"If any man had come along just then, I probably would have taken him on the spot."

"Madeleine," Antoinette admonished jokingly. "You wouldn't."

"I would too," the young lady responded.

"And just how can you be so sure it was the seneschal?" Antoinette probed.

"It is well-known he comes to the Court of Anjou precisely because he is one of the duchess' lovers.

"And rumor has it he purposely detached himself from the hunting party yesterday to have his way with some wench."

"Lucky wench," Antoinette sighed. "But from what I heard around here yesterday, he would have enough jism left over, even after a whole afternoon of fucking, to last nearly all night long with Her Grace."

"But, that's hardly the best part," Madeleine continued. "I managed to come down the hall from my room hours later. And guess what?"

"I'm sure I could guess," Antoinette laughed.

"I'm sure you could," Madeleine giggled. "The two of them were still fucking away like a couple of minivers. I could hardly contain myself."

Agnes was actually made ill hearing all this.

"What's the matter, Agnes? Aren't you feeling well? You look so pale," Antoinette observed.

"Oh, Antoinette. It's nothing," Agnes replied weakly. "Merely a case of the vapors. Like Madeleine, I didn't sleep well last night. Perhaps we both over-ate servings of the wild boar with bitter vetch. I'm just going to return to my room for a bit of a nap. I'm sure I'll be fine."

Agnes did return to her room and lay down in her bed. Visions of Breze fucking Duchess Isabelle for hours tortured her. Not that she had any more desire for him for herself. The very idea was anathema to her. But it was the disrespect to herself that hurt.

"I will never again be a tool for him," Agnes vowed. "He will be my tool to power. Never again, for any reason, will I place myself in jeopardy with Pierre. Or with any other man. I have but one love and one lover in my life. Chatz."

But even with this resolve, the hurt and humiliation lingered on.

The rest of the day, and part of the following morning, Agnes remained in her room, declaring she was overwhelmed with a case of the vapors. She thus assured that her path would not cross that of Pierre de Breze. If she suffered physically, it was only during the hours of the night when she was sure the seneschal was fucking the voluptuous duchess.

Master Poictevin, the court physician, was dispatched to Agnes' chambers to diagnose her delicate condition. He affirmed that she had all the symptoms of the female vapors, and sent up doses of purgatives and emetics that were known to clear up the problem.

Agnes managed to dispose of the obnoxious medicines, and declared herself cured the following morning. Her rapid recovery was hailed as affirmation of the skills of Master Poictevin.

Agnes made sure she was cured in time to ascend the parapets to observe Pierre de Breze riding across the wooden bridge, heading for Poitou. He left behind a happy and well-satisfied duchess and a much wiser matron-of-honor.

As the robust purple and gold clad figure faded towards the horizon, all the ladies watched him leave. And many of them sighed in wistful admiration of his virility.

Agnes sighed as well. But it was a sigh of relief that Pierre de Breze was riding out of her romantic life, forever.

A little over a week after Breze's departure from Saumur, Agnes received a letter from the sovereign.

"My dearest and well-beloved Beauté. I will be leaving Basel tomorrow morning. The Council of Basel has concluded satisfactorily. I can tell you about the resolution of the conflict when I am blessed to again hold your luxurious self in my arms.

"Unfortunately, I will not be able to come directly to Saumur. I have just been informed that my new-born son is in great jeopardy for his life. Duty and paternal concern dictate that I must proceed forthwith to Poitiers to be present at the side of the queen during this trying time.

"Believe me, my darling, I long for you. Nay, I ache for you as I write this. You know I will be with you as soon as I possibly can.

"C"

Charles pressed his destrier hard to attempt to get to Poitiers in time to be present during his new son's crisis.

"Marie, my dearest," he said when he arrived at the queen's bedside. "Tell me first, is all well with you?"

"It was not a difficult birth, Chatz," Marie lied. "I am physically in good enough shape. But it does give me enormous comfort to have you here holding my hand."

"And the child, my dear. What of little Charles?"

"Like so many of our…"

Marie's answer was lost in sobs. Charles kissed away a tear and patted her hand. His love and tenderness for his queen was not diminished by his love for his mistress.

Master Morat, the queen's physician, entered the room, saluted the sovereigns, and went directly to the crib by the window. Charles left Marie's side to address the physician.

"How goes my son?" the sovereign asked.

"I regret to have to inform Your Majesty that the infant appears to be losing his struggle."

"His struggle?"

"His lungs are unable to pull much air into the little body."

"What are you telling me, Master Morat?" Charles asked. "In plain words now. I want to know what the chances are of my son's survival."

The two men looked down at the poor red wizened creature that was gasping for breath between whimpers. Charles reached into the crib and lifted the child to his chest, patting its back gently.

"Your Majesty," the doctor replied. "The sad truth is that your son is slowly drowning. There is nothing in the world we can do to save him. It appears to be the will of God that his soul return to dwell among the angels."

The king held the gasping infant up in front of him, looking sadly at his pathetic little face. He carried the child over to the bed where Queen Marie was lying.

"Has he been baptized yet?" Charles asked.

"Yes, Chatz. Shortly after he was born," Marie assured him.

The queen's confessor was summoned and arrived within minutes to administer last rites to the child.

"*In nomine Patris, et Filii, et Spiritus Sancti, Amen.*"

By nightfall, there remained but one clear heir to the throne of France – the dauphin, who had just defeated the English at Dieppe.

Charles remained at Poitiers through the funeral of his son, and stayed yet another week with Marie grieving with her for their loss.

At length, Marie told him to go to Saumur.

"Chatz, I am fully resigned to accept the will of God. He has called another of our progeny to His Bosom. I grieve for all the children we have lost, but thank and praise Him that our son Louis is alive, well, and strong. Now it is time for you to go to the Court of Anjou."

"Yes, my dear," Charles agreed. "I really do have an obligation to the lady there."

"God go with you," said the queen.

Charles felt his heart swell with love for this woman who had been his companion from childhood. And who understood him so well.

The Court of Anjou was quivering with excitement. News had spread that the sovereign was approaching Saumur.

As all the ladies at court were hurrying to the ramparts to observe the royal approach, Duchess Isabelle nabbed Agnes by the elbow.

"Not so fast there, my dear. I prefer that you not go up to the parapet with the others."

"Why, Your Grace...Isabelle? What would you have me do?"

"We need not dissemble with each other, Agnes. I was the first to suggest to you what your relationship to the king might be. He has been away from you for weeks. Now, he approaches the one place he most wants to be."

"And that is...?" Agnes asked with a smile, knowing what the duchess' next words would be.

"And that is wherever you reside," Isabelle finished. "So, clearly, he doesn't want you high atop some wall. When he arrives, let us regale him with the sight of his love awaiting him at the castle gate itself."

She gave Agnes a playful shove towards the gate as she herself hastened away towards the steps leading to the barbican.

It was not as though Agnes had not anticipated this moment. She had attired herself in a sheer white robe with a bodice that revealed the outlines of her justly famous tits. Over her shoulders was a scarf of cloth of gold that set off her luscious cream-colored skin. She had purposely dressed to meet her king... her lover.

As the royal procession approached Saumur Castle, the verger led. At his sides were two swordsmen and two archers. Behind them were three trumpeters, their silver trumpets bedecked with black pennons displaying golden fleurs-de-lys.

The procession approached the drawbridge that was lowered over the Loire River. The trumpets blasted the royal tattoo.

Verger, swordsmen, archers, and trumpeters removed themselves to the sides of the road. In the center of the highway, mounted on his white destrier, attired in his suit of green, wearing a black felt hat festooned with a tall golden feather, was His Majesty, the King of France, Charles VII the Victorious. Behind him rode the Royal Council, the twelve men who were advisors to the king on all matters political, legal, military, and diplomatic. And trailing behind them could be seen a military guard of some thirty men attired in the royal livery.

When Charles spied Agnes awaiting him, standing on the other end of the bridge, his face shone like that of an adolescent boy gazing love-struck at his first sweetheart.

What happened next pleased and gladdened Agnes' heart beyond belief. The victorious king, who had feared crossing a wooden bridge on horseback, who always dismounted and crossed the span afoot, instead sat even straighter and more regally in his saddle, spurred his horse onward, and rode proudly, majestically, over the wooden planks.

At the entrance to the castle, he doffed his hat, bent down, encircled his paramour's waist, and lifted her to ride before him, clasped in his arms, through the castle gates.

This act of heroism, overcoming his fears in his love for his woman, won the last bit of reluctance from Agnes' heart. Charles was her true valiant knight. She knew no one else would ever be able to displace him as her only lover.

Before the banquet to be held in honor of the sovereign's arrival, the king called a council of state.

In the Great Hall, sitting at a table with his twelve councilors, and observed by the entire Court of Anjou that stood against the walls, Charles made his proclamation.

"My lords of the council. We have made a decision that will establish a new precedent for France. Nay, not only for our beloved France, but for all Europe.

"I, Charles VII, by the grace of God King of France, declare that I will honor the woman I love with an official title. I pronounce Agnes Sorel, formerly Demoiselle of Picardy, to be officially known and accepted hereafter as Royal Mistress (*Maîtresse en titre*).

"The official relationship that the king holds with Agnes Sorel, who henceforth shall be known as Dame Agnes, does not in any way diminish the deep and holy love I hold for Her Majesty, Queen Marie. She dwells in my esteem, as in that of all her subjects, as my legitimate and well beloved wife.

"But as God created men both spiritual and carnal beings, we must recognize that our spiritual and carnal needs exist in separate domains.

"Thus, with this Seal of France, I affix my affirmation to this document and declare Agnes Sorel Royal Mistress."

The councilors were nonplused. They had not anticipated this action at all. Indeed, they could not have foreseen it, since it was unprecedented.

The members of the Court of Anjou who were witness to the astounding proclamation were not as taken aback by the pronouncement as the councilors. The king's relationship with his favorite was more than gossip. It had become acknowledged fact in the Court of Anjou.

So, on June 12, 1434, Agnes Sorel, a member of the lesser nobility of Picardy, became the official mistress of the king of France.

A precedent was set that would exist for as long as France would remain a monarchy.

Chapter Seventeen

At the banquet given that evening by the Duke and Duchess of Anjou, Agnes Sorel, the king's mistress, sat at the right hand of the sovereign. In the absence of the queen, it was thus established that the royal distaff side was to be represented by Dame Agnes.

Amidst the general festivity and gaiety, the lovers discussed, oddly enough, not love, but politics.

"How sad," Agnes said, "that you had to cut short your mission in Basel because of the tragic event in Poitiers."

"The grave state of the new-born prince did make it necessary to come back to France, of course. But, as it turned out, it was time for me to leave Basel anyway."

"Because the discussions were going well or poorly?"

"The representatives of all the states in Roman Christendom were gathered there with the cardinals and the two men who claimed to be pope," Charles told her. "The arguments back and forth were all in Latin of course. That was a disadvantage for the delegate from the Duchy of Bohemia. But the rest of us were comfortable enough in the language of the Church.

"Just days before I received news of the birth of Prince Charles, I had a meeting with Lord Suffolk, the delegate from King Henry of England and with Philippe of Burgundy."

"Hardly a meeting of friends," Agnes remarked.

"Everyone was quite surprised," Charles answered. "Though France has been fighting England and Burgundy now for decades, we have come to a new understanding. Philippe is ready to abandon the English cause, and the English

137

are being driven out of France and acknowledge the fact. So the three of us met without rancor."

"Another sign that we live in new and better times, Chatz."

"So it is," the king acknowledged. "We agreed to give our full support to Pope Eugene, and urged him to close the debate about the papacy. We asked him to announce at the Council that he was transferring the venue from Basel to Farrara. He did so. The cardinals supporting his cause left Basel with him, leaving Felix behind with only a handful of cardinals and hardly any heads of state.

"With Suffolk, Philippe, and me working behind the scenes with the other rulers, we had managed to convince all but the margraves of three German states and the duke of Bohemia to accompany Eugene.

"It was at that point that I learned of the crisis in Poitiers. The dauphin had just won his victory in Dieppe, so I sent him to Ferrara to represent me."

"Then the Church is spared a schism?" Agnes asked.

"Yes. Louis sent word just two days ago that he is returning to France. Felix' last supporters abandoned his cause, and we are left with one single pope."

"Thanks be to God," Agnes said.

"Yes," Charles assented. "Thank God. And, I must add, thank God the rulers of the individual states in Christianity are beginning to emerge as more powerful than the papacy itself."

A new era had begun to dawn in Europe.

When Agnes returned to her room, she was surprised to discover that it was redolent of roses and wild thyme. The flowers were banked up along two walls and the herbs were scattered about the floor. The result was a scent that served as a mighty aphrodisiac.

Although Raimbaut remained her personal bodyguard, he also continued to serve as go-between for her and Charles. So Raimbaut knocked on her door and Nini answered the call. The time for the king's arrival at Agnes' chambers was discussed, and at the time agreed on.

Agnes thought about the differences between King Charles and Seneschal de Breze.

She considered that Breze was certainly a brave and worthy knight. But her royal lover, who had overcome a deep-seated fear of crossing a bridge while mounted on his horse, had come to her a victor over his own dark anxieties.

Charles the Victorious – In her eyes, he was the nobler knight.

Charles entered her room wearing a green velvet jacket, a pair of blue tights, and a radiant grin.

The difference now was that there was nothing whatsoever furtive about the procedure. As sovereign to royal mistress there was perfect openness about the king sleeping in his own chambers or in Agnes'. Agnes felt quite secure with the new arrangement, as did Charles.

Agnes received her lover-king attired in a diaphanous peignoir. The effect was more sexually stimulating than if she had been stark naked.

Her gorgeous boobs were veiled in a gossamer screen that gave a soft, sensuous vision of the round, gorgeous orbs crowned with delicious, appealing pink nipples.

The sight had an immediate effect on the royal scepter.

Chatz' eyes caught sight of the concave sweep of the female hips and his vision flowed naturally to the Venus mount embellished by the glimmer of the golden triangular bush pointing invitingly down to the most luscious cunt in all Europe.

The royal scepter had transformed from wooden to steel.

Agnes ambled over to her royal lover and with sensuous touch removed his garments one by one.

When he was facing his mistress bare-ass nude, Agnes removed a soft, lustrous silk morning robe that was draped over a near-by chair and slipped his arms through it.

Before closing over the front of the robe, she reached behind him, took gentle purchase on his ass with her left hand, cradled his balls with her right, and guided him forward while holding her lips up for a welcoming kiss.

As she stepped away from him to approach the bed, Chatz addressed her.

"Stop right there, Beauté," he called. "While I was in Basel, discussing the politics of the Holy See, my mind was continually envisioning your divine ass. Keep your back to me, that I may take full view of the loveliest rounded ass in all Christendom. And I include both the Roman and the Greek bishoprics."

Agnes held her pose, and then, slowly, seductively, removed the peignoir, revealing to her lover in full light what was, possibly, the most seductive ass on the entire planet.

She suggestively swayed her hips from side to side, causing her butt to suggest 'come hither, Love'.

When the king had satisfied his soul with an eyeful worthy of a monarch, he approached her, knelt down, and conferred kiss after kiss on those buttocks that had pleasured his imagination while he was engaging in holy discussions in Basel.

With arms about each other's waists, the king and his *maîtresse en titre* enjoyed a night devoted to the full enjoyments that hands, lips, tongues, prick, balls, ass, and cunt can be employed in by a couple truly in love.

After they had made love in its many forms, Agnes thanked Charles for managing to bring Antoinette to Saumur.

"Oh, Chatz. It was so wonderful of you to arrange for my cousin, who is my best friend in the world – except you, of course – to come visit me."

"It was no great feat on my part, my dear," he answered. "My good sister-in-law welcomed my request for her to host your lovely friend. I have made further arrangements for her to be with you in the future. But enough of that for now."

"I believe you will find reason to be happy you made provision for Antoinette to visit here," Agnes pressed on with a coy smile. "While she and I are very much alike, on one point we have been quite different."

"How so?"

"I kept my flower chaste for your plucking, my lord, as you know. I never allowed intimacies until you and I were united. However, Antoinette enjoyed sexual adventures and learned many ways to pleasure her swains."

"You seem to have come by that ability naturally, my dear," Chatz chided.

"You have taught me everything I know in that regard, Chatz. With, however, one exception," Agnes told him.

"And what might that exception be?" he asked.

"Antoinette told me of an act of love that I could not have even imagined."

"And what, pray tell, it that?" Charles asked with interest.

"It's a technique she learned from a Byzantine sailor."

"I have heard that Constantinople is noted for the erotic repertoire of its hetaerae," Chatz commented.

"That's what Antoinette told me," Agnes continued. "I've wanted to try out the technique with you. To see whether it would really pleasure you."

"When would you like to demonstrate this new art form, Beauté?" Chatz asked intrigued.

His mistress told him she was not only ready, but enthusiastic to try out the sexual exercise of pompoir right then.

Chatz responded with a lascivious smile.

With moist, velvet smooth lips, Agnes guided her lover's dong into a throbbing hardon.

Her koozie was warm, moist, and fragrant.

She wordlessly let him know that he was to mount her as she lay languidly on her back with her legs spread wide to invite loving penetration into her yawning cunt.

As the king's peckerhead made its entrance, Agnes' labial sphincters gently encircled the bulb. The effect caused Chatz to murmur with delight.

After a pause to savor the experience, he slowly and lovingly slipped his cock farther into the hole. But as he did so, Agnes' vaginal muscles gave a massage to the stiff pole.

When he was fully inside her, those moist cunt muscles pulled his dick up and down, slowly, relentlessly, as though grasped by a gentle jack-offing fist. While at the same time, there was a sensation as though her womb was sucking, sucking, sucking the cum right up out of his balls.

She had practiced the strategy diligently while the king was off in Basal, with her own finger and then with Antoinette's. But she found there was no pleasure like doing pompoir with the hard prick of her lover responding with erotic excitement.

When the king came, his orgasm was reciprocated by the most exuberant come she had ever experienced.

During the process, Charles VII murmured in ecstasy in a manner such as Agnes had never heard before. But his murmur was echoed, and even exceeded, by her own cries of joy.

Each testified afterward that it was the most excruciatingly satisfying experience they had ever known.

It was during the early morning hours, when neither was able to sustain any more erotic play, that Agnes had Nini bring in a light repast of fruit, cheese, and wine.

As king and mistress were enjoying the repast, Charles told Agnes the news he had been saving for her.

"I would like you to return with me to Poitiers next Monday."

"But what of my status with Duchess Isabelle?" Agnes inquired.

"Don't you realize you have a new status?" Chatz asked. "I have discussed the situation with Queen Marie. She is quite amenable to it. You will become one of her ladies-in-waiting. The position in the royal court has no requirement of virginity. It not only puts you in the royal household. It will demonstrate that the queen holds no resentment about our relationship."

"I am thrilled, of course, Chatz. But the situation will feel so strange."

"The times are strange," the king declared. "So is it any surprise that we should feel strange in them?"

Agnes expressed her appreciation with a kiss.

"And as a further surprise," Charles said when he recovered from the embrace. "I will see to it that your friend, your cousin Antoinette, shall join the queen's menage as well."

Agnes was pleased. But deep inside she felt misgivings. Suppose the king's attention should turn to his mistress' best friend?

The procession from Saumur to Poitiers lasted three days. At mid-day, the summer heat was fatiguing, and the cortege halted its progress in consideration of the ladies.

As the royal procession wended its way down the highway, Agnes rode on a white palfrey next to the king. Riding along with the other nobles, Duke René was mounted on a dappled gray gelding. He was resplendent in a gold and silver suit. The massive perspiration that perpetually dripped over his expensive clothing revealed the physical price he was paying for his show of splendor. Following the procession of the nobles, Antoinette rode in a carriage. Duchess Isabelle remained in Saumur.

As they passed through the villages and towns of Loudun, Mirebeau, and Neuville, the sides of the highways were lined with Charles' subjects. The people of Anjou and Poitou were there to cheer their victorious king. But also, word had spread that the king's mistress, now his official mistress, was accompanying him. That curiosity alone was enough to excite the villagers. But, additionally, it was said that the mistress was a lady of exquisite beauty. It seemed that everyone wanted to get a glimpse of her.

When the royal procession reached the gates of Poitiers, the crowds were enormous. Shouts of "Vive le Roi," "Vive la France," and even though it was now mid-summer, "Noël," greeted the king and his mistress all along the way to the castle.

When they had arrived at the castle, and entered the Great Hall, Charles and Agnes were well greeted by everyone.

Everyone, that is, except the Dauphin. The crown prince of France observed his father and his father's mistress with a murderous look in his eye.

Chapter Eighteen

The court did not remain much longer in Poitiers. The memory of the death and burial of the infant prince hung heavily over the court there. Besides, Charles VII's tactic of an ever moving court was popular with his people. He was accessible to a much larger constituency than would have been possible had there been a fixed, immovable capital. And he was able to see, firsthand, the manner in which the various provinces were being governed in his name.

So when Charles announced that the court would move on to Tours, or, more specifically, to Ambroise Castle, it was no surprise to anyone.

It was on that peregrination to Tours that Nini tearfully informed Agnes that she had just discovered that she was not pregnant with Raimbaut's child after all.

Raimbaut himself happened to be riding near Agnes and Nini at the time. Agnes saw that he was aware of the conversation and scanned his face for evidence of how he felt about the situation. His smile was clearly one of relief. It was quite evident that the young man did not have marriage, paternity, or, indeed, any amatory commitment in mind. She rightly read in this that his sole commitment was to his king, to be a buffer and protection for the royal mistress.

When the court retinue reached the city of Tours, Charles chose to remain in the town for several days to receive petitions from the inhabitants. Agnes attended mass at the cathedral every morning.

One day, after mass, she visited a shop across the parvis from the cathedral. The shop sold religious items. A statue of Mary Magdalene, the Madeleine, caught Agnes' eye. This was a saint, she felt, who would understand her own situation. A saint she could pray to to intercede on her behalf. A saint who understood carnality.

She purchased the statue, along with an alabaster vase and a prie-dieu, and had them delivered to her chambers in Tours. She vowed to pray to the Madeleine every morning before breaking fast.

And she further vowed to present fresh-cut roses for the vase in front of the saint, whenever they were available.

She felt great comfort in this decision.

Three days later, the court moved on to Ambroise.

Ambroise Castle had a magnificent sweeping view of that loveliest of rivers of France, the Loire. Agnes had grown very fond of the beautiful river when she was staying in Saumur. Looking down on the Loire from the embankment and the parapets of Ambroise reminded her constantly of her single-minded devotion to her lover, her king, her hero.

The court had not settled into Ambroise more than a week when it was visited by Pierre de Breze, Jacques Coeur, and Etienne Chevalier. Since Isabelle d'Anjou was still back in Saumur, Agnes knew Breze had not come to entertain the duchess with his singular charms. When he arrived, Agnes had no inclination to observe his approach. There were quite enough twittering females at court to take care of the stir the dashing knight caused everywhere he went.

At his welcoming dinner, Queen Marie sat at the king's right and Breze at his left. Whenever the queen was present at court, Agnes sat among the ladies-in-waiting, and never in a conspicuous position there. So there appeared no reason to have to encounter Breze.

However, after dinner, the courtiers gathered in the Great Hall to play cards and dice. Playing-cards had been brought to France from the Near-Orient by the crusaders, and had become quite a popular pastime at court during the reign of Charles VII. The two card games played at Ambroise were triomphe and ombre.

Dice games had been popular in France from the time of the Roman conquest of Gaul.

The ladies at court never played at dice. Most of the men preferred dice, although there were a number of gentlemen who did prefer cards. Particularly the game of ombre.

Agnes took a seat at a triomphe table with three other ladies-in-waiting.

There remained an empty chair next to her. Breze approached the table.

"My complements, Mesdames," the seneschal smiled. "Would it be an imposition were a gentleman to join your game?"

"It would be an honor, *Messire le sénéchal,*" answered Dame Suzanne, with a greater show of enthusiasm than Agnes thought necessary.

From the ensuing game, Agnes surmised that Breze was not particularly skilled in card playing. That would be understandable enough. Any evening that there was not a special entertainment, like a musicale or a ball, the ladies-in-waiting played cards while the men tended to play dice. Agnes noticed that Breze's companions, Coeur and Chevalier, were at the dice tables. Breze was undoubtedly a dice, not a card, player.

Queen Marie had retired for the night. The king and his brother-in-law Charles d'Anjou wandered from table to table to greet the players, joke, and compliment the ladies. Guilhem Raimbaut was the only person in the room who was not walking about or engaged in play. He quietly, and rather unobtrusively, was sitting comfortably near the door, observing the proceedings.

After a couple of hours, the various tables of cards were finishing their play. Agnes' table was one of the last to complete. The dice tables were still going strong, and, influenced by the wine consumed during the throwing of the dice, the game had become rather loud and boisterous.

When the scores were settled at Agnes' table, Dames Suzanne and Marie-France arose and bid good evening to Breze. He of course rose with them to bow and make a flattering remark. Agnes got up just after them when Breze whispered, "Wait, Agnes. A moment, please."

Startled, she paused and looked at him in surprise.

"I have to see you," he whispered.

Aloud, in a normal voice, Agnes answered him.

"*Messire le sénéchal.* I would be delighted to have an audience with you. I will contact you further."

It was time for Breze to show surprise. He made a very formal bow and extended his hand as if to grace hers with a courtly kiss.

Agnes pretended not to see the gesture, called out to her other two table companions to wait for her, and joined them on the way back to their quarters.

At noon the next day, Raimbaut knocked at the door of Pierre de Breze's chambers. Breze's scrawny page answered the door.

"I bear a message for Messire de Breze," Raimbaut stated.

The page said not a word, grabbed the note Raimbaut had in his hand, and closed the door.

The page brought the letter to his master, Breze.

Breze read it.

"*Messire le sénéchal.* I will be in the Great Hall this morning following Nones[1]. I will be happy to attend your visit there. A."

"Who brought this letter?" Breze asked crossly.

"A young man attired in the livery of the Royal Guard."

"Bring him to me so I may return an answer!" Breze commanded.

The page rushed to the door, opened it, and found no one there. He hurried back to his master.

"The person is not there, Master."

"Not there!? What do you mean 'not there'?! Breze shouted."

"He appears to have left, Messire."

"Fool!" Breze bellowed and struck the wretch full force across the face, knocking him down.

"How stupid of you. Didn't you tell him to wait for my answer?"

With that he delivered a kick to the page's ribs, and stamped into the adjoining room. Breze did not wait for or expect an answer from his page.

Agnes went to the chapel at nones, and following the brief service proceeded to the Great Hall. When she arrived, three men were standing there waiting for her.

She acknowledged them, sat down, and they then took seats on the other side of the table. The three men clearly were aware of the appearance of a member of the Royal Guard at the door.

"Dame Agnes," Breze began. "We thank you for meeting with us."

"When you indicated you desired an audience, Messire, I was only too happy to oblige," Agnes answered in a neutral tone.

"May I present two distinguished gentlemen: Messire Jacques Coeur and Messire Etienne Chevalier?" Breze asked.

The two stood and bowed.

"It is an honor, gentlemen," Agnes said politely. "Messire Coeur's well deserved fame and fortune are legendary. And I have previously met Master Chevalier at court when he has come at the request of His Majesty. His learning is the envy of the universities."

---

1 The liturgical service nine hours after sunrise.

The two men made courteous replies and sat again. They appeared at ease. Breze, on the other hand, was clearly uncomfortable.

"I would have sent an answer back to you with your man, Madame. But he did not wait for me to do so," Breze told her.

"Raimbaut is an honored member of the Royal Guard, Messire. He is not a servant who is accustomed to be kept waiting in corridors," Agnes answered.

"I noticed that your letter to me was not sealed," Breze went on. "The carrier could have read your private correspondence."

"I have no secrets to disguise, Messire," Agnes responded coldly. "Do you?"

Breze was irritated at himself. He was starting this matter out all wrong. He was accustomed to being in control of all situations. This Agnes woman seemed to have usurped leadership of the conversation. He changed course abruptly.

"Of course, Dame Agnes. Your openness does you credit," he said, flashing that famous smile that had melted so many hearts.

Agnes nodded her head agreeably and stared at him wide-eyed waiting for him to get to the point.

"I felt you would like to have the chance to converse with my two friends," Breze continued. "In ordinary circumstances, court procedures being so formal, it would be difficult for the four of us to hold a serious conversation. So I presumed to bring them to Ambroise so you could converse with two of His Majesty's most worthy subjects in this informal manner."

Agnes realized that this meeting was very important to her plans. Although she now disliked Breze personally, he and his two friends were essential to her aim of influencing the king politically.

Her conversation with the three men lasted two hours. At the end of the audience, she knew everything she then needed to know about each of them. Without ever saying so overtly, a pact was formed among the four people.

Agnes, as the person who had the king's ear, would suggest that Breze, Coeur, and Chevalier become members of the Royal Council. There had never before been commoners on the Council. Coeur and Chevalier would be the first. And Breze was of the petty nobility, a rank too low to have been considered for the honor. But, though never stated, Agnes made it clear that if she managed to convince the king to take the revolutionary step of admitting such as these three men to the seat of power in the monarchy, she would be the one to call the shots.

The three men, without saying so directly, agreed with her.

Raimbaut, who was at the door the entire time, was out of earshot of the discussion that led, finally, to the awakening of Europe to a new era.

Agnes was cautious about discussing state matters with the king. She knew none of his previous lovers or favorites would have presumed to do so. She doubted that even Queen Marie ventured much into affairs of state, other than matters that touched upon the dauphin or other specifically family oriented concerns.

Bit by bit, she asked Charles about members of his Council. But always as though she was merely a curious woman seeking crumbs of gossip. Charles was pleased to tell her countless details about the people who sat in positions of power. He had never before had anyone with whom he felt comfortable revealing his innermost thoughts about such matters. In time, Agnes knew more about the inner workings of the court of France than anyone beside the king himself.

But Agnes knew she should not rush her suggestion to admit Breze, Coeur, and Chevalier to the Royal Council. She would move her plan along slowly, one sure step at a time. To begin to attempt to suggest matters of policy to the king prematurely would certainly be ill-advised. Her power-hungry friends would just have to wait until she, herself, decided the time was ripe.

Chapter Nineteen

In April of 1436, Agnes discovered that she was pregnant. She and Charles were delighted. A child would unite them in love in a way that declared to the world their love for each other.

So, in October, Agnes' confinement was occasion for joy, not only both for her and Charles, but also for most members of the court. The only person who was openly hostile to the impending birth was the dauphin.

The summer that year had lingered on well into October. But despite the unseasonable heat, the enormous fireplace in Agnes' bedroom at Ambroise Castle was blazing. Suspended in that fire was a copper kettle full of boiling water. In front of the fire was an exotic oriental cradle constructed completely of beeswax impregnated with sandalwood. A gift from Jacques Coeur.

Agnes' mother, Catherine, had come to Ambroise for the birth. And she brought Hortense Lauvain, the midwife, with her. Hortense had assisted in all of Catherine's births, including that of Agnes herself.

Agnes began feeling labor pains two hours after dawn. Nini was sleeping in Agnes' room at the time. When she awoke, she flew about calling Catherine, Hortense, and Antoinette to gather at the bedroom at once.

As soon as she arrived, Hortense took charge of the situation.

"You, Nini. Is that copper kettle filled with water? Make sure it's boiling. We're going to need cold water, too. Where is it? Oh, good. Now you stand over there watching the water. And while you're at it, fold those linens."

"There, there, Agnes, dear. Are you comfortable?"

"I guess so," Agnes answered. "I'm feeling contractions."

"Here, I'll massage your legs. That'll help. My, my, my. I brought you into this world. And your brothers as well. I've assisted at enough births to fill a good-sized town, I have. And of all those souls who saw light as I eased them into this world, you were the most beautiful.

"So many infants come squirming into this world looking no more handsome than wizened rats. Not you, my dear. Beautiful from the moment you were born. And still a beauty, eh? My, my.

"There. Does that feel better? Good. Dame Catherine, are the statues of Saint Britte and Saint Maure up on the mantle facing this precious lamb here? The saints assure a healthy delivery. That is, of course, unless God decides to call the new-born souls back to His Bosom up in Heaven. Tsk, tsk. Glory be to God and all His saints, eh?

"Antoinette, you see the birthing stool over there? When I say the word, bring it over here near the bed. Would you believe it's the very stool our little Agnes here was born on? In the last twenty something years it's assisted hundreds, yes hundreds of births. Praise God.

"Here, Dame Catherine. You take over massaging our little angel's legs. Are you comfortable, dearie? The contractions are far apart. It will be a long while yet before they come close enough together to get you out of bed and onto the stool. We want to keep this room nice and warm. Here, Antoinette. You massage Agnes's right leg while her mother massages the left. Now where are those herbs we want to toss into the boiling pots?..."

For the next eight hours, Hortense Louvain kept up a constant stream of commands, observations, exhortations, reminiscences, and grumbles.

Mid-morning, the king came to the door of Agnes' chambers. He was met by Midwife Hortense.

"I came to see how Agnes is doing."

"She's doing fine, Your Majesty," Hortense replied. "Now go away! No men allowed!"

Charles VII had never been told to "Go away" since well before his coronation at Rheims. He was taken aback.

"I have been present," he said, "At many of the births of the queen. Mightn't I just come in and greet Agnes?"

Hortense told him, "I have been present, Majesty, at more births than you can count. And no male has ever been present during labor at any of them. It would be most unlucky for you to enter. Go away!"

Charles was amused at the absolute sureness of this rural midwife.

152

"I just wish I had more advisors as sure of what they say as you, Madame. Please let me know when the baby is born. I will post a messenger outside the door. Inform him so I will know if all goes well."

"You do that, Sire. And rest assured. With me in charge, all *will* go well," Hortense assured the king.

When Agnes' time was at hand, the birthing stool was brought close to the bed. Hortense directed Agnes how to breathe, when to press, and when to relax her muscles. The room filled with the odor of sweat, blood, and boiling herbs.

"It is a girl, Agnes," Hortense exulted. "A beautiful, beautiful girl. The image of you when you were born. Ah, what a beauty!"

Hortense cut the cord.

"You, Dame Catherine," Hortense continued. "Here, take the child and bathe it in the warm Bordeaux wine. Antoinette, bring the swaddling clothes. Nini, quick with the linens. Clean up this mess. Someone come here and help me get Agnes back into her bed. Hurry now! Where are the warm damp cloths to bathe the new mother, eh? Here, while I massage her belly, Dame Catherine, spoon some poppy wine into the little mother's mouth. You, Nini! Tell that person outside the door he can notify the king that it is a healthy little girl and he can come see the mother and child in a half hour."

Hortense then got the child, who was now bathed and swaddled, and placed her at Agnes' breast.

"Her name is Marie," Agnes smiled, looking into the face of her first-born.

She looked at her mother.

"Charles and I agreed that if the child was a girl, we would name her Marie."

Two weeks later, Catherine Sorel took the baby, the midwife, and a wet nurse with her back north. She left Marie with her own parents and a wet nurse in Maignelay. It had been agreed that the child would be raised there until further arrangements should be made.

In November, the cold weather found its way into France. And through the crisp, but not yet snowy fields, roads, villages, and towns, the court moved towards Nancy in the province of Lorraine. En route, the traveling court stopped for three days at a retreat the king's grandfather, Charles V, had build beside the Marne River on the edge of the Bois de Vincennes. He had named it Beauté-sur-Marne. It was an extensive estate with its own woods, gardens, and fountains. Even in the winter with the exfoliated trees and the gloomy skies, it lived up to its name.

"But Charles," Agnes exclaimed. "This is one of the loveliest spots I've seen. It is clear that you get your sense of good taste from your grandfather."

"I purposely led the cavalcade in this direction so we would be able to spend a few days here," Charles answered. "I had a very special reason for doing so."

"So we could soak in the beauty of the spot in the midst of the difficult traveling," Agnes surmised.

"In part, Beauté. But more for another reason as well. I have always been fond of the estate. And it has very consistent revenues that I enjoy as well. Most of all, the name of the estate reminds of…what?"

"What?"

"Or I should say 'whom'".

Charles let the conversation stop there.

On the last day of the stop at Beauté-sur-Marne, Charles asked:

"Do you really fancy this estate, Beauté?"

"I am ravished by it," Agnes enthused.

"I am so happy," Chatz told her. "For I have had my notary draw up the documents. As of today, you are the owner."

"Chatz!" Agnes shrieked with joy. "You wouldn't! You shouldn't! You didn't!"

"I would. I should. I did," the king declared. "It is yours. With all the revenues attached. This gift is in partial thanks for the great gifts you have given me."

Agnes looked puzzled. What gifts?

Charles answered her look.

"Yourself, Beauté. That would be gift enough. And my own new self that owes its existence to you. And, of course, our daughter Marie. This estate is so little compared to those presents."

Charles had lavished many gifts on Agnes. Silver, furs, jewelry, clothing. But the gift of Beauté-sur-Marne made her independently wealthy. Although not titled, Agnes was now a lady.

A few days later, when they all arrived in Nancy, Agnes loved the city at first sight. The ducal palace belonged to Duchess Isabelle's family, since she was, in her own right, not only Duchess of Anjou by marriage, but Duchess of Lorraine by birth. But, of course, as long as the king was in residence, the palace was the Royal Court of France.

The day the royal cavalcade arrived at Nancy Palace, the snows made their appearance. Snowfall on the elegant city was enchanting. The Christmas Court would be held there. Agnes could not think of a better place for the great event.

Agnes had regained her alluring shape. It seemed that maternity had left her lovelier than ever. Her complexion, always textured sublimely, now seemed to have an additional luster. Her breasts and hips were somehow more voluptuous. She was truly stunning.

Viscount Castellain, ambassador from the court of Burgundy to the king of France, sent a critical letter to his liege, Duke Philippe;

"Your Grace. I write to you from the Ducal Palace of Lorraine, where your cousin Charles is holding his Christmas Court. The French court becomes more sumptuous every year. It seems to have pretensions to rival our magnificent Burgundian see. And there might be those so vulgar s to believe these creatures of France compare with those who inhabit the lands along the Rhone.

"But Your Grace. How wrong they would be. For the style here is vulgar beyond imagination.

"Feminine style is set not by the queen, but...can you imagine?...by the king's mistress. The dissoluteness in the matter of her costume would be shocking enough. But it is aped by the other young ladies. The dresses are low-cut in the bodice and lightly veiled. One can see not only the breasts, but the nipples as well.

"The lady herself, a so-called *maîtresse en titre*, shows off her enticing form, and particularly her gorgeous breasts, to perfection.

"Disgusting! Thank Heavens there is still good taste displayed in Your Grace's realm.

"Castellain."

The Christmas Court of 1436 was the gayest in memory. Isabelle and René provided balls, banquets, minstrelsy, and a continuous round of gambling games.

On Christmas morning, Agnes was awake before Chatz.

The large fireplace had somewhat over-warmed the bedroom. As a result, the king had thrown off the blankets on his side of the bed.

On the previous night, Christmas Eve, after the banquet and the court ball, the couple had repaired to their room and had frolicked about on the bed naked. Neither had put on nightclothes before falling asleep.

As Agnes awoke, she snuggled around a bit under the covers. Her first sight on peeking out of the covers, when she looked towards her lover, was a vibrant hardon.

Chatz was apparently reliving some of the previous evening's merriment in an erotic dream he was enjoying.

Very stealthily, so as not to awaken him, Agnes sneaked out from under the covers and inched towards the throbbing prick.

Raising herself on an elbow and steadying herself on the sheet on the other side of Chatz, she lowered her head over the boner.

Slowly she inched her mouth down over the item, smiling widely as she wondered what the effect of what she was about to do would have on the monarch and his dream.

First she breathed over it, inhaling that musky fragrance that surrounds the penile area.

The royal prickhead had emerged from its foreskin, presenting a perfect target for the encroaching lips.

Agnes surrounded the bulb with her mouth and ran her soft tongue around the circumference.

As she lowered her mouth down onto his shaft, running her lips up and down, Chatz feigned a continuance of his sleep.

Indeed, he pretended to himself that he was dreaming the most vivid sex dream he had ever experienced.

Even when he came in her mouth, he continued to breathe as if still asleep.

As she was swallowing his cum, Agnes began to laugh.

As if just awakening, Chatz opened his eyes and rubbed them, yawned, and addressed the love of his life.

"Oh, Beauté," he said as if just seeing her. "You won't believe what a beautiful dream I just had."

"Really, Chatz," Agnes teased. "What were you dreaming of?"

He sat up suddenly and encircled her left nipple and sucked lasciviously.

When he came up for air he answered her question.

"I was dreaming I was fucking you, Dear. And guess what?"

"What?" Agnes teased.

"Here I am awake, and I can't make my dream come true...until..."

'Until what?" Agnes asked faux-naïvely.

"Until you can get my cock hard again. It seems I had a wet dream and will need a few minutes to revive."

"I'll bet we can get it up in seconds rather than minutes," his mistress said.

And, with her expert mouth music, she proved herself right.

"This is the happiest Christmas in my life," the king declared. "Tell me, Beauté. Name any gift. It is yours."

Agnes had been waiting for this opportunity. She took a deep breath and said it as calmly as she was able.

"Chatz. Would it be too presumptuous to ask to be able to sit at your side during the meetings of the Royal Council?"

Charles was surprised at the request. He thought it over and then laughed a deep, hearty laugh.

"Beauté," he responded. "I can think of no one in the world I would rather have by my side to steady me at the Council table. Merry Christmas, my dear."

Three days after the New Year's celebration, Charles VII called a meeting of the Royal Council. He had received a very important message from London – from the court of Henry VI. When the Council met to hear the contents of the letter, the members were astounded to see the king's mistress sitting by his side. As novel as the contents of Henry VI's letter to Charles VII was, the appearance of a woman in the council chambers was more surprising still.

The new year apparently was starting out in a most unusual manner.

Chapter Twenty

The session of the Royal Council was extraordinary in more ways than one. None of the august members were able to take their eyes off the lady who sat confidently at the side of the sovereign.

That many, if not all of the council members were shocked, there could be no doubt. Yet not one word was raised about the propriety of a female sitting at the meeting. No one asked whether the king's mistress would be sitting in on meetings in the future. Only Agnes and the king knew she would be a permanent fixture from then on.

Without comment about the person sitting at his side, Charles presented a letter he had received to the council secretary, Guillaume Mariette, to read aloud.

"To our Brother Charles de Valois, by the Grace of God, King of France, from Henry Lancaster, King of England: Greeting.

"As we are approaching an age when prudence and policy dictate that we should be considering entering into the holy estate of matrimony, our attention has been called to consider asking for the hand of Marguerite d'Anjou, the daughter of Your Majesty's brother and sister, the Duke and Duchess of Anjou and Lorraine. The lovely young lady has found much favor in our eyes. And, as a secondary consideration, the binding of the Houses of Valois and of Lancaster in marriage may hopefully lead to terminate the differences between our two nations that have so grievously separated us in the past.

"We would invite you, Dear Brother, to send to our court a representative empowered to discuss this matter at your early convenience.

"With the utmost respect and admiration, etc., etc., etc.

"H VI"

"Let's see, now. As I recall, the young king was born in 1422. The very year our father, Charles VI departed this earth. How old, then, is the young king at present?" Charles asked the members of the council. One of the members answered immediately.

"Your Majesty. That would make him fifteen years old, sometime this year. He should, indeed, be thinking of taking a wife."

The council members all nodded in agreement.

Agnes knew that Marguerite d'Anjou had recently celebrated her twelfth birthday. And she knew that King Charles knew that as well.

"Do the members of the Council have any suggestions or recommendations concerning what action we should take on this letter from the King of England?" Charles asked.

It was agreed that Charles should send an envoy forthwith to London to discuss the matter at court there. It was hoped that this proposed marriage might secure the peace that both England and France sought.

No further action was taken by the Council that day.

The word most exchanged at court that day was "Extraordinary." It applied to more than the welcome chance of a closer alliance between the two countries through a royal wedding. Word that Agnes Sorel sat in the council chamber was an even more astounding piece of news.

Agnes had not uttered a word at Council. Nor would she ever. But having been present at the deliberations, it immediately became natural for her and Charles to discuss what happened there when they were together in the evening.

"Well, Chatz," Agnes commented. "It appears there will be a royal wedding in the near future."

"I was hoping Henry would broach the subject," Chatz said. "Or rather, that his advisors would. It would have been impolitic for me to have advanced the idea."

"Then it came as no shock to you?" Agnes asked. "You had already thought of marrying little Marguerite to the boy king?"

"Of course," the king told her. "Thinking people in both France and England want to put an end to this senseless war. True, we have all but won back our land. But there remain pockets of English soldiers who cannot bear to see us get back our country. The boy king's father, Henry V, married my sister Catherine with the hope of securing his right to usurp our throne."

"Yes," Agnes said. "I knew that the young king was your nephew."

"Exactly," Chatz said. "So now that the English court sees that it's useless to try to hold on to France, another English-French royal wedding is seen as a way of re-establishing friendly relations. And since Marguerite, while my niece, is not a blood relative of young Henry, there is no reason why the two young people should not marry."

"What will René and Isabelle have to say about their twelve year old daughter marrying an English boy?" Agnes asked.

"That English boy is, after all, half French by birth," Charles stated. "And their son-in-law would give immense prestige to René and Isabelle. I saw them this afternoon. But since I have discussed the possibility with them for years, they were not surprised. Years ago it was they who first suggested this to me."

Agnes was amazed at what had been going on behind the scenes before the letter from London had arrived at Nancy.

"Whom do you have in mind to send to London to work out preliminary plans for the wedding?" Agnes asked.

"I've been considering a couple of names," Charles said. "There's Poton, of course. He was the one I sent to Scotland to represent me in the matter of Louis and the Scottish princess. He did a very commendable job. It is a shame that the dauphin is bungling the possible diplomatic benefits of that marriage. And then there's Bishop Cartier of Toul to consider sending to London. He is quite dignified, and speaks well, don't you think?"

"I wonder about Poton," Agnes said. "I am very fond of the general and am impressed by his courtliness and his intelligence. But since he represented you in the Scottish matter, and Scotland is still a firm enemy of the English throne..."

"I see what you mean, Beauté. Poton might not be the best choice as leader of the delegation."

"Bishop Cartier is an impressive man," Agnes said. "But he seems to be somewhat...religious? That's not the word. But although holy and righteous, he so often sounds..."

"Sanctimonious?" Charles chuckled.

"That's the word I wanted."

"Yes," Charles agreed. "Perhaps Cartier would be better officiating in the cathedral than in the role of diplomat. But, as a member of the envoys…"

"Chatz," Agnes essayed. "Had you considered Seneschal de Breze?"

"Breze? No, not at all. Why Breze?"

"Oh, I don't know," Agnes said off-hand. "I hear he's conversant in English. But I've never actually heard him speak it."

"The English court speaks fluent French, my dear," Charles informed her. "Norman French, to be sure. But still quite understandable. That's not a concern. But, yet…I believe I will consider Breze along with others. He certainly is the best speaker in France. An imposing warrior. That could be important. Yes, thank you for mentioning him."

Other matters more pressing at the moment than the special ambassadorship to London occupied the lovers. Agnes never again mentioned the subject of who might negotiate the details of the proposed royal wedding.

Not too much later, a delegation was sent to the court of Henry VI. The group consisted of Pierre de Breze, Poton de Xantrailles, and Aiméry Cartier. Breze was spokesperson for the ambassadorial group.

Lord Suffolk spoke for King Henry and the court of England. His pronouncements were accompanied by nods of assent from the young king. Satisfactory agreements were made concerning most of the arrangements. The English found most of Breze's proposals acceptable, but wanted time to consider the minute details. It was decided that Lord Suffolk would come to Nancy in February to meet directly with Charles VII and the Duke and Duchess of Anjou and Lorraine.

Before the French delegation left London to return to France, Breze received instructions from his king. He was to proceed directly to Treves to met with the German emperor to attempt to resolve the conflict at Metz through diplomacy rather than by war.

When Breze finally returned to Nancy, he brought with him the Treaty of Treves, which guaranteed there would be no war with the German emperor. He had also satisfactorily concluded the important diplomatic relations with the English. Breze's value as a skillful ambassadorial representative of Charles VII was assured. Agnes felt the way was now well paved to introduce Pierre de Breze into the Royal Council, where he could voice her opinions in matters of state.

Not only the court, but all France was delighted with the prospect of a wedding that would bring a formal, definite halt to the war that had inflicted such grief on the country for over a hundred years. The populace was proud of its victorious monarch. There was much to rejoice about.

In mid-January, Lord Suffolk landed at Harfleur. He carried plenipotentiary powers to complete all arrangements attendant on the marriage of Henry and Marguerite.

He had not yet left Harfleur for Nancy when tragedy struck at the Court of France.

Charles VII fell deathly ill.

The king was in agony. His internal organs and his limbs were in spasm. He had a raging fever. He was incontinent. He mumbled constantly and was incoherent.

Speculations ran wild at Nancy Palace.

"The king has been poisoned."

"It sounds like the dauphin has finally…"

"Didn't this happen to his father as prelude to his madness?"

"A spell has been cast on him by Philippe of Burgundy."

"The Anti-Pope is behind this. Just you wait and see."

In her chambers, Agnes knelt before the statue of the Madeleine that dominated the eastern wall.

"Holy Saint Mary Magdalene. You know me to be but a humble sinner. My prayers to you have been, I know, selfish and unworthy. But now, in this hour of sadness, pray for me. Intercede for me, a sinner, but one who loves.

"Our sovereign was surely not rescued from his dark days of doubt and indecision by Joan of Arc to lead our nation to victory and then to die before the task is completed.

"You, who found favor in the eyes of Our Lord, even though you were a sinner, intercede with Him not on my poor behalf but on behalf of Holy France.

"Our sovereign is the heir of his grandfather, Saint Louis. He leads France to a righteous glory in the name of Our Lord and all his saints.

"If our Charles recovers from this egregious illness, I offer this vow. I will have a statue made, dedicated to you, O Saint. It will be cast in pure silver and overlaid with gold. You need but to guide me to the church or chapel of your desire and I will have your statue erected there.

"I promise from the depths of my heart that I will acquire the funds for your holy image to be located wherever you choose to be honored.

"So, on my knees, I implore you, Great Madeleine, to restore King Charles to vigorous health.

"Amen."

Agnes' prayers, both public and private, were constant. At the king's bedside, she sat vigil every night.

And three days after her vow to the Madeleine, Charles showed the first signs of recovery. His fever abated. Moments of consciousness reappeared. The tremors and thrashing of his limbs quieted.

After a night of calm sleep, a night when neither Agnes nor Queen Marie stirred from his bedside, the court physician declared that Charles could sip some clear broth.

Agnes was confident that the king's recovery was a true miracle. A miracle wrought by the Madeleine. She, Agnes, had a vow to fulfill. She would see to it that the statue be made and installed wherever and whenever the saint decreed.

A week later, Charles VII was well enough to receive the English ambassador, and Lord Suffolk set out from Harfleur for Nancy.

Breze met Lord Suffolk and his retinue at the gates of the palace. The two men knew each other quite well by now. There was more than mutual respect. Their friendship was clear to all observers.

The final details of the wedding were worked out. The ceremony would take place at Nancy Cathedral and would be officiated by Bishop Aiméry Cartier of Toul. Gregory Lane, Arch Deacon of Canterbury, would celebrate the choral portions of the nuptial mass. Duke René would be accompanied by King Charles in presenting the bride.

Henry VI's council decided it was not advisable for the boy king to come to France in person at the time. It was recognized that a great deal of animosity still dwelt in the hearts of the French people. Lord Suffolk would stand in for the English king.

Marguerite would return with Lord Suffolk to London after the celebrations in Nancy. There she would dwell with the Dowager Queen Catherine, who was, after all, not only French but the sister of the king of France, which made her nearly an aunt.

Marguerite would be Queen of England, but would not join Henry VI in the royal bed until her flowering. It would be the dowager queen who would proclaim Marguerite's readiness for the carnal coupling of England and France when the time came.

It was settled, then, that the royal wedding would take place on March seventh. It would be a day of rejoicing on both sides of the Channel.

In due time, Charles VII, under Agnes' gentle persuasion, invited Pierre de Breze, Jacques Coeur, and Etienne Chevalier to sit in on the meetings of the Royal Council. Each of these men had proved his worth to the country and to the king's cause. The noblemen and prelates who sat as privileged members of the Council had become accustomed to Agnes' presence at their sessions. They simply had ignored her, pretending she was nothing more than a new fixture in the room.

But the three gentlemen, one renowned as the king's successful ambassador and point man in recent international negotiations and a popular military figure, another the most wealthy man in Europe and the nation's financier, and the third the most distinguished non-theologian scholar in the land – these were difficult to ignore.

Very soon after their presence at the meetings had been allowed by the sovereign, he began to ask for their opinions. At first, unlike the actual members of the council, the three did not speak unless or until specifically invited to do so by Charles. But their responses to the royal queries were so clearly cogent and based on the contemporary scene that Charles eventually made them full participants.

For the first time in history, the King's Council included members of the petty nobility and the bourgeois class. These newcomers held esteemed positions therein. And it was believed by the old aristocracy that these upstarts were controlled by the lady who quietly sat at the king's side during the sessions – his official mistress.

The new situation engendered jealousies aplenty. Rumors were circulated about a romantic liaison between Agnes and Breze. But when Pierre de Breze became engaged to be married to the ravishingly beautiful Countess Dominique d'Evreux, the rumors were squelched. Breze and Dominique were so clearly an enamored couple that no questions survived concerning any romantic entanglements between the seneschal and the king's mistress.

Agnes felt that the destiny prophesied for her by the sorcière in Picardy had been fulfilled. She did indeed rule a great nation. Publicly, she was not really seen as a political creature. She was certainly an arbiter of style, and her taste in dress and coiffure was widely copied by the smart younger set not only in France, but throughout Europe. Her political influence was quietly exerted through her intimate Thursday dinners.

On Thursdays, when all the participants were available at the royal palace, Agnes was hostess at her *petites soirées*. She and Charles hosted Pierre de Breze and his fiancé Dominique, Jacques Coeur and his wife Florence, and Etienne Chevalier and Poton de Xantrailles, both of whom arrived unaccompanied.

To all appearances, it was a gathering for a lovely dinner followed by card games. The seneschal, however, whose ability at cards was greatly inferior to his renown on the field of battle, on the jousting lists, or in the diplomatic conference, played chess with Etienne Chevalier. When it came to chess strategy, Chevalier proved as skillful as the seneschal. All other guests at the gathering engaged avidly in the card games.

But Breze was very much a part of the discussions that occurred at the dinner table and at the card and chess tables. And those discussions were where decisions were made about the political and military situations confronting France. Very few of the positions taken by the three new members of the Council were forwarded publicly until they had been well discussed at one of Agnes' *petites soirées*.

One evening, Poton asked to be allowed to bring Colonel Jean Bureau, the nation's master of artillery to a *soirée*. It was in that venue that the colonel explained his views on the wartime use of cannon using gunpowder and a moveable catapult. It was an idea that revolutionized warfare forever. The colonel needed time and funds to develop the new technology. The group organized by Agnes Sorel made that possible.

Under Agnes' astute eye, Europe was undergoing unprecedented changes. One age was melding into another. The Middle Ages were yielding to Modern Times.

Chapter Twenty-One

In March, Nancy was completely consumed by the royal wedding. Even in Agnes' boudoir, it was a subject of conversation.

Agnes and Charles were seated before the fireplace. They had removed their clothes and were sipping muscadet wine. Neither felt a care in the world.

"Isn't Marguerite radiant, Chatz?" Agnes enthused. "She will be such a gorgeous bride."

"She has been the apple of my eye from the time she was born" Charles answered. "I have to admit that I hate to see her leave for England."

"She'll be with your sister, anyway, Chatz."

"My sister. Yes," Chatz considered. "My father sacrificed her and half of France to Henry V after the Battle of Agincourt. I wish I could see Catherine again. But it would not do for either of us to cross the Channel."

"Have you ever forgiven your father?"

"There is that Commandment about honoring one's father. I have struggled with it all my life. Father betrayed me, my sister, and France. He made my life Hell. My legacy from him consisted of doubts, indecision, and fear."

Charles pondered a moment.

"Then you came into my life. All that changed. And I recently told my confessor that I think I really can find it in my heart to forgive Father."

Agnes caressed her lover, and he smiled into her eyes.

The couple was content to sit quietly and simply enjoy the comfort of being close to each other and caring.

The smile did not fade from Chatz' face.

"Is there meaning in your smile, Chatz?" Agnes asked, returning his smile.

"As a matter of fact, there is," Chatz responded.

He didn't follow up, and the two again sat silently facing the fire.

"Well?" Agnes asked.

"Well what?"

"Well, Chatz. Would you care to tell me the meaning that lurks behind your smile?"

"Yes," he replied enigmatically.

Again they sat in silence, each smiling at the crackling fireplace.

At length, Agnes broke the silence.

"All right, Chatz," she demanded. "No more of your provocative games. Tell me right now what is behind your suggestive smirk or I will have to take charge myself."

"That's what the smile's about," the king answered.

"What what's about?" Ages demanded.

"I'd like you to take charge," was his laconic answer.

"Tell me what you mean," Agnes said, a glimmer of understanding shining through.

"Back when I returned to you from Basel, you told me about a...technique your cousin Antoinette had learned from a Byzantine sailor."

"Pompoir," Agnes suggested.

"Yes, pompoir. And you pleasured me with that practice then, and countless times since."

"Are you just telling me you want me to do you with pompoir, *Cheri*? Is that all that mysterious smile is about? Let's get in bed then right now. My pussy is ripe for a pompoir session."

"Not so fast," Chatz responded. "That's not what I was smiling about. Your cousin Antoinette has had numerous swains. She obviously has taught them a lot. But she has also learned a lot from some of the true connoisseurs she has bedded.

"Surely she has revealed to you some of the more exotic practices she has been taught. Pompoir cannot be the only one."

"And you would like me to try out one of the more...tantalizing of the approaches she has told me about?"

"Yes, Beauté. Perhaps a technique you thought might shock me were you to tell me about it," her lover responded, with a devilish twinkle in his eye.

"Well," Agnes pondered. "There's ligottage. I'm not sure that the king and master of the French monarchy would want to subject himself to it."

"Beauté," Chatz told her. "I am, indeed, the master of the kingdom. But here in your boudoir, you are the mistress of my body and soul.

"So I humbly petition my mistress, captivate your subject's body with this 'ligottage'."

With a sly smile of her own, Agnes got up from the couch and went to her wardrobe closet.

She retrieved four long silk sashes she had stored in there. When she returned with the items, the king was puzzled. But he said not a word.

Agnes had her lover lie spread-eagle on his back on the four-poster bed. She had him raise his butt so she could slip a pillow under it, raising his pelvic section.

She then skillfully tied a sash around each of his ankles and wrists and secured the other ends of the sashes to the bedposts. The king was now restrained, fully exposed, and captive to the restraints Agnes had fastened to him.

He instinctively struggled against the bonds, and found himself helpless. The feeling, for the master of a nation, was vaguely frightening and definitely erotic. He felt a tingling in his balls as his peter began a pleasurable ascent.

He looked at his lover with new, fascinated eyes.

She lowered her face over his and kissed him deeply on the mouth. And in this kiss, it was well established who was in total charge of the situation.

Agnes stepped back, and as he watched in stupefied amazement, she began to rub her cunt slowly and provocatively. As her fingers caressed her clit, the moisture from her twat began to flow.

Sticking a finger up her damp hole, she ran the digit up and down, up and down.

She removed her finger, sniffed the cassolette fragrance, approached the bound monarch, and smeared the cunt-juice across his upper lip where its perfume would linger with his every breath.

She re-inserted her finger up her vagina, pulled it out, and slipped the finger into her subject's mouth.

He sucked her scented finger as she pulled it back and forth. The effect on the king's dong was excruciatingly sensual.

He squirmed, he struggled, he sighed, he moaned. He was in an ecstasy.

Agnes climbed up onto the bed.

She ran her tits slowly, sensuously, over his entire exposed body, so that her nipples grazed him from his face to his toes.

As those nipples ran over his cock and balls, he involuntarily struggled against his restraints in an agony of joy.

Having caressed his body with her nipples, Agnes straddled her lover's body, a knee on each side of his hips, facing his feet.

She gracefully lowered her koozie down onto his mouth as she reached down to his cock to jack him off slowly. Ever so slowly.

As he lapped at her hovering cunt, she slipped down his foreskin and skillfully manipulated it over his glans.

For the next hour, she manually brought Chatz to the point of coming, then desisted from allowing the ejaculation, again and again. His tongue licking her cunt and clit kept time with the ministration of her educated fist.

The time came when he could withstand the awaiting pleasure no longer.

He struggled against his restraints.

He pleaded, "Let me come."

"That is up to *me* to decide," Agnes replied.

Again and again he pleaded as he worked ever more spasmodically against his restraints

When she knew the moment was right, Agnes pumped lightly but rapidly. And the royal prick spurted its regal jism with an explosion that left the monarch limp in more ways than one.

Agnes released her lover from his restraints.

Chatz thanked Agnes for demonstrating ligottage.

He *loved* the experience.

But he told her they would have to reserve it for special occasions.

"You mean it took a lot out of you, Dear?" Agnes smiled.

"In more ways than one," he answered.

They fell all over each other with laughter.

When they recovered, they put on lounging robes.

Agnes called for Nini.

"His Majesty and I would like some oysters and a new bottle of muscadet," she ordered.

Nini wondered what the silk sashes were doing on the bed.

She knew better than to ask.

Over the oysters and wine, Agnes said, "René has certainly organized the grandest round of entertainments I've ever seen, Chatz. With all the English Milords and Miladies from England here for the wedding. And I believe the whole court of Burgundy is here in attendance. And I've never seen so many of our own French dukes, duchesses, counts, countesses... Well, every title in the land must be here.

"And René is putting on banquets, balls, games, concerts, jousts...even contests of the trovères organized like the jocs florals of the troubadours in the South."

"René does love to entertain," Charles agreed. "And since I've authorized Jacques Coeur to pay from the treasury whatever René has in mind, the festivities do seem, indeed, lavish."

"The balls, Chatz," Agnes gushed. "All of the dances are now French. None Italian. And how beautifully and gracefully you dance with me."

Agnes hummed the tune of a passepied. Charles took her by the hand, danced her around the room, and led her to the edge of the bed.

But he did not make love to her. They both needed time to recover from the excesses of the morning's romp.

They dozed off into a nap in each other's arms.

The English and Burgundians who had come to Nancy for the wedding expected to be shocked by the habiliments of the ladies of the Court of Charles VII. They were not disappointed. The younger ladies had, indeed, succumbed to the fashions set by the king's notorious mistress.

On the morning of the wedding, Nini was assisting Agnes with her toilette and her apparel.

"Shall we give the *milords* and *miladies* something to really set their tongues a-wagging, Nini?" Agnes asked.

"You have never been reticent about shocking the strangers, Madame."

"For little Marguerite's wedding, I am thinking of something bright and gay. She has always been delighted with colorful things."

"Very appropriate, I'm sure, Madame." Nini agreed.

"Yes, I think the bright red muslin robe, the one with the black silk bodice."

"Very décolleté, Madame. And so revealing of your every...curve."

"Do you think it might shock our visitors from across the Channel?"

Agnes asked with a wicked smile.

"It nearly shocks me, Madame. And I have had occasion to grow accustomed to the new styles Madame as introduced to France."

"The perfect train, I believe, would be the blue one," Agnes decided. "You know. The one encrusted with rubies and pearls. Bring it to me."

While Nini went to fetch the train, Agnes put on the fleur-de-lys ring of tiny diamonds and rubies and the sapphire and emerald bracelet that had been the king's first gifts to her.

Nini helped her don the train.

Agnes placed on her head a particularly tall hennin. These conical hats had been popular throughout the chivalric age. But none before had ever been so precariously tall.

Agnes was now dressed for the sacred ceremony that would hopefully, at long last, bind France and England into a state of political and diplomatic harmony and peace.

Her jewelry was in place. But she was acutely aware that her finest jewelry, her dazzling breasts, outshone anything she wore.

And she knew that every young and attractive demoiselle and dame of Charles VII's court would be displaying her own "jewels" on this festive day. Let the Goddams click their tongues if they so chose.

The wedding procession wended its way through the streets of Nancy accompanied by cheers from the crowd all along the way.

First came the standards, the standard of France and then that of the king, followed by those of the House of Anjou and the House of Lorraine. The king rode on his white destrier, directly behind the standards. Duke René and Duchess Isabelle were in a gilded coach with the queen and with the bride, their daughter Marguerite.

Archers marched on each side of the procession, followed by the dauphin, the dauphine, and all the dukes, duchesses, counts, and countesses of the kingdom. Drummers and trumpeters followed, and could be heard the length of the procession except when the clanging of all the church bells of Nancy drowned them out.

Behind the drummers and trumpeters, in silver coaches, the ladies-in-waiting and the maids-of-honor rode.

The knights of France awaited the cortege at the Parvis, where Lord Suffolk and his retinue also waited. There was no English parade since no soldiers or armed representatives of the English crown were permitted to enter free France.

King Charles and Lord Suffolk met in the center of the Parvis. Amid enthusiastic shouts from the enormous crowd that had come to view the spectacle, Suffolk knelt before the king. The two then entered the cathedral to wait for René and Isabelle to escort Marguerite up the aisle. The cathedral choir sang a glorious Te Deum.

The English retinue then entered, followed by the French.

The crowd at this point was intent on the garments worn by the ladies of Charles' court. Never had they seen the like. The wedding represented the greatest fashion statement ever seen in France. And the gorgeous lady in the red gown, the black décolleté, and the tall hennin caused the greatest stir.

Once all the invitees were in the cathedral, Charles VII stepped aside from the altar and René and Isabelle d'Anjou walked their daughter up the aisle. Isabelle joined the king and René presented Marguerite to Lord Suffolk, who represented the groom, the King of England.

The Bishop of Toul, before God, joined the House of Lancaster to the houses of Anjou and Lorraine.

Was peace assured?

That was the hope and prayer of two nations.

Once the wedding and the festivities that followed the ceremony were completed, Charles sent the dauphin off to Alsace. Since his return from the Dauphiné, Louis had constantly stirred up trouble in court. On his campaign against the Alsatians the dauphin was accompanied by twenty thousand mercenaries who had served France in its constant battle with the English. These were soldiers trained in rape and pillage, known as *écorcheurs*. The dauphin led them north to Alsace where they had a grand time raping, murdering, and pillaging to their hearts' content.

Louis had his troops capture blond Alsatian boys who became the dauphin's unwilling objects of sensual pleasure.

At times he had to be satisfied with just one boy per night. But more often he entertained himself with two or three at a time. For Louis, the campaign was heavenly.

His mercenaries scoured the Alsatian countryside to capture the blondest, prettiest adolescent youths they could find. Louis rewarded his troops in accordance with the attractiveness of the prey they caught.

Louis would suck the captive's cock and slap him hard across the face if he did not smile and say, "*Merci, Messire*" to the prince.

Then the boy was privileged to suck Louis' cock while jacking himself off.

As the finale, the lad was sodomized, caused to thank the dauphin, given a Louis d'Or, and pushed out the door.

The mercenaries hanging around the door laughed and shouted obscenities as the victims exited hollow-eyed and staggering as in a trance.

The troops took their pleasure with their prince's cast-offs as they chose.

One day, an Alsatian crossbowman unleashed a quarrel that found a home in the dauphin's right leg. The *écorcheurs* captured an Alsatian they claimed to have been the one who shot the bolt. The man they captured did not have a crossbow, and appeared to be simply a dairyman attempting to drive his herd out of the way of the invaders. Whether he was or was not the marksman, he was the one chosen to pay for the dauphin's discomfort. His punishment was dismemberment that lasted for ten days. The comedy of the Alsatian's discomfort helped divert Louis' concern about his wound.

Back in Nancy, the king was distraught when he heard that his son had been wounded. He sought solace in the comfort of his mistress.

Agnes was seated on the floor with her head on Charles' knees. Charles was seated at his desk. He had goose quill in hand and was attempting to put ink to vellum.

"Who are you writing to, my love?" Agnes asked coquettishly.

"I am concerned about Louis. He is wounded and I want him to return to court."

"It seems to me," Agnes said. "That Louis has shown he can take good care of himself wherever he is."

"I know," Charles agreed. "But he is the Grand Dauphin of France. It is God's will that he rule France after my demise. When I sent him off to fight the Alsatians, I didn't think he would meet real danger..."

Agnes tugged at Charles' jacket and urged him down onto the floor beside her.

The letter never got finished.

Louis returned to court soon anyway. His amusements in Alsace were beginning to bore him, and his wounded leg was bothering him enough to seek the ministrations of the court physicians. The *écorcheurs* were left in Alsace to divert themselves however they pleased.

Jean Bureau continued his experiments to improve the portable catapult and to construct a workable cannon. Although gunpowder had been known and used in Europe for a hundred years, no nation had provided the resources to its ordnance to construct a cannon that did not explode, killing the gunners rather than the enemy.

Paris still remained in the hands of the English, despite the treaty and promises of the Goddams both in London and in Nancy. Charles was preparing to set out to liberate the great city.

He consulted Bureau.

"Bureau, the walls of Paris are formidable," the king stated. "Is the catapult you've been working on up to the task of knocking down those massive walls? And tell me about the cannon. Is it safe?"

"Sire," the inventor replied. "Come to the field outside the city where we have been testing the new armaments. I would like you to draw your own conclusions."

When Charles and Agnes visited the field, Bureau's men shot the cannon at trees in the surrounding forest. Agnes had been the strongest proponent in the land for the development of a safe cannon. She was confident that Bureau could and would perfect the weapon.

When he saw the demonstration in the field, no doubt was left in the king's mind. With this weapon, he had the means to break down any wall that might stand in the way of entering Paris. He consulted with General Poton, and a battle plan was formulated.

Due to Agnes Sorel's influence, France was the first nation in history to add cannon to its artillery. And, as a consequence, warfare was changed forever.

By May, the dauphin's leg wound was healed. Charles was ready to liberate Paris from its long occupation by the English. He would allow his son to participate in the siege. By rights, and by recent treaty, Paris was part of Charles' kingdom. But despite rights and treaty, the English remained in control of the great city.

Charles planned to lead an army of knights, archers, crossbowmen, and his newly modernized artillery, south and west from Nancy. He would cross the Seine at Villeneuve and approach Paris' Saint-Jacques Gate with his cannon and catapult to lay siege to the Left Bank.

He reluctantly commissioned the dauphin to return to Alsace and gather the *écorcheurs* into an army again. The *écorcheurs* had managed to lay waste most of Alsace and had crossed the Rhine to raise havoc in the German territories. The German princes were threatening to attack France if Charles did nothing to halt the ravage.

It was better to harness the wild men and aim them at Paris under the leadership of Louis than provoke war with the Germans.

Louis, then, would lead his troops up through Picardy and then direct them to Paris from the North to liberate the Right Bank. The dauphin started out to collect his troops on the first of May. Charles remained in Nancy for another two weeks to oversee his army and to test out his newly created ordnance.

Finally, the king's troops were ready to march on Paris. The liberation of the great city was seen as symbolic of the fulfillment of the liberation of France from the English.

Agnes watched as Charles donned his battle armor. She smiled as he put on the brassards and gauntlets. His valet assisted him in pulling the huque over the armor. It was deep blue velvet appliquéd with golden fleurs-de-lys. The bagpipers sent by the Scottish king were playing their infernal music in the courtyard.

"Oh, Chatz," Agnes said. "You look magnificent."

"You think so?" Chatz answered. "I believe I look ridiculous. War will never again be fought by knights in armor led by kings in huques. Never more. And it is you, my dear, who wrought this change."

"Not me, Dear. You," Agnes insisted. "And, you still are a very imposing figure in your armor. But Poton and Bureau do predict that this battle you're setting out on is either the last battle of the ancient art of war or the first battle of a new era of warfare."

Before the king put on his helmet, Agnes gave him a kiss that he treasured in his mind all the way to the Ile-de-France.

As Charles led his troops, he met English at Villeneuve. However, rather than fighting, the English surrendered to the French commanders. They were taken prisoner and were dispatched willingly back to England.

Louis' *écorcheurs* were allowed to rape and pillage in Picardy, although the province was firmly loyal to Charles VII. As the *écorcheurs* headed south towards Paris, the English who held the outskirts of the city surrendered without resistance. Unlike his father, though, Louis hanged all the English soldiers who surrendered.

When Agnes heard of what had happened in Picardy, and about the hanging of the English prisoners, she shuddered. She knew the dauphin would love to hang her as well. She was aware that he considered her a greater enemy than the English.

The dauphin and his *écorcheurs* were not able to breach the north walls of Paris. In frustration, Louis rode post haste around the city walls to join his father's forces in the south.

As Charles approached the St.-Jacques Gates to Paris, he did not have a chance to set up his cannon and catapult. For, as his army came into sight of the great gate, it was opened and a delegation marched out of the city to greet and welcome him as a liberator. Not a single arrow was shot in defense of Paris. The liberator had arrived.

At the moment of the bloodless victory, the dauphin had arrived to join his father's forces.

Charles VII entered Paris in triumph. The king was in full armor, mounted on his white destrier. The horse itself was draped in blue velvet with appliquéd fleurs-de-lys. Before the king rode General Poton de Xantrailles on a black destrier covered with cloth on which was seen the device of the winged stag. Poton carried Charles VII's great helm surmounted by a gold crown emblazoned with the fleur-de-lys.

Behind Poton rode Jean Bureau, carrying the king's sword of state, worked with a golden fleur-de-lys.

The king himself followed, surrounded by the Royal Guard and the King's Archers.

Behind followed the king's pages, the dauphin, and the lords.

At the end of the procession came a battalion of eight hundred soldiers bearing lances.

As the cortege marched though the city, there did not appear to be a single vestige of any English. The Goddams had apparently left the city entirely. The Parisians hailed Charles, but the shouting was half-hearted at best. During the long English occupation, the Parisians had fared well. Food was cheap and abundant, the English kept crime down and justice was fair. There was no haughtiness of the nobility as there had been under Charles VI and his court.

The Parisians had had to learn some English, it was true, to deal with the people in charge. The English did not seem able to learn the language of the Parisians, so the Parisians acquired a slight ability to speak and comprehend the language of the occupiers.

The reverse situation applied when the Norman French occupied London back in 1066.

The last king the Parisians remembered was this king's father. Completely mad. Unpredictable. He had given their city to the English rather than to his own son. *His own son – that's who we're cheering today. Well, we'd better cheer. His people are in charge now.*

During the triumphal entrance to Paris, the sanctification at Notre Dame was a high point. The bishop had been a partisan of the English and Burgundians. He had approved the death at the stake of Joan of Arc. Now he welcomed the king. Charles nearly gagged. As he entered Notre Dame every church bell in Paris rang out.

Despite his feeling of revulsion at the churchmen who changed allegiance with every shift in the wind, Charles felt the exhilaration he had felt when Joan of Arc led him into the cathedral at Rheims for his coronation.

After the ceremonies at Notre Dame, the royal cortege proceeded on to the Basilica of Saint-Denis. It was there that the king was met by the representatives of the city. The city provost presented the keys to the city to the king who, in turn, gave them to General Poton. This was the official gesture of the submission of the Parisian officials to the Crown.

Charles felt as little warmth for these city officials as he did for the church officials at Notre Dame. In both cases, there were people who had sided against him during the English occupation. But that did not lessen his pleasure of being publicly hailed as the King of France there in the city of Paris.

The provost informed Charles that the Parisian residence of the former English viceroy, Les Tournelles, had been prepared for him as his residence. He acknowledged the fact with a nod of his head. He was aware that the Louvre would be less comfortable living quarters at the time.

The procession continued on to Les Tournelles. Charles did not feel comfortable yet for his own safety in Paris, even in this heavily fortified palace. His archers and cross-bowmen slept fully armed in every hallway leading to the king.

But, Paris was now, once again, a part of France. And for this, Charles VII was truly grateful.

Chapter Twenty-Two

On his return procession from Paris to Nancy, Charles passed through Chalons-sur-Marne. He found the area charming, and since it was closer to Paris than Nancy, he thought it wise for the present to be within easy commute of the great city. He was aware that the bishop of Chalons had a vacation mansion about a league from Chalons itself. The king made a trip to the retreat, Sarry Mansion, and felt it would be just the place to bring the court.

When Charles arrived back in Nancy, Agnes had delightful news for him. She was pregnant with their second child. Charles was overjoyed at the news. He then told her about Sarry Mansion and she accompanied him to inspect it.

Agnes agreed that the mansion was indeed charming. The great hall and the dining room were large enough to house large numbers of visitors. Ambassadors, ministers of foreign states, and even the nobility of the realm who were not regular courtiers would have to lodge in Chalons, making for more intimate living conditions for the court itself in Sarry. It seemed to both Charles and Agnes to be an ideal spot for the summer court.

During the first week of June, the court moved from Nancy to Sarry Mansion.

Charles had become the most renowned monarch in Europe. He was master of the most disciplined and most technologically advanced army in the world. He was now self-assured, gallant, strong, forceful, bold, and majestic.

And Agnes Sorel was the most talked-about woman in the Western world.

Charles decided to hold a Plenary Assembly at Sarry. It seemed that his fellow monarchs were now anxious to show that they were on good terms with the King of France and sent representatives to the Grand Plenary Session held during the second week of July, 1437. It was the most important international event of the year.

Duchess Isabella of Burgundy came to the session to work out final differences between the duchy and the kingdom. Ambassadors arrived from the Duke of Savoy, from the Emperor of the Holy Roman Empire, from the King of Castile, the Duke of York, and even from the Patriarch of Constantinople. The court of France had become the power center of the continent.

Charles used the occasion to signal to his own court the new power structure of his government.

He announced that Pierre de Breze was now elevated in rank. With his marriage to the countess of Evreux, the king declared him Count of Evreux and Grand Seneschal of France. He informed the court and the world that the Royal Council would now include as full participating members Count Pierre de Breze, Jacques Coeur, and Etienne Chevalier, with full voting rights.

Soon after being elevated to full membership, Breze became speaker of the council and Coeur, who was personally wealthier than the royal treasury itself, was made master of the treasury. Chevalier was not made the secretary of the council. Guillaume Mariette, who was the king's notary and secretary, kept that position. But Mariette worked well with the three "upstarts."

During the Plenary Session, Dauphin Louis was not much in evidence at court. More often than not he was off in the northern provinces, where he was said to be hunting. But when the foreigners left Chalons, Louis was very much back at court.

His animosity towards both his wife and towards Agnes was even more evident than it had been heretofore.

Upon entering the dining hall for the Midsummer's Day Banquet, the dauphin arrived last, even after the entry of the king and the queen. He was accompanied by five of his toadies, all of them smirking.

The six young men proceeded directly to a group of young ladies who were discussing poetry. Among the ladies were Agnes, the dauphine, and Antoinette. Louis bowed gracefully to Agnes and said:

"My deepest respects, Dame, to my father's whore."

His companions all then bowed as well, and said in unison:

"Long live the king's whore."

Agnes smiled frostily and responded, "My lord Dauphin. Gentlemen. How kind of you to part with your lovers to join us. I trust the lads are all well."

The dauphin smiled and addressed his toadies.

"My lady, the royal whore, knows how to use her tongue, does she not? I'm sure that pretty pink tongue keeps our royal sire deliciously happy in more ways than one."

He then looked surprised as his eye fell upon the dauphine.

"My word," he said. "I do believe it is my wanton wife. Forgive me, Madame. I did not notice you among these lovely ladies. You will excuse me. I should have recognized you immediately. You're the one who has no bust line."

Marguerite blushed and could find no word to say.

Louis continued to talk, but addressed himself to his toadies.

"Do not be deceived by the princess' lack of physical charms, my friends. There is not a poet or troubadour who visits the court who has not enjoyed the charms of Her Highness' bed. I understand all it takes is a stanza or two to cause the freckled Scottish legs to spread in welcome."

The dauphin and his group bowed and withdrew.

Dauphine Marguerite burst into tears.

"I do not know why he hates me so," she wept. "I have never done anything at all to offend him. He says awful things like that about me constantly. And what's worse, there are many in court who gossip about what he says."

"My dear dauphine," Antoinette replied. "No one really believes his wicked remarks. You surely know that."

"But at least a few do pretend to believe Louis," Marguerite sobbed. "It's just too awful."

It was clear to see the toll the dauphin's spitefulness was taking on the princess. She was visibly losing weight. And she was so thin anyway that she could ill afford the loss. Her pale Celtic complexion was turning ever more sallow.

"You must not allow His Highness' slanders to undermine your health, Princess," Marie de Belleville admonished.

"The only thing that supports me at all," Marguerite said, amid her tears, "is my love of poetry. And I do thank God that there is poetry, minstrelsy, troubadours, and trovères always present in His Majesty's court."

The dauphin could be seen across the room relishing his wife's discomfort and sneering at the presence of the king's mistress.

Raimbaut advised the king that Agnes required increased security and recommended that her brothers Vincent and Cyrille be brought to court with orders to keep tight surveillance on the activities of the dauphin. The king sent for the two young men. In addition, a permanent spy was placed in the kitchen to see that no poison was slipped into Agnes' food.

In July, it was evident that the dauphine had lost weight constantly. Her health was of concern to the king and queen who consulted the court physician about what could be done.

"I have prescribed every medicine known to man to reverse her highness' alarming deteriorating physical condition," the physician said. "I suggest that the dauphine consider a pilgrimage to Notre-Dame-de-l'Epine. Her condition is, in my opinion, spiritually rather than physically based. The shrine of the Epine has been known to work wonders for the spiritual crises that inflict the lesser sex."

The queen was much taken with Master Poictevin's words and insisted that the dauphine set out immediately for the shrine. Marie de Belleville, who had become one of the queen's ladies-in-waiting, and one of the most judicious, inserted a contrary voice.

"Your Majesty," she said. "With all due respect to Master Poictevin, and with confidence in the efficacy of holy intervention, I would urge delay in this matter."

Queen Marie was always courteous even when hearing dissent from her own judgments.

"Indeed, Dame Marie. I honor your views. Pray tell, why, in your opinion, should the dauphine delay setting out to seek the intervention of Our Lady of the Epine forthwith?"

"Your Majesty has noted, yourself, that this is the most inclement July in recent memory," Antoinette observed. "The temperature has enervated even the most robust.

"Perhaps her highness might better delay her pilgrimage until the insufferable heat abates."

"We will consider your counsel, my dear," the queen replied.

And consider it she did. But Master Poictevin's advice won out over that of the lady-in-waiting. And Marguerite of Scotland set out in a royal carriage on the very hottest day of the year. She was accompanied in her carriage by Agnes Sorel, Marie de Belleville, Master Poictevin, and her confessor, Abbé Pelletier.

The first evening, the travelers stopped back in Nancy in familiar surroundings. The next morning Marguerite could scarcely get herself out of bed. Before she could get dressed, she fainted, turning a deathly gray ashen color. Master Poictevin saw that she was very feverish and decided she should be rushed back to Sarry.

By the time the dauphine arrived back at her chambers at Sarry Mansion she had a severe fever, was perspiring profusely, could not hold down any food, had raspy breathing and a wracking cough.

Master Poictevin bled her, applied suction cups, immersed her in cold water, applied plasters, and administered herbal enemas. Each treatment seemed to worsen her condition.

When the queen was not at the princess' bedside, Agnes was there. She recited poetry. She brought in musicians. Marguerite's suffering clearly grew worse and worse. But she seemed to take comfort in the poetry and the music.

Her husband, the dauphin, did not visit her once during her illness.

Marguerite of Scotland, Dauphine of France, faded away into death surrounded by the king and queen, Agnes Sorel, all the ladies-in-waiting and maids of honor, a dozen poets, and her favorite musicians. She was twenty years of age.

The court was in deep mourning for the fragile princess. There was no gaiety, no frolics, no festivities of any kind. For two months, Sarry Mansion was somber indeed.

In September, the king felt that affairs of state dictated that the mourning period be lessened, and that court life revive again. To that end, he decided to move the court.

Agnes suggested a move to Loches, in Touraine.

Chapter Twenty-Three

Charles had spoken to Agnes often about Loches, and they had visited the locale several times. Agnes found the area exceedingly pleasing.

She was particularly intrigued by Loches Castle.

During his time of trial, Charles had considered the castle his retreat. After meeting Joan of Arc at Chinon, he took refuge at Loches. It was there that the Maid met him after the victory at Orleans. It was from Loches Castle that she led him to Rheims to be crowned King of France.

The castle was, then, doubly dear to him. It had been his retreat in time of stress. And it was from this place that his destiny took its new positive lease.

For those reasons, Agnes loved the place. But it also appealed to her for other reasons as well. It was a fortified castle on a rocky point overlooking the forest and the valley of the Indre River. It was beautiful, romantic, and historic. She somehow felt "at home" there.

Agnes and Charles were walking hand in hand through the castle grounds.

"Oh, Chatz," she exclaimed. "No wonder you sought solace here in your retreat during the dark days. I believe this is the most dramatic and most wildly romantic spot on earth."

"Do you mean that, Beauté? This castle truly affects you emotionally, as it always has me?"

"Every place we have been together holds a warm and lovely place in my heart," Agnes informed him. "And I have loved them all. But this spot holds absolute magic for me. It was here that your life changed and you became the great man you are today. Oh, I know the seeds of greatness were always there. But it was here that those seeds germinated. And, as I love you with all my heart, Loches Castle is a concrete representation of the overwhelming passion I feel for you."

Charles was greatly moved by Agnes' words. So much so he could not find words to express what was in his heart. So he merely gave her hand a squeeze, then pulled her to him to kiss her deeply and passionately.

The next evening, Charles and Agnes supped privately in her elegantly appointed rooms in the castle.

As they were finishing the salad course, Agnes asked, "Shall I ring for the dessert yet, dear?"

"Not yet, Beauté. I have brought a surprise dessert this evening myself."

"A dessert, Chatz? How delightful. Where in the world have you kept it hidden?"

"Here in the sleeve of my robe," Chatz teased. "I hope it has not been ruined there."

"Let me see! Let me taste! Chatz, what is it?" Agnes exclaimed.

Charles removed a folded piece of vellum from his sleeve pocket and presented it to his mistress.

Agnes couldn't imagine what kind of dessert could be inside a sheet of vellum. She opened it and read. She squealed in delight.

"Chatz, Chatz! Is this real?"

"Real and official. I had my notary, Guillaume Mariette, draw up the deed this very morning. Loches Castle belongs to you now, exclusively, my dear. I am truly your guest this evening."

"But Chatz," she protested. "It is too much. Why ever would you relinquish ownership of a place so dear to you?"

"Merely on a whim," he responded. "Merely on a whim."

The fruit compote Agnes had prepared as dessert was forgotten.

Agnes never tired of pumping her cousin Antoinette about her sensual experiences. Indeed, Antoinette's sporting activities did not come to a halt when she came south to join Agnes at court.

When the Patriarch of Constantinople had come to Sarry Castle for the plenary session, he brought with him a hetaera for his fucking pleasure. She blended in with his entourage, appearing to be merely another servant.

Antoinette spotted her for what she was. And she and Penelope learned a great deal from each other.

As always, Antoinette taught Agnes the erotic practices she learned from her novel acquaintances.

This evening, at Loches, Agnes plied some of the Byzantine teachings on her lover who had just regaled her with her dream castle.

Penelope had brought a good supply of Indian hemp, which she called ganja, with her from Byzantium. She taught Antoinette how to place a small amount of it in a tiny pipe, ignite it, and inhale the smoke. Antoinette found the effect to be a heightening erotic pleasure.

A whole erotic ballet of sorts called *rahat* is built around the ingestion of ganja.

Antoinette had given Agnes a miniature pipe and a pouch of ganja to pleasure her king with on a special occasion.

The evening of the gift of Loches Castle was just such an occasion.

As preparation for a special sexual engagement, Chatz always preferred that Agnes disrobe slowly and salaciously as he sat in his overstuffed chair and gazed.

Agnes was very adept at disrobing in a provocative manner that always elicited a firm royal boner on the part of her sovereign

Once she had teasingly disrobed, she stood before him in all her naked female glory, he stood and waited for her to remove his garb as sensuously as she had divested herself of hers. She got him unclothed and excited. He was ready to go, but she sat him back in his chair and produced the loaded pipe. It contained just enough ganja for two puffs.

She lit a taper from the fireplace and instructed her swain how to draw the smoke from the pipe into his lungs. The first drag caused him to cough. The second went down smoothly.

Following that inhalation the king's balls felt a rush of exquisite sensation and his hardon fairly bloomed.

His lover took him by the hand and led him to the four-poster and laid him down on the silk sheets to await his treat in whatever form it might take.

Chatz was aware of a tingling sensation at every erogenous zone of his body. He was soon to learn that there were more of such zones than he had imagined.

Agnes urged him to stretch out on the bed to the greatest extension possible, causing a lengthening of his hardon.

She then slithered down his body, leaving a saliva tongue trail from under his chin, across his nipples, making a leap from his naval to the tip of his dong, down the shaft to his nuts, with a sweep under the scrotum to the fleur-de-lys birthmark at his perineum, down the left thigh, to the instep at the sole of his right foot.

As her tongue tickled, in turn, the soles of his feet, his dick began to quiver excitedly. Whatever that ganja was, it seemed to have caused his soles to become extremely erotically sensitive.

When he was at a heightened state, Agnes brought her own soles together around his pulsating prick and caressed that organ with her feet. When he came, he marveled that he had been jacked off by the loveliest feet in France.

Agnes moved up on the bed and snuggled against her lover.

They discussed the amazing erotic experience that the ganja had enhanced.

When she knew her lover had rejuvenated, and while he was still affected by the ganja, she employed the ear caresses that Antoinette had taught her.

As Chatz lay contentedly, his mistress at his side, he was startled to feel her caress his earlobes.

He was further aroused as Agnes nibbled and tongued the back of the lobes. The moist nibbling, licking, and sucking ran from the lobe down to the adjacent sensitive area of the neck.

He found his pecker responding joyously to whatever Agnes was doing up there.

He was the proud possessor of a mighty hardon.

Agnes left her loveplay at the ear and neck, got up from the bed, and straddled her king at his hips. With her back to him, she slid her cunt down over his pulsating boner and rode it up and down as he caressed her gorgeous buns.

When they both came, Agnes sighed and Chatz let out a whoop.

Charles VII felt he was very well rewarded that night for his generosity. Very well rewarded indeed.

Agnes knew in her heart that she now had found her home. She had acquired other properties, Beauté-sur-Marne chief among them. But Loches would forever be her true home. As it had previously been a refuge for her lover, Charles, it would now be her refuge from her public life at court.

Within easy walking distance of Loches Castle is the Collegiate Church of St.-Ours. Three times a day, every day, Agnes walked to the church, accompanied by no one but Raimbaut. And Raimbaut, always armed and alert, remained a respectful and usually inconspicuous distance from the woman he was sworn to protect with his life.

When she entered the church, Agnes went directly to the Madeleine Chapel to pray.

"Holy Saint Mary Magdalene. You have watched over me and the king, and for that my gratitude is beyond expression. When your servant Charles was deathly ill, he was cured by your intercession. At that time, I promised I would erect a silver and gold statue of you in a location you would indicate to me. You have directed my feet to your chapel here in Loches. Is this the spot you have chosen for me to honor my vow?"

An absolute sense of assurance enveloped Agnes Sorel. She knew this place was the one the Madeleine was telling her to sanctify with the silver and gold image.

Agnes arranged an audience with Abbé Raimon.

"Father, you know who I am. A sinner, but a lover of Our Lord, His Blessèd Mother, and of the Madeleine who found forgiveness in the eyes of the Son of God."

"I see you here every day, my daughter. Your devotion does you credit," the priest replied.

"I made a vow to the Madeleine to erect a statue of her in a chapel of her choosing."

"And the saint has directed you to Saint-Ours, and to the chapel here dedicated to her."

"Yes, father."

"The statue of the saint in her chapel here is of fine workmanship already, my daughter."

"So it is," Agnes agreed. "But I have reason to believe that the Madeleine seeks to be honored by a representation of solid silver, chased in gold. Providing, of course, that you feel such a gift on my part would be appropriate and acceptable."

"Let us pray for guidance together," the abbé advised.

After prayerful consideration of Agnes' proposed gift, as the abbé knelt before the figure in the Madeleine Chapel, Father Raimon invited her into his study.

"I believe, my daughter, that your vow has been heard by the saint, and that she has chosen Saint-Ours as the favored location for you to fulfill your vow.

"Also, in prayer, the thought came to me that it would be right and proper that your gifts to our poor church not to be limited to the statue. We have many needs and responsibilities here in Loches. Our charities to the poor, the sick, the halt, and the blind could be greatly extended by gifts from those in favored positions in the court. There are also many mundane needs at Saint-Ours that are not being met due to the shortage of funds. A new reredos behind the altar is one crying need that you may have noticed."

"Father," Agnes replied. "I understand what you are saying. I intend for Loches to be my home. I will certainly not neglect my responsibilities, my financial responsibilities, to my home church."

The abbé smiled what he believed to be a beatific smile at her words.

"God will bless you for your generosity. Now, do you have a sculptor in mind to create the statue?"

"I was in hopes you could advise me on that," Agnes smiled.

"In Tours, there dwells a master sculptor," Abbé Raimon told her. "He is renowned throughout France, nay, throughout Christianity, for the excellence of his work in precious metals. His name is Master Honoré de Montluçon. Would you care for me to write you a letter of introduction to him?"

Agnes did, indeed, desire such a letter.

Three days later Agnes appeared at the artist's studio. Master Honoré had been contacted by the Abbé of St.-Ours and already knew what Agnes wanted and had drawn sketches of his concept for the statue. Agnes was thrilled.

And on that September day in 1437, one of the great sculptural masterpieces of the late Middle Ages was commissioned.

One of the luxuries of Loches Castle was a steam room. Agnes and her cousin Antoinette were accustomed to enjoy the pleasure of a steam bath every afternoon.

The two beautiful women luxuriated in the sensuousness of the enveloping steam. They used the time to confide completely with one another.

"How goes your affair with Duke René?" Agnes asked.

"Since Duchess Isabelle returned to Lorraine to look over her holdings there, he has been able to devote himself nearly exclusively to me," Antoinette confessed.

"To her holdings, you say," Agnes pressed. "From what I hear, what she's been looking after is Count Aristide de Caillaux."

"Apparently," Antoinette told her. "They say that since Pierre de Breze got married, he has not been servicing his flock as before."

Agnes was pleased that she could hear tidings of Pierre de Breze without any emotional twinges. She had but one love. And that love was for Chatz.

What Agnes wanted to hear about was her cousin's fling with Duke René.

"Give with the dirt on René," she urged.

"Well, René says I am the only one he truly loves. And that with Isabelle off in Lorraine, he can fully express his deep devotion to me."

"Pretty much the same line he used on Thérèse," Agnes observed.

"And on Anne, Dominique, Yvette, and…Since Her Grace lifted the requirement for her ladies-in-waiting to be *virgo intacta*, the field is wide open to the count."

"Apparently he doesn't know how the duchess's ladies-in-waiting talk behind his back," Agnes mentioned.

"And laugh behind his back as well," Antoinette added. "I keep demanding that he show me more and more tangible proof of his devotion. He, of course, pleads poverty. But when I hold out on him, and he goes fishing in old familiar waters, and can't get what I can give him, I end up with some very pretty baubles."

"Such as?"

"A pearl necklace, a ruby and emerald broach, and a hundred gold coins to send to my poor sick mother."

"Aunt Gertrude is ill?" Agnes asked.

"Don't be naïve, dearie," Antoinette answered with a wink.

The laughter started all over again, but not as intense as before.

"Oh, 'Toinette," Agnes chided. "What a very naughty girl you are."

Then Agnes began giggling.

The two ladies hugged each other in laughter.

The conversation had been most amusing.

As November approached, Charles grew restless again. Now that Loches belonged to Agnes, he wanted the court to be held elsewhere, so as not to intrude on her new refuge. Chinon was not far distant, and the court moved there.

Chapter Twenty-Four

The king had many dear memories of Chinon Castle. And the court was quite content there. But Charles felt uneasy at the time with the hubbub of court life, and sought a near-by retreat for himself and his intimates.

Charles' chamberlain, Jean de Razilly, owned a property two leagues away from Chinon in a thick sylvan park in the valley of the Vienne. When the king mentioned his need to have a place to relax, Jean invited him to explore Razilly.

Charles rode out to the property accompanied by Jean de Razilly, Agnes, and two of Charles' good friends, Antoine d'Aubusson and André de Villequier.

Jean addressed the king:

"As I told you, Sire. It is a small castle. Perhaps too small to even be called a castle. It would scarcely accommodate the entire court."

"How well you read my needs, Jean," Charles replied. "It is a thoroughly charming dwelling. And in a paradisiacal locale. And, as you point out, it would be impossible for the court to gather here. Which makes it absolutely perfect."

"I am happy it pleases Your Majesty," Jean replied.

"Your generosity in granting my use of it will not go unrewarded, Jean."

"My only hoped-for reward," Jean told him, "is Your Majesty's pleasure."

As they were walking though Razilly Castle, exploring the rooms, Charles asked Agnes what she thought of the place.

"It is just too perfect, Chatz. The affairs of state can be carried on at Chinon. But we know that you cannot relax and restore yourself surrounded by the pomp and circumstance of courtly life.

"My time of confinement is at hand. I can remain here, away from the demands of court. When you come to Razilly, there will be just the two of us and a few friends.

"Being here now, I can fully imagine what it will be like. No gossip. No intrigues. No daily petitions. All the time in the world for picnics on the banks of the Vienne, for romping through the woods. We can hunt, make love, laugh, play..."

Agnes realized she was getting carried away and stopped her monologue with a self-deprecating laugh.

"Yes, Beauté," Charles smiled. "I believe you see it all even more vividly than I do."

So it was settled. Razilly would be their refuge from court life.

The group that gathered regularly at Razilly consisted of André de Villequier and his wife, Antoine d'Aubusson and Madame, Breze and his wife, Agnes' brothers Jean, Charles, Vincent, and Cyrille, Raimbaut, Nini, Antoinette de Maignelay, and, of course, Jean de Razilly.

When their duties allowed, Jacques Coeur, Etienne Chevalier, and Guillaume Mariette joined the select group.

Charles and most of the others from the Razilly ensemble traveled regularly to Chinon. And not only to take care of affairs of state there. Queen Marie stayed at Chinon, so Charles had duties to perform with her as host and hostess at formal and festive occasions. His conjugal duties in the queen's bed were, of course, performed as well. At Chinon, the king presided over the Royal Council, and the petitions, diplomatic obligations and litigations as well.

Agnes remained behind at Razilly, attended by Nini and protected by Raimbaut and her brothers. Cooks and household servants attended to the needs of the small Razilly contingent as well.

Charles was always happy to return to Razilly with his close friends after his duties at Chinon were fulfilled. Back in the Vienne Valley life consisted of sylvan walks and simple musical evenings, or games of cards, chess, or forfeits. And, of course, for lovemaking before a roaring fire.

Razilly truly was Charles and Agnes' love nest.

As the Christmas Season approached, Charles' presence was required more and more at Chinon. For Christmas Court would be held there. But more intimate family festivities were held back at Razilly.

It was during this season that Catherine Sorel and Nurse Hortense Louvain were brought to Razilly to celebrate Christmas with Agnes and to assist at the birth expected in January.

The two ladies from Picardy were visibly aging. The winter trip was difficult for them. Agnes was concerned about Catherine and Hortense's declining health, and decided that she would never allow them to ever again make a voyage in the wintertime.

With Christmas behind, as well as the festivities involved in greeting the New Year of 1438, Charles was able to spend more time at the love nest in Razilly.

Hortense felt no compunction against scolding Agnes. Any of the children who had been delivered into her hands at birth were still her concern. And Agnes most of all.

Her scoldings became part of the routine of Razilly.

"Agnes, you are not going out on that hunting party with the king," Hortense admonished.

"And why not, Madame Hortense?"

"Your condition, child," Hortense explained.

"I see no reason why my condition should keep me from falconing."

"Really! Riding a horse in your condition! It is not to be done."

"But I do not ride a horse," Agnes insisted. "The king has arranged for me to travel by sedan chair and litter."

"Pulled by horses..."

"No!" Agnes corrected. "Carried by four brawny, broad-chested lads."

"Even so, child," the aging nurse replied. "I do not approve."

But Agnes did go hunting with Charles and his party as often as she chose. Despite Midwife Hortense's disapproval.

The king was particularly skilled with the crossbow. But he was also a better than average falconer. Agnes was skilled with the short-bow. She had often gone hunting with her brothers back in Picardy in her youth. She was not interested in the crossbow. But Charles had bought her a peregrine and delighted in teaching her how to hunt with it. She found, surprisingly, that she grew quite adept at falconry. To her midwife's dismay.

The hunting parties bagged wild game several times a week. Agnes particularly enjoyed practicing her culinary expertise with game dishes.

"Agnes, child. You are not going into the kitchen again," Hortense scolded.

"Why not, Madame Hortense?"

"In the first place, it's not appropriate," the midwife claimed. "In the second place, it is too hot in there for your condition. And third, you stand too long for your own good as you prepare food. There are cooks and scullions enough in this castle to take care of our needs, I warrant."

But Agnes had assembled spices from all over the world, thanks to Jacques Coeur. She delighted in combining them to create savory dishes. Her sauces were the rival of any in France. Everyone but Hortense, and sometimes Catherine, was delighted by the cuisine prepared by France's mistress. And Charles was her most avid gourmet enthusiast. Agnes' wine mulled with exotic spices was a winter delight even the grouchy midwife raved about.

Meals taken before the fireplaces were one of the delights of the castle. Entire walnut and oak trunks burned day and night in the hearth. Winter in Razilly was truly a delight.

On January 28, Agnes bore her second child, Charlotte de Valois, named after her father, the king. Catherine, Hortense, Antoinette, and Nini were present at the birth.

As before, Charles strove to be present when his daughter was born.

"No, no, no!" Hortense chided His Majesty. "I told you last time the child was giving birth. And I tell you again. You may not enter the birthing room."

"But at all the queen's deliveries..." Charles began to argue.

"I've heard it all before, you know," Hortense was adamant. "Stay out!"

Charles was amused at the rural midwife's brashness. But, as she had demanded, he did not enter the birthing room until the infant was bathed in wine and swaddled, and until the mother was cleaned, groomed, and in bed away from the birthing stool.

After the birth of their second child, Charles worshiped Agnes even more than before, if that were possible.

He brought a special gift to her when she was recovered from the birthing experience enough to participate again in the activities of Razilly Castle.

"I have brought you a bauble, Beauté, to celebrate your return to health."

"Return to health, Chatz?" Agnes questioned. "I was not unhealthy at all, you know. It was an easy pregnancy and an easy birth."

"Be that as it may," Charles continued. "Will you receive a little token of my love and esteem?"

When Agnes opened the casket she was delighted.

Inside was a tiara comprised of perfectly matched pearls of a variety of hues from brilliant white to ebony black.

No such array of pearls had ever been seen in Europe before.

Jacques Coeur had imported them from a near mythical island in the Indian Ocean called Ceylon. No European had ever visited that far-away island.

Its pearls, brought precariously by canoe from the island to India, were extremely rare.

The tiara was worth a fortune. And Agnes loved it dearly.

But she never wore it in public.

It was too regal and Agnes never wanted anyone to accuse her of desiring to be a queen. Her love for Queen Marie was too great for such a consideration.

Chapter Twenty-Five

In April, 1447, there was a new crisis within the Church.

"I have to go off to Bourges," Charles told Agnes.

"What is happening in Bourges, Chatz?"

"Well, you know that after Pope Eugene's death, Nicolas was elected pope."

"Everyone in Christendom knows about our new pope," Agnes replied. "Is he coming to Bourges for some reason?"

"Yes he is."

"So, of course you must go pay your respects," Agnes said. "Bourges is only a couple of days' ride from here."

"It's more serious than that, Beauté. Felix' partisans are at it again," Charles told her.

"You mean there's a new possibility of schism?" Agnes asked.

"Exactly. Both Nicolas and Felix have agreed to meet in Bourges, along with the cardinals and the heads of state from all over Europe."

"Why these constant problems of popes and anti-popes, Chatz?" Agnes asked.

"Church politics, my dear," Charles sighed. "It's becoming increasingly necessary for the kings, princes, and dukes to resolve the petty conflicts within the papacy."

"The very fact that they chose a city in your kingdom to resolve the difficulty is a further proof that you are the most important ruler in the world," Agnes asserted.

Charles chose, modestly, not to respond. Agnes changed the subject.

"Will you be gone long this time, Chatz?"

"I fear the deliberations may take a couple of months."

"I'll miss you."

"Bourges isn't so far away," Charles mentioned. "I will manage to return to see you every couple of weeks."

"But, in the meantime, dear, you'll be away. And you do have your physical needs."

"I'll take my secretary, Guillaume Mariette with me. He'll not only serve as my secretary, but will warm my bed as my *mignon* as well. I'll be all right while I'm away from you."

"You've only had one *mignon* since we met," Agnes replied. "And that was when you were away in Basel."

"After I return from this conclave in Bourges, I hope I will never need one again."

The two were silent for a while.

"You'll be fine during my absence, Beauté," Charles assured Agnes. "I'm sure you will be quite safe here in Razilly."

Agnes thought about that for a moment.

"With you off in Bourges, dear, I don't really want to stay here. I would prefer to wait at home."

"Home? Oh, Loches?"

"That's where our children, Marie and Charlotte are," Agnes responded. "My mother lives there with them, and that's where I really want to be while you're away."

"Of course," Charles agreed. "With the children."

"My cousin, Antoinette, would like to get away from all the excitement of the court, Chatz," Agnes told him. "She'd like to take over the education of the children. And being with Marie and Charlotte all the time has become very tiring for maman."

"I had wondered if your mother wasn't getting a bit worn out with the children," Charles answered. "When your father died, she wanted to come down this way to be with her grand-children. But I wondered, myself, if it might not be too much for her. It might do her good to move from the castle to someplace near-by. There's that residence at Montresor, the hunting lodge...?"

"Chatz," Agnes exulted. "That would be just too perfect for maman. She would have her own home, and would be close enough to the children, and to Antoinette, to come and go as she pleased."

Before Charles set out for Bourges, Guillaume Mariette drew up the papers transferring ownership of Montresor into Catherine Sorel's name.

Charles himself accompanied Agnes and Antoinette to Loches.

Agnes was home again.

Catherine Sorel was dubious about the new residence being offered to her.

"A hunting lodge?" she asked. "Agnes, why would I want to go live in a hunting lodge? Don't you think I'm a bit old to go out every morning with my little bow and arrow looking for bunnies to toss into my stew?"

"Maman, maman. How you do put things," Agnes laughed. "Let's just go out to Montresor. Wouldn't you like to at least take a look at the property that's now yours?"

"If that's what you want me to do, I'll look," Catherine said resignedly. "But don't expect me to get myself a bow and some arrows before I go."

Agnes knew her mother. And understood her sense of humor. She had a pretty good idea of how this would all play out.

Charles left the whole matter in Agnes' hands. But as he left for Bourges, he was still chuckling at Dame Catherine's response to the offer of the property.

Dame Catherine, Agnes, and Antoinette rode out to Montresor, accompanied by Agnes' two oldest brothers. It was a half-hour ride.

As they approached the lodge, the servants — a major-domo, three maids, a cook, and two scullions — observed the group and hastily rushed outside. They lined up in greeting.

"Well, maman. What do you think?" Agnes asked.

"It looks charming, Agnes," Catherine answered. "But appearances can be deceiving you know."

The major-domo introduced Catherine to the staff.

Agnes could see that her mother was pleased.

"Let's go inside and look around, maman."

The major-domo, Alexandre, conducted them from room to room.

"What do you think now, maman?"

Catherine smiled a mischievous smile.

"It has possibilities, child," she said. "Quite livable as a matter of fact. And close enough to Loches that I can see my grand-children...and you too, of course...whenever I have a mind to pay a visit."

The truth was, Catherine Sorel was delighted with the residence at Montresor.

Back in Loches, a new situation arose. Nini was quite flustered. Agnes grew annoyed at her dithering.

"For Heaven's sake, Nini. You're driving me mad with your dithering. What's the matter with you?"

"Oh, Madame. I believe I'm in a family way."

"Nonsense, Nini," Agnes scolded. "You've thought you were in a 'family way' at least, let me think,...five times since I've known you. It's been a false signal every time."

"This time it's different, Madame," Nini answered.

"Different? How can it be different?"

"This time, I have missed my flux not for just one month, but for two."

"I grant you, that sounds more serious," Agnes agreed. "I'll contact one of the local midwives for a consultation."

A certain Nurse Emilie held a consultation with Nini and pronounced her pregnant.

So, afterward, Raimbaut asked for an audience with Agnes.

"Yes, Raimbaut. What is it?"

"You are aware, Madame, of Nini's condition," Raimbaut declared solemnly.

"Of course," Agnes agreed. "I remember that you have never particularly enjoyed the prospect of fatherhood."

"Madame is correct."

"And yet, you were perfectly aware that intimacies can produce families."

"Yes, Madame. The possible consequences were always quite clear to me."

"So, what is it you wish to say to me?" Agnes asked.

"If God has seen fit to bring a soul into this world through my agency, I wish to do the right and proper thing."

"You are saying you wish to marry Nini?"

"It is only right, Madame," Raimbaut affirmed.

"And do you love Nini, Raimbaut?"

"I am asking permission to marry her, Madame," Was Raimbaut's matter-of-fact answer.

Agnes did not wish to press the point any further.

"Is there any impediment to your marrying her?" Agnes asked.

"I would need the permission of my liege lord. And also of you, Madame."

"I see," Agnes informed him. "Of course. Well, rest assured, Raimbaut, that I give such a union my blessing. And when I next see the king I will urge him to agree to your request as well."

"Thank you, Madame," Raimbaut answered with a bow.

During Charles' next visit to Loches, Agnes told him about Raimbaut's petition to marry Nini.

"You say he really wants to marry her?" Charles asked.

"I didn't say he *wants* to marry her. I said he is asking for permission to marry her."

"I see," the king smiled. "And everyone is convinced that Nini has, indeed, conceived?"

"Considering how long the two of them have been gamboling in their two bedrooms, I'd say it was about time," Agnes stated. "But the answer to your question is a simple 'yes'."

"Then, of course I grant my permission," Charles agreed. "And, considering the two of them really are dear to us, what do you suggest we give them as a wedding present?"

"Have you ever visited their quarters here in Loches Castle, my dear?" Agnes asked.

"No, I can't say that I have."

"In each of their rooms, there is a narrow bed, suitable for only one person to sleep in," Agnes suggested.

Charles laughed his deep, hearty laugh.

"The poor dears. How uncomfortable they must have been all this time. It's a wonder Nini got pregnant at all."

Agnes made the necessary arrangements at Saint-Ours for the ceremony. It took place the next time the king was in Loches. The bride and bridegroom were very pleased to have the king and Agnes present to bless their union.

But they were even more pleased with the gift of the enormous bed that graced their new bedroom.

Part of Agnes' feeling of safety when residing at her home in Loches was the proximity of the Collegial Church of Saint-Ours. Even the gently falling rain that dominated springtime in the Indre Valley that year did not keep Agnes from visiting Saint-Ours several times a day. She still felt the special draw towards this church that had enticed her within its portals several years before.

It wasn't just the conical domes of the edifice that drew her, although they were lovely. It was a spirit that the building exuded. The same spirit she felt emanating from Loches Castle with its elegant turrets.

When she entered the portals of the church, she headed directly for the Chapel of the Madeleine. She had contributed generously to the church, and the results of her largesse were evident at every turn. But this chapel had been particularly blessed by her lavish contributions. The gilt-encrusted solid silver statue of Saint Mary-Magdalene was the most meaningful of the gifts. Agnes felt sheltered from the vicissitudes of fame and defamation under the saint's protection.

She would occasionally return from her sessions of prayer at Saint-Ours drenched from the rain. But she always felt a serenity that resulted from her devotions.

The Council of Bourges continued to hold sessions through the spring and summer. The meeting lasted five months. Months of intense and heated debate. But in September, all parties ended up agreeing with Charles that Nicholas V was truly pope. Felix publicly renounced his claim to the throne of Saint Peter.

With schism within the church averted again by the intervention of the secular rulers of Europe, Charles returned to Razilly.

There were many clerical type tasks left to be undertaken in Bourges. Guillaume Mariette remained there to take care of such details in the king's name.

Agnes left Loches Castle and her children in charge of her cousin Antoinette and proceeded back to Razilly.

It was in Razilly that Nini gave birth to a daughter. Agnes was present in the birthing room, and actively assisted the midwife.

The midwife handed the infant to one of her assistants to bathe in wine. Once the child was bathed and swaddled, she was handed to Agnes. The midwife and her other assistant got Nini cleaned up and back into bed from the birthing stool. Agnes brought the child and laid it in Nini's arms.

"Oh, Madame. She is lovely, is she not?"

"A very beautiful child, Nini," Agnes agreed.

"May I ask a favor of you, Madame?"

"Of course, Nini."

"Would it be improper of me to ask you if I could name her Agnes?" Nini requested.

Agnes was thrilled and flattered.

"I would be honored, Nini."

Nini pulled her daughter onto her breast and smiled down at her.

"So, little Agnes. Wouldn't you like your papa to visit you?"

Agnes stepped outside the door and ushered Raimbaut in to meet his daughter.

Chapter Twenty-Six

Charles felt that it was time to move the court back to Tours, to Ambroise Castle. Queen Marie was nearing the term of her next pregnancy, and had asked that the child be born at Ambroise.

So, early in the month of October, the court moved from Chinon to Ambroise.

The court had barely settled into Ambroise Castle when Charles was called upon by General Poton de Xantrailles who was serving the kingdom as Constable of France.

"Poton, old friend," Charles addressed him. "You appear distraught. Unusual for you, who always show such sangfroid in spite of every obstacle. I trust you are not unwell."

"Majesty. I'm not the one who is ill. There is a rottenness in your kingdom which none of us could have predicted."

"Let us be seated, then, Poton," the king invited. "It is clearly bad news you bring me."

The two men sat. Poton was clearly uncomfortable.

"Well, Poton," the king began. "I am ready to hear whatever it is you must tell me."

"Treason, my lord. High treason."

"And who is the culprit?"

"Your secretary, Majesty. Your notary."

"Not Mariette!" the king exclaimed.

"It seems incredible. But yes. Guillaume Mariette."

"Treason you say. Of what nature?" Charles asked.

Charles was clearly flustered. Mariette was one of his most trusted advisors. He was very intimate with his secretary. Treason on the part of such a person was unthinkable. Monstrous. Detestable.

"Tell me the nature of this accusation," Charles demanded, in a voice of despair that had not been heard from him since he had met Agnes.

"Guillaume left Bourges two days ago," Poton narrated. "Quite suddenly. He had been observed conferring with Gilles de Bozel at a tavern in Bourges, the Laurier d'Or."

"I know Gilles," the king said.

"A close friend of the dauphin," Poton added.

"Let us speak clearly, old friend. It is said that Gilles is my son's current 'favorite.'"

"So it is said," Constable Poton agreed. "For that reason, when he was spotted by my men as he sneaked surreptitiously into Bourges, he was under constant surveillance."

"I assume that the meeting between Mariette and Bozel raised suspicions," Charles opined.

"My agents are very alert, and can be very inconspicuous," Poton said. "And they have been very suspicious of Messire Gilles de Bozel."

"What then?"

"The next morning, Mariette abruptly left Bourges. Once he had departed, we...detained Bozel and subjected him to interrogation. Our agents also followed Mariette, who was arrested in your name in Montils."

"Come, come, Poton," Charles insisted. "Get right to the point."

"Your secretary, indeed the secretary of the Royal Council, was carrying very compromising papers."

"Which were...Come out with it man."

"They consisted, among other things, of a note from the dauphin to Duke Philippe of Burgundy," Poton explained. "In the letter, His Highness accuses the count of Evreux, Pierre de Breze, of attempting to govern the kingdom through the intermediation of Dame Agnes. To save the kingdom, the dauphin proposes to eliminate Breze and Dame Agnes, and to place Your Majesty in a monastery. He then plans to take over the crown himself. But to these ends, he solicits the assistance of Burgundy."

"Monstrous," the king moaned. "Good God! Louis, I know, is anxious for power. And he has done many things that even I, his father, find despicable. But this smacks of slander. I cannot believe my son would sink so low."

"I regret to bring this information to you, Sire," Poton stated. "I have seen the documents. And the interrogation of Messire Gilles in Bourges yielded the same information. That is of the dauphin's accusations against Breze and Dame Agnes. And...the rest of it as well."

"Very well, Poton," Charles informed him. "We shall get to the bottom of this. Have Mariette and Bozel brought to court. And summon the dauphin."

"Mariette and Bozel are in Tours already," Poton told him. "Under strict detention. Techniques of persuasion have already been applied. I will have the confessions available when Your Majesty may wish to review them."

"I want them now," Charles said.

"And Poton."

"Yes, Sire."

"I will personally preside at a trial concerning this matter to be held in the Throne Room Tuesday next."

"It will be done, Majesty."

The second Tuesday in November, 1447, the trial of one of the most notorious traitors in the history of France was held at Ambroise Castle.

Mariette and Bozel were brought into the Throne Room in chains. The dauphin appeared attired in his ceremonial garb as the Grand Dauphin de France. Poton de Xantrailles was in his uniform as Constable of France. Etienne Chevalier, who, for the present, had been elevated to the position of court secretary, was simply dressed as a clerk.

"Messire Chevalier," Poton said. "Please read the confession of Messire Guillaume Mariette."

Chevalier read the document.

"Is that, indeed, your confession, Messire Mariette?" the king asked.

"It is, Sire," Mariette admitted.

"And what do you have to say?"

"Sire, I ask for mercy," Secretary Mariette pleaded. "The dauphin, for years, has solicited me to commit treasonous acts against Your Majesty. He promised me great preferment if I were to aid and abet his plans. I always resisted his entreaties. Even his threats. His agent told me that if I carried certain documents to the Duke of Burgundy, I would be free of any further treasonous requests on his part. I did not know the nature of the documents and would have refused had I known."

The dauphin burst into tears.

"Father, father," he sighed. "Such lies. It is exactly the reverse. Over the years, Messire Mariette has pleaded with me to take the crown from you. He claimed he could prepare the way. I scoffed. It was beneath my dignity to even report his treason to you."

In the midst of Louis' sobs, Mariette, who had clearly been worn down by torture to secure his confession burst out:

"Liar, liar. His Highness lies. It was he who solicited me!"

"Silence!" Poton roared. "There will be suitable decorum before the person of His Majesty."

Charles was visibly shaken by the outbursts of his trusted secretary and his only legitimate son.

"Constable de Xantrailles," he ordered. "Let us hear the confession of Messire Gilles de Bozel."

Poton nodded to Chevalier to read this confession, which implicated both Mariette and Dauphin Louis.

Louis broke out in sobs again.

"Lies, lies, lies," Louis insisted. "General Poton has always hated me. He tortured Gilles to force him to say such things. It is not true, papa. It is not true."

When all the evidence had been presented, the king declared his sentence.

"Messire Gilles de Bozel."

Gilles dropped down on his knees and bowed his head.

"I find you guilty of treason against the Crown. Being a clement ruler, I spare your life. You had a treacherous hand in this infamous affair. Your right hand will be severed at the wrist. Your tongue was infamous in this affair. It shall be torn out by its roots. And your face, that has fronted this treachery shall be disfigured by having your nose severed from its base. You will, in such condition, be turned loose upon the world to fend as best you can. Your properties are confiscated to become part of the holdings of the Crown."

Gilles was hauled away, apparently in a daze.

"Guillaume Mariette!" the king called out.

Guillaume fell to his knees and bowed his head.

"Your conduct is the most despicable I have ever encountered. You have been the secretary of your king and of the Royal Council. All matters of state, both public and private, were entrusted to you over many years. Your treason is reprehensible. One week from today, in the city of Tours, at Place Charlemagne, before the assemblage of the court, I sentence you to be drawn and quartered."

"But the dauphin made me do it," Mariette sobbed as he was dragged from the room.

"And to you, Dauphin Louis," the king continued.

Louis did not drop to his knees, but his legs quivered so that he could scarcely stand.

"As Grand Dauphin of France, you may suffer no physical harm, regardless of your actions. But I banish you from my kingdom to the Dauphiné for four months, the full extent of punishment allowable in the Kingdom of France."

"Not exile, Father!" Louis pled.

"Be warned, Dauphin Louis," his father ordered. "If you are not quit of our domain prior to the commencement of the new year, you will suffer house arrest for the full term of this sentence."

The dauphin was in tears as he left the courtroom, saying, "I am innocent. It is Pierre de Breze who should be punished."

The entire court gathered in Tours, at Place Charlemagne, which was shadowed by Charlemagne's Tower and the Vieux Horloge. The center of the square was left clear except for four black destriers and their grooms. In addition to the courtiers present, as many townspeople as could crowd into the additional space were allowed as spectators to the grand event.

A hush fell over the crowd as a pathway was cleared for the horse-drawn open cart to pass through. In the cart, bound by ropes tied securely to his wrists and ankles, stood Guillaume Mariette, stripped naked before the crowd.

Mariette was rudely hauled off the cart to the jeers of the crowd. The horses were led to the condemned, and the ropes attached to the horses.

At a drumroll, the horses were led, very slowly, away from Mariette, one to the North, one to the South, one to the East, and one to the West. As the ropes tightened, Mariette fell hard on the pavement of the square. Soon, the drumbeats could not be heard over the shouts of the assemblage. Mariette's screams were muffled. As his joints were pulled apart, no one but the grooms could hear the snapping. As his limbs were torn from his body, those closest to the scene of the execution could hear his agonized screams.

Many in the crowd laughed hard at the spectacle. But no one laughed as heartily as the dauphin.

Two weeks after Mariette's execution, Queen Marie gave birth to a son.

King Charles rushed to the birthing room. Marie was already back in her bed from the birthing stool.

"Marie, Marie, my dear. You are all right?"

"I am fine, Charles," Queen Marie assured him. "And what is even more important, our son is robust and healthy."

Charles shot a glance at the physician and at the midwife. They nodded their heads in agreement.

Mistress Alyce, the midwife, beckoned the monarch towards the cradle. The king looked down at his newborn son and was mightily pleased.

He returned to the queen's bedside.

"The child does appear to be healthy, my love."

"Let us name him Charles," the queen said.

The newborn prince was baptized the next week at Tours Cathedral amid great pomp. He was declared Duke of Berry and was to be called Charles of France.

Poton was in attendance at the ceremony with Etienne Chevalier.

"How good it is to have a second prince in the land, is it not, Poton?" Chevalier asked.

"Yes," Poton agreed. "And a fearsome thing. The dauphin does not leave for two more days. In the interim, I have placed the tightest security possible about the Duke of Berry."

"Yes," Chevalier observed. "The mortality rate of Louis' rivals to the throne has been extraordinary, has it not?"

On the last day of December, 1447, the dauphin left Tours for his province. He did not take leave of his father before he left.

At the city gates, a crowd gathered around him. He rose up on his horse and removed his hood from his head.

Addressing the awed crowd, he proclaimed:

"I swear by this unhooded head, I will avenge myself against those who have driven me from my home!"

And with those words, Dauphin Louis rode through the great gates towards his province in the mountainous eastern region of France. He rode on to Grenoble, the capital of the Dauphiné.

Everyone at court took Louis' threat seriously.

Chapter Twenty-Seven

Dauphin Louis was able to carry out his vendetta against his enemies from his capital in Grenoble. His weapon was one of the most effective in courtly politics — calumny.

A stream of slanderous rumors oozed out of the Dauphiné. The juicier and the more wicked the libels, the better. Dauphin Louis had agents, friends, and toadies throughout the kingdom. And, of course, they were rife at court.

The treasonous letter carried by Mariette did, of course, show the dauphin's treachery. But the accusation contained in it that suggested Breze's overweening lust for power struck many of the king's subjects as having some validity. Therefore Louis directed his calumnies principally against Breze. He reasoned that if Breze could be brought down, Agnes, Coeur, and Chevalier would be easy to destroy.

Louis also spread canards linking Agnes and Breze sexually, Agnes and Coeur in financial chicanery, and Agnes and Chevalier in treasonous communication with France's enemies. Myriad permutations on those themes abounded not only at the royal court but at all the provincial courts as well. But the most persistent theme was that Breze was preparing to overthrow the monarchy and rule the state himself as a despot.

Poton and Breze were at Evreux Castle, strolling in the rose garden. It was April, 1448.

"And do your agents sense any lessening of these slanders, Poton?" Breze was asking.

"The malice is growing stronger, Breze, not weaker," Poton informed

Pierre. "Our Lord Dauphin has cells in every court. The network consists of attractive, witty, unprincipled young men. Each one a rumor factory in himself. I fear you are being very greatly maligned. There is more resentment against your rise in power than anyone could have forecast."

"And somehow Coeur, Chevalier, and Dame Agnes are being besmirched at the same time?" Breze asked.

"The dauphin swore to punish those he sees as his enemies. He is very effective," Poton affirmed.

"You have been close to the seat of power from the outset of the king's own ascendance. What would you suggest I do to encounter this enemy?" Breze asked. "I understand warfare well. But I am not skilled in this kind of battle."

"Your best recourse is to drive this whole matter out into the open," Poton suggested. "As long as it is waged in surreptitious gossip, you cannot win."

"And how do I do that?"

"Insist on being tried," Poton advised. "Ask to have your case tried by the Parliament of Paris. Have all accusations against you presented there."

"I understand," Breze informed the constable. "If I have committed any crime, let it be proved."

"Right. If claims against you be not proved, suspicion against you will be openly, publicly expunged."

"The problem, Poton, is that, as you so well know, there are still pockets of English resistance in the North. The king has sent orders dispatching me to launch another phase of the reconquest of our land."

"No matter," Poton advised. "Declare you are prepared and ready to be made a prisoner that you may face all accusations against you. The king will do what he has to do. Leave all in the hands of our sovereign."

Breze went directly to the royal court and explained his desire.

"My dear count," the king said. "I understand your need to uphold your honor. You are as noble a knight as any in the kingdom of France. I will submit your case to the Parliament of Paris as you ask. I am absolutely sure of your innocence against any charge of treason. And I am confident the Parliament will find you innocent as well. Your courage in choosing this course is most commendable.

"But I will not agree that you be made a prisoner during the trial. The kingdom needs you leading our troops in the North to put an end to the long, unjust occupation of our territories.

"Therefore, the trial shall be held. But you will be serving France militarily, with distinction, during the session."

The trial was ordered by the king. And even before the session began, Breze was leading his troops north.

The matter was not much discussed between Agnes and Charles. The details were well known and the outcome of the trial a foregone conclusion.

The king and his mistress were sensually whiling away a Sunday afternoon in a sylvan meadow in the countryside. The meadow was located in the royal deer preserve that was not only fenced off for some miles around but that was further protected from intrusion by posted guards.

The couple had brought a picnic basket containing cheese, fruit, bread, and wine.

It was a bright sunny day and for their *déjeuner dans l'herbe* they had removed their clothing.

"How free it feels," Agnes declared. "No one around for miles. It's quite freeing for the soul. Don't you think so Chatz?"

Chatz was slathering some cheese on a slice of bread.

"No one around, you say Beauté? When I was a boy, I used to run around naked in the royal preserves. And I pretended that I was not the dauphin. That I was a wild animal, free of the problems imposed on me by my mad father and the fawning courtiers. I was an animal. A wild animal. And I believed I had a bond with the other animals in the preserve. Those were healing sessions for me."

"It is true, Chatz," Agnes opined. "After all, we *are* animals."

Chatz ogled her gorgeous tits. "Ah, yes," he sighed. "We are most definitely mammals."

He set his slathered bread down on the blanket.

He crawled towards her, exclaiming, "And I *do* love being a mammal."

He encircled her with his arms and suckled those tasty nipples.

She lowered herself onto the grass as he climbed atop her. He allowed himself an orgy of sucking first on one tit, then on another.

"Since we're animals," he suggested. "Let's do it like the other animals do. We humans are the only animals I know of that can fuck belly to belly. Let's forget we're humans for now."

Agnes realized what he was hinting at.

"All right," she squealed. "That sounds like fun. Just one thing, though, Chatz. I don't think any of the other male animals ever hits the wrong hole."

"If my prick cannot find your cunt from the rear, Beauté, I will surrender my crown."

The tit sucking had aroused them both enough that no further foreplay was needed. Agnes' twat was well saturated and primed for entry.

Agnes rolled over onto all fours, wiggling her ass, playing the female animal in heat.

Chat assumed the all-fours position and made growling noises at her as he stalked around on the ground. She answered with mewing, come-and-get-me tones.

When he was in reaching distance, he dropped character since he could not resist rising up on his knees so he could caress the sweetest ass in Christendom.

"Down boy," Agnes snarled.

Chatz returned to character and brought his hands down onto the ground as he grandly mounted her.

As he penetrated her cunt he emitted a loud roar.

As he pumped away, however, his left hand left the ground, encircled her, and his finger found purchase on her clit.

Ever so gently, as always, the king massaged that lovely nub and, with a duet of growls, the couple came simultaneously.

The act completed, they lay on the grass on their backs and broke out in joyous laughter.

When they recovered, they were in an expansive mood.

It was the right moment to bring up a subject that was very much on Agnes' mind.

Agnes said, "Chatz. My dear Chatz. I would very much like to go on pilgrimage to the Shrine of Saint Genevieve in Paris. I yearn to pray there. And, besides, I need to check on how things are being managed at my estate of Beauté-sur-Marne."

Charles understood the request. He knew that Agnes was aware that Breze's trial in Paris was equally a trial about her, even though it was not so stated.

"It is a very courageous thing you are proposing, you know, my dear," Charles replied. "In all the kingdom there is no city, no region, less loyal to myself and to my interests than Paris.

"When Joan of Arc was captured by the Burgundians, the powers in Paris supported Burgundy and England against the Maid. The Parisians always found life sweet under English occupation. They collaborated with the enemy quite openly and cheerfully. Now that we have won the war against the Goddams, there is resentment toward us. And that means you may not be well received in Paris."

"I know, Chatz," Agnes said. "I did not make the decision that I wanted to go there whimsically. But I don't believe I should live in fear of anyone or any place in France. And I truly desire to do this."

Charles agreed with her:

"Then God go with you, Beauté. I would like you to talk to Jacques Coeur before you go. He has many commercial contacts in Paris. You might find them helpful."

Chatz and Agnes put their clothes back on, finished off the picnic, and returned to court.

Charles insisted that an enormous retinue accompany Agnes. Guilhem Raimbaut was present, as always, as her personal guard. There were soldiers, knights, ladies, abundant servants including Nini, grooms, and porters.

On the way to the great city, the group stopped at Beauté-sur-Marne. At the estate, there was barely enough room to accommodate the party.

Agnes made a minute inspection of her estate with the major-domo. She was disappointed at the many inefficiencies that she perceived. The grounds were somewhat shabby in places. The kitchen was improperly stocked. There was even dust in some corners of the guest quarters.

Her disappointment was apparent. But she took no action at the time. She planned to discuss the problems with the king when she returned.

From Beauté-sur-Marne, the cavalcade moved on to Paris. It entered by the great gate of Saint Jacques. The city was protected at that gate by a double moat and a wall thirty feet high.

Once through the city gate, the large party had difficulty moving up Rue Saint Jacques. The street was crowded with mobs of people about their daily business. No attempt had been made by the city authorities to clear the way. Rowdy students shouted abuse at Agnes and her party. Among the phrases she heard hurled at her were, "Behold the king's bitch." "The bitch is dressed like the queen of the whores," "Let's see some more of those titties, Sweetie."

The guard accompanying Agnes began to club the protesters, but Agnes intervened demanding no violence against the mobs. She felt that violence would merely incite the Parisians against her even more.

Agnes had not expected such overt antagonism. Nowhere else in France had the opposition to her been so obvious. The entire party was nervous. The response of the Parisian populace had been sadly underestimated. It seemed these people still must feel more sympathy for the English enemy than respect for the court of France.

The retinue continued on, crossed the Seine, and proceeded on to Les Tournelles, the previous residence of the Duke of Bedford where Charles had stayed at his triumphal entrance to Paris. It was the most elegant residence in Paris by far.

The neighborhood around the residence was quiet, respectful, and genteel. A relief to Agnes' whole party. The building itself was enormous and very well fortified.

Once inside, Agnes felt safe. She spent the rest of the first day, and all of the next, resting in her elegant suite.

Les Tournelles had twelve inner courtyards with cloistered galleries. There was a steam room, a library, and a zoo inside the walls. The gardens, pools, and even woods constituted a world quite apart from the bustling city outside. In this enclosed space, Agnes regained her composure. She realized that it had been a mistake to enter Paris dressed elaborately. When she walked out the well guarded side gate the next day, accompanied only by Raimbaut, she was simply dressed and Raimbaut wore neither uniform nor livery. An unpretentious carriage awaited them. No one would suspect Agnes and Raimbaut of being the notorious royal mistress and her personal guard.

They visited the showplaces of the city. First, Agnes wanted to go to Notre-Dame de Paris, and then to the exquisite Sainte-Chapelle. Her carriage next took her to the Louvre, which was the most beautiful castle she had ever seen. But she agreed that Les Tournelles was much more livable.

She returned to the student neighborhood of the Latin Quarter where she had been so rudely received just days before. She was not recognized. She purposely avoided visiting the Parliament. That would be a separate trip, and not a pleasure jaunt.

On her outing the next day, Agnes visited the marketplaces of the city. They were unrivaled anywhere in Europe. At the Halle aux Champeaux she made herself known to the merchants who were associates of Jacques Coeur. She shopped for gloves, lace, headdresses, furs, and perfumes. She purchased dolls and toys for her daughters. Everything would be delivered to Beauté-sur-Marne for her to re-examine later. She wandered along the maze of narrow streets on the Ile-de-la-Cité, admiring the wares of the perfumeries, flower merchants, bookbinders, bird-sellers, and bootmakers. She found that she loved much of Paris. But she was still wary of the Parisians.

On the following day, accompanied by a coterie of knights and ladies, Agnes visited Parliament Palace. She was quite gratified by her reception there by the judges and lawyers. It seemed these functionaries knew quite well that their loyalty had better show itself well disposed towards the House of Valois. Agnes was fawned over even more lavishly by the members of the Parliament than by the merchants.

She invited key members to Les Tournelles for dinner and entertainments. She was less than subtle in letting them know what the decision needed to be in the Breze case. That is, if they wanted to retain hold of their judgeships.

Agnes devoted a full two weeks to politicking, lobbying, entertaining, and cajoling the influential judges. At the end of the first week in May, the Parliament not only found Pierre de Breze innocent. It wrote accolades. The verdict included praise for his excellence as a military commander and for his many services rendered to the kingdom. It refuted, in detail, each of the slanders that had been spread against him.

The day after the favorable verdict, Agnes made the pilgrimage that had been the announced purpose of her trip to Paris. She proceeded to the Abbey of Saint Genevieve, the city's patron saint. She prayed, gave thanks, and left a very generous donation.

On May 10th she and her retinue left Paris. Her trip had been very successful.

The cortege returned to Beauté-sur-Marne. Her criticisms of the procedures of the staff had clearly found their way to the king. For every single irregularity had already been righted. She took a full day to review the purchases she had made in Paris, and had those items not destined for Beauté-sur-Marne forwarded to Loches.

After a week of relaxation and entertainments at Beauté, the cavalcade returned to Touraine.

In May, 1449, Agnes found that she was pregnant again. She was delighted and Charles was overjoyed. Their children constituted a tangible expression of the immense love the king felt for the woman who truly made him feel like a king. He knew he was the victorious hero his people believed him to be because the woman he loved had made him kingly.

As France grew stronger and more opulent in the peace, the English interest in re-occupying the continent returned. Henry VI and his French royal wife were interested in maintaining the peace. But public opinion waxed stronger and stronger for the English troops that still lingered in France to remain, and be reinforced.

The incident that renewed conflict was the non-evacuation of the Goddams from Le Mans.

The English had promised, at Marguerite d'Anjou's wedding to Henry VI, to remove their troops from Le Mans. But the English Captain Townsend, governor of Le Mans, was both intractable and cantankerous. He remained there with his troops. Pierre de Breze was sent to liberate the city. He drove the English out, but the English went on a rampage, pillaging the countryside, proceeded to Brittany, laid siege to the city of Fougeres, and sacked it.

Charles VII was holding court at Chinon. He decided that a renewal of full hostilities was inevitable. Under General Poton, France had built up a formidable infantry during the "peace." The 8,000 well-trained archers were superb and ready for action.

And Jacques Bureau, whom Agnes had championed, had developed the first safe cannon ever produced. Unlike the previous firearms, these war engines did not blow up killing the troops rather than the enemy. They brought unrivaled fire power to France. And Bureau had developed a light catapult, easily maneuverable, called the Snake. It could rapid-fire eighty pound cannon balls. The artillery combination surpassed any weaponry yet developed anywhere. Charles called the infantry, archers, artillery, and cavalry to action.

The English troops that still remained in France were tired, discouraged, poorly armed, and underpaid.

Charles decided on all-out war against the remnant of the English occupation.

Chapter Twenty-Eight

On August 6, Charles VII personally led his army to fight the final battles of the Hundred Years War. In every battle, Pont-Audemer, Pont-l'Eveque, Lisieux, Bernay, Mantes, Vernon, and Rouen, the French were victorious. When the city of Vernon fell, Charles declared his mistress, Agnes Sorel, Lady of Vernon-sur-Seine and sent her the keys to the city.

Most of the English had by then been driven from French soil. Charles VII the Victorious was hailed throughout the land. Even in Paris. He had re-earned the laurels that declared him "The Victorious." There remained but one pocket of English resistance. And that was the stronghold of Harfleur, that had been under English domination for a hundred years.

Charles VII spent Christmas in Jumièges, in the north of France, within striking distance of Harfleur. He was there as leader of the finest army in the world. The most advanced military technology was at his disposal. His army's morale was at an all-time high since it had consistently won one battle after another over a demoralized enemy.

News of her lover's string of victories heartened Agnes at her comfortable, beloved home in Loches.

The Feast of the Epiphany, January 6, 1450 began as the most joyful of days. On Christmas Eve, a fierce snowstorm had assailed France. The intense cold had lingered on. A severe snowstorm still raged outside. But inside Loches Castle every fireplace was ablaze. Agnes had prepared special seasonal sweetmeats for the children. Agnes' mother was spending the holiday season at the castle with Agnes, the children, and Antoinette. Master Poictevin and Midwife Louise

Malherbe were staying at the castle to attend to Agnes' approaching parturition. They were accepted in the festivities as though part of the family. Loches Castle was alive with laughter and the joys of the Noël season. Marie was fourteen years old and Charlotte would soon be twelve. They were much too old to believe that the gifts piled up in the Great Hall had been left by the Magi. But they knew that real kings had, indeed, been responsible for the lovely presents.

The family group was enjoying the mid-day feast when Jules, the major-domo entered the dining room.

"Madame. Messire Antoine de Chabannes has arrived and seeks audience with you."

Agnes was astonished.

"Chabannes has come to Loches through this blizzard?! Astounding. Show him in immediately, Jules."

Chabannes had been left by the king at Chinon to be in charge of security of the castle there. It seemed incredible that he would choose to travel from Chinon to Loches in such weather.

When Chabannes entered the room, he was clearly not only still trembling from the cold, he was disheveled from travel and appeared distraught. Agnes determined it would not be wise to talk to him in front of the children.

"Come, Antoine," she said to him. "Let us repair to the library. Jules. Bring a pitcher of hot mulled wine and some viands to the library for Messire de Chabannes."

When they arrived at the library, Raimbaut was already there. He was always within range when anyone who might cause harm to Agnes was present. Since the Mariette case, no one was above suspicion.

Chabannes stood before the fireplace warming himself. He soon had the hot wine in hand and took a moment while sipping to regain his composure. Agnes sat at a table and patiently waited for her visitor to refresh himself from what had clearly been an arduous voyage.

"Dame Agnes," Chabannes began. "I have come in haste to warn you that there is a plot afoot to assassinate both you and the king."

"There are always suspected plots, Antoine," Agnes replied. "What is special about this one that caused you to brave this dreadful weather?"

"This time, there is more than suspicion and rumors, Madame," Chabannes told her. "I have spies in the Dauphiné. I just received intelligence from them that the dauphin has gained access within the Royal Guard. The plan is to have the king killed by officers His Majesty trusts implicitly.

"And the dauphin's agents are attempting to suborn even those on the staff here at Loches Castle. I am not able to get word to the king yet concerning the plot. But I felt impelled to let you know immediately that your life is in danger."

"I appreciate your concern, Antoine," Agnes replied. "I am confident of my own safety with Raimbaut in attendance here. He will be doubly alert now. But when will you be able to inform the king about the imminent danger to his person?"

"As soon as humanly possible, Madame," Chabannes assured her. "But with the weather such as it is? I cannot really say when."

Agnes panicked at Chabannes' news about the danger to the king. She invited him to accompany her to the dining room to explain to the family the news that he brought.

"I would be honored, Madame," he said. "But I must return immediately to Chinon to see if there is any way to inform the king of the danger he is in."

"Back out into the storm, Antoine?"

"Regretfully, yes," he answered. "I must brook no delay."

With that, Chabannes took his leave.

Agnes was very emotional when she returned to the dining room. Raimbaut accompanied her.

"Mother, children," she began. "I have just been informed that the king is in grave danger. I must go to Jumièges to warn him."

"Go to Jumièges, child!?" her mother exclaimed. "You can't go traipsing off. Not in this weather. Not in your condition."

Raimbaut entered his concern:

"Madame, I do not trust Messire Chabannes. There is something that does not ring true here. I beg you to trust His Majesty's intelligence sources to warn him if he is in danger. A trip to Jumièges by you poses a far greater danger to you than anything confronting the king."

"No, no, Raimbaut. I know what I must do. Inform Jules that I desire a coach to be prepared for me."

"But Madame..."

"Do not argue with me, Raimbaut," Agnes replied curtly. "Be so kind as to remember your place."

Raimbaut obeyed Agnes' order and reluctantly went to inform the major-domo of the wishes of the lady of the castle. But he harbored great doubts concerning Chabannes and his real intentions.

"Madame, I protest," Master Poictevin said. "To attempt a voyage of such length and difficulty in this inclement weather will not only jeopardize your health, but that of your unborn child...The child of our sovereign. I plead with you, Madame. Heed Raimbaut's advice. The king is well protected, I am sure."

"I will do what I will do, Master Poictevin," Agnes snapped. "If you are reticent to accompany me, I will go save the king without you. And, if necessary, without midwife. But go to Jumièges I will."

There was no arguing with the mistress of the castle. She was in a frenzy and would not listen to reason.

Charlotte began to cry and ran to her grandmother.

"Agnes," Catherine protested. "See how you're frightening the children. You are needed here, not in some remote place far from your little ones. As your mother, I..."

"No, mother," Agnes retorted. "You are the one frightening the children. While I am gone, you and Antoinette will be here to take care of them."

"All right then, Agnes," Antoinette said firmly. "If you insist on this mad and senseless trip, I will not remain behind. I see you are determined. Very well. So am I."

Two carriages were prepared. Agnes and Antoinette shared the lead carriage. Master Poictevin, Nurse Louise, Raimbaut and Nini followed. Raimbaut chose six of the archers who were protecting Loches Castle to ride beside the carriage to provide protection for the king's mistress. The archers did not complain or grumble, but knew that to ride their horses through such weather was likely to be more lethal than service in the front lines against the English.

The group, covered with furs and wool carpets, huddled in their carriages. They had charcoal heated foot warmers. The leather curtains, however, could not keep out the bitter cold. Agnes shivered every moment of the trip.

The voyage lasted eight days. Some nights, their stay was in peasant hovels. Once they were fortunate enough to stop at an inn. That was at Chateaudun. Another night they stayed at the castle at Beauvais, a place Agnes knew from her youth.

At length, the party arrived at Jumièges. Three of the archers had been left behind along the way, close to death from exposure. New drivers for the carriages had to be conscripted four times for the same reason.

Agnes was in a physical condition that alarmed Master Poictevin greatly.

She was very pale, emaciated looking, and could not stop shivering. The others in the group were not in much better shape. They were frozen, chapped, and in dismal spirits.

The king's headquarters were at the Abbey of Jumièges. The carriages pulled up before the abbey door. Raimbaut jumped out of the carriage, charged up to the door, and knocked repeatedly. It took a good quarter of an hour before anyone answered from inside. The door finally creaked open and an elderly Benedictine monk peered out.

"Come, come now," he said. "Such a racket out there. It is not becoming."

"Open the door, Brother," Raimbaut ordered. "We have some ill and weary pilgrims out here."

"What is the nature of these pilgrims?"

"Dame Agnes Sorel and her companions."

"Dame...? A female?" the monk replied, alarmed. "No, no. It is impossible. No women are allowed within the abbey. There never have been, nor can there be."

The brother attempted to close the crack, but Raimbaut butted himself against the door, knocking the elderly monk back. The monk came very close to falling.

"Bring the lady inside," Raimbaut commanded the archers.

With great difficulty, they got Agnes out of the carriage and lifted her into the abbey. The monk kept protesting that what was happening was quite improper.

Raimbaut demanded of the protesting monk, "Is His Majesty here at present?"

"Yes," the alarmed friar replied. "He cannot be disturbed."

"Go! Immediately!" Raimbaut demanded. "Tell him Agnes Sorel is here in a most parlous condition. Hurry old man. It is the king's mistress you are keeping waiting."

"The king's mistress? Dear, dear." the elderly monk muttered.

The monk ran off mightily distressed.

The entry room the arriving group was in gave protection from the intense cold outside. But warm it was not.

The harried monk went directly to Charles to complain.

"Agnes? Agnes Sorel?" King Charles asked.

"That's what the young man said," the monk answered. "I told him you were not to be disturbed. And that no women are ever allowed..."

Charles didn't let the Benedictine finish his sentence, but rushed to the entry vestibule.

"Agnes! Are you all right?" he called out.

"Dame Agnes has immediate need for warmth," Master Poictevin explained without invoking any royal protocol.

"What are you waiting for? Get her to the refectory immediately," the king ordered.

As the archers literally carried Agnes into the inner rooms of the abbey, Charles was rubbing Agnes' hands and saying endearing words to her.

"You!" Charles commanded a novitiate. "Throw more logs into the fireplace! Now! Can't you hear? Move!"

The befuddled young man scarcely knew what to do when ordered by the king. One of the brothers took him by the hand and led him to the pile of wood and helped him throw logs on the fire.

Master Poictevin went directly to the kitchen to get hot water to mix with wine, honey, and camphor. He began spooning the potion into Agnes' mouth.

Antoinette talked to the abbot who made his entrance as the hubbub was going on. She asked where she could find blankets that were at least room temperature or warmer.

Agnes couldn't utter a word, her teeth were chattering so. Charles remained at her side, holding her hand. Gradually she became warmer and her trembling stopped. Then she fell into a very deep sleep.

She was taken to the king's quarters and tucked into his bed.

Charles sat up the whole afternoon and night as his mistress slept.

Master Poictevin entered the chambers every couple of hours.

"Will she be all right?" the king asked.

"Your Majesty," the physician answered. "I must inform you that her situation is grave. I warned her that a voyage in her condition and in this weather was most ill-advised. But she insisted she had to inform Your Majesty of some possible threatened harm."

Poictevin was not reassured by the routine examinations he made during the night.

Dom Xavier, the abbot, came to check on Agnes' condition and to talk to Charles.

"How goes our patient, Sire?" he asked.

"The physician seems concerned," Charles answered. "But she seems to me to be resting well, thank you."

"We are most gratified by Your Majesty's choice to grace our abbey with your presence during your military campaign, Sire. But..."

"You needn't explain, Dom Xavier," the king advised the abbot. "I know that the rule of your order prohibits the presence of women within the abbey."

"Your Majesty, the rule of Christian charity always overrides the rules of our order," Dom Xavier explained. "Of course we offer succor to the ill lady.

"What I was going to say is that our order has a retreat house, Mesnil Manor, less than a league from here."

"Of course," Charles answered. "I am well aware of Mesnil Manor. I believe that it would be an ideal spot for Dame Agnes to recuperate in."

"I came here to your quarters this evening to declare that the manor is at your disposal whenever the physician feels it is safe to move the lady," the abbot informed the king.

"A very generous offer, Father," Charles replied. "Thank you."

The next morning, when Agnes awoke, Charles was still by her side. She was very pale and too weak to get out of bed. Nurse Louise came to take care of her morning needs. Antoinette brought in some porridge. Agnes was able to swallow four spoonfuls. Master Poictevin brought in a goblet of a steaming potion. She was not able to swallow any of it.

When Poictevin, Louise, and Antoinette left the room, Agnes summoned the strength to tell Charles of her concerns. She told him about Chabannes' visit to Loches, and about the dauphin's plot.

Charles patted her hand.

"Oh, my Beauté! That you should have made this perilous trip because of that fool Chabannes. He did a very foolish thing coming to you with such a tale and upsetting you. Alarming you so much that you felt obliged to risk your life because of a rumor.

"I hear a dozen rumors a day that there are plots against me. And, it turns out that some of them are true. This one about my son having suborned my highest officers — that one has been checked very carefully.

"There was, indeed, an attempt to turn my closest officers against me. My own spies became aware of the plot and the perpetrators have been apprehended, tortured, and executed. The dauphin remains banished in the Dauphiné. I assure you, there is no need for you to be concerned."

Agnes listened and clung on to every word. She felt assured that her lover was safe from harm. She was relieved.

By noon, the weather had cleared somewhat. Master Poictevin declared that if the patient were wrapped up sufficiently, she could be moved.

At noon, Agnes, Antoinette, Midwife Louise, Nini, Master Poictevin and Raimbaut were moved to Mesnil Manor. A guard of twenty archers accompanied the convoy.

The king rode in the carriage with Agnes, clasping her tightly the whole way.

Chapter Twenty-Nine

Mesnil Manor was a long, open-beamed, two story edifice with a slate roof. It was flanked by eight turrets. As the group entered, the warmth of the place was felt immediately.

Agnes was carried to her room on the second floor. It was simple but warm and comfortable. The bed had silk sheets, wool blankets, and extensive furs on it.

Antoinette and Nini bathed, lotioned, and perfumed Agnes and positioned her in bed. Then the king entered, kissed her, and told her he had to return to the siege of Harfleur, but would return to her bedside every evening.

The kitchen staff had prepared a rich nourishing soup for Agnes and a hearty meal for the rest of the company. Agnes was able to sip some of the soup.

Before he left the manor, the king asked Master Poictevin about Agnes' condition. He was told that the trip had been devastating to a woman close to term in her pregnancy. The cold, the jerkiness of the route, the uncomfortable layovers, and the length of the trip were all contributors to undermining her health. The king was very concerned. But he had a war to wage, and had to go attend to the battle.

After a few days, Agnes began to feel better. She was still pale and weak, and spent most of the day in bed. But she got out of bed and walked some around the Manor at the end of a week. Every evening Charles came to see her and told her about the progress of the siege. Bureau's cannons and catapults continued to hammer at the walls of Harfleur. There was no defense against them.

When Charles was not with her, Agnes gave in to her lethargy and despondency. Around her lover, she made the effort to appear alert and cheerful.

On February 2, Agnes felt the first labor pains.

Nini fetched Master Poictevin and Louise Malherbe, the midwife.

Agnes' previous deliveries had not really been difficult. The labor this time was hard. She was still very fatigued from her traveling and unable to help much. The labor lasted hours, painful, wretched hours. Eventually, a very frail daughter, weighing less than four pounds, entered the world.

Master Poictevin doubted the infant would live. Midwife Louise knew for a certainty the little girl would not survive.

Nini, Antoinette, and Louise bathed, perfumed, and lotioned Agnes. Nini scoured away every trace of blood. Antoinette arranged the fresh silk sheets on the bed and Louise, with Antoinette's assistance, led Agnes to the bed. The fragile new-born girl in the crib was losing her battle to stay alive.

Agnes was exhausted and despondent.

It was evening before the king was able to get to Agnes' side. He glanced at the crib and then at Master Poictevin. The crib was empty. In response to the king's unanswered question, the physician nodded "yes." The child had died.

Charles sat up with Agnes until she fell asleep, then left to return to Jumièges.

About four hours after midnight, Agnes' moans aroused the midwife who felt Agnes' forehead. Agnes was obviously feverish and perspiring heavily. Master Poictevin was summoned. He called for snow to be brought in from outside to be placed on Agnes' abdomen. The cold caused her to cringe with pain. Master Poictevin gave her warm milk steeped in poppy pods. The potion lessened the discomfort and allowed her to sleep.

The following days were filled with pain. The king asked what was ailing Agnes.

"It is puerperal fever," Master Poictevin replied.

"What can be done?"

"There is no cure. Few survive. We are doing everything we can," the physician responded.

The king, who under Agnes' guidance, had become strong, a leader, even a warrior, could not bring himself to come see his mistress under these woeful conditions.

On the morning of February 14, 1450, before dawn, Agnes called for a confessor. After confession, the last rites were received. As the sun rose, the most beautiful woman in the world became one with Eternity. She was thirty-four years old.

Afterword

By order of the king, Agnes Sorel was buried in the crypt of the Collegial Church of Saint-Ours in Loches. Her heart and breasts were interred beneath the statue of Saint Mary Magdalene in the Madeleine Chapel.

Every Valentine's Day, for the rest of his life, Charles VII repaired to the Chapel and placed flowers in the alabaster vase brought there from Agnes' oratory at Loches Castle.

Six months after Agnes' death, her cousin, Antoinette de Maignelay, became Royal Mistress of Charles VII.

Dauphin Louis introduced accusations against Jacques Coeur, Pierre de Breze, and Etienne Chevalier to the Parliament of Paris through Count François de Montberon. Montberon presented evidence that Jacques Coeur had poisoned Agnes Sorel. Master Poictevin presented contrary evidence that it was puerperal fever that had been the cause of her death. Montberon, the more powerful man, prevailed and Jacques Coeur was sentenced to prison and his extensive wealth and holdings were transferred into the royal treasury.

With Coeur's fall in power, Pierre de Breze and Etienne Chevalier continued to be suspect, but were never prosecuted. De Breze retreated to his castle in Evreux, retiring from public service. Chevalier became a professor at the University of Poitiers.

Antoine de Chabannes was suspected by many of treachery against Agnes Sorel. The true motivation of his trip to Loches Castle in the winter storm was never determined. He became a member of the "inner circle" when the dauphin became king.

In 1461, Charles VII died. The Dauphin ascended the throne as Louis XI, known to history as Louis the Cruel and as "the Spider King."

Louis XI converted Loches Castle into an infamous prison that housed anyone who displeased him. No prisoner, once committed, ever was released. The iron cages within Loches Prison remain in place to this day as testimony to the dark reign of Louis the Cruel.

About the Author

Tim Desmondes and his wife live in a beach community in Southern California.

He has been known to look favorably upon la Veuve Cliquot, M. Courvoissier, the Chivas Brothers, Mr. Jim Beam, the Sapphire Empress, Señor Bacardi...

(But only in moderation.)

Cheers, fair reader.

Tim is the author of eight previous books published by the Nazca Plains Publishing Company:

- Sex and Loathing in Hollywood
- Sexual Diversity and Perversity in California
- Dracula Sucks Hollywood Dudes
- Venus Does Adonis While Apollo Shags a Tree
- Arthur Does Camelot
- Whores, Love and Pistols in the Wild West
- Robin's Too Tight Tights
- Sex and Love in Paris and Frisco

If you have missed any of them, Tim suggests you run out right now and buy a few. You won't want to miss a word.

Desmondes

Arthur Does Camelot

Arthur
Does Camelot

a novel by
Tim Desmondes

Dracula Sucks
Hollywood Dudes

Desmondes

Dracula Sucks Hollywood Dudes

Tim Desmondes

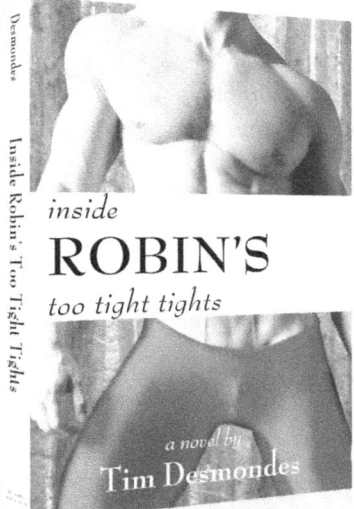

Desmondes

Inside Robin's Too Tight Tights

inside
ROBIN'S
too tight tights

a novel by
Tim Desmondes

Desmondes   SEX AND LOATHING IN HOLLYWOOD

Sex and
Loathing in
HOLLYWOOD

Tim Desmondes

Sex and Love in Paris and Frisco

Tim Desmondes

Sexual Diversity and Perversity in California

Tim Desmondes

Desmondes

SEXUAL DIVERSITY AND PERVERSITY IN CALIFORNIA

Tim Desmondes

Venus Does Adonis while Apollo Shags a Tree

Desmondes

VENUS DOES ADONIS WHILE APOLLO SHAGS A TREE

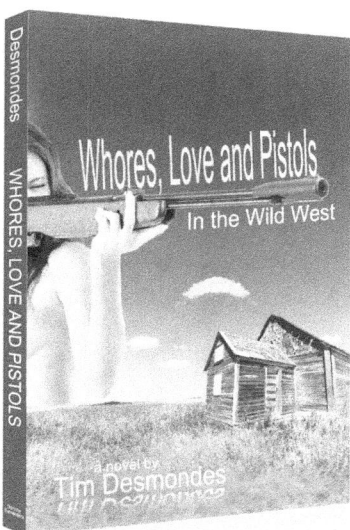

Whores, Love and Pistols

In the Wild West

a novel by
Tim Desmondes

Desmondes

WHORES, LOVE AND PISTOLS

www.ingramcontent.com/pod-product-compliance
Lightning Source LLC
Chambersburg PA
CBHW051639260626
47170CB00004B/1245